THE LITTLE TOWN OF MARROWVILLE

JOHN ROBERTSON

ILLUSTRATED BY LOUIS GHIBAULT

PUFFIN

PUFFIN BOOKS

UK | USA | Canada | Ireland | Australia
India | New Zealand | South Africa

Puffin Books is part of the Penguin Random House group of companies
whose addresses can be found at global.penguinrandomhouse.com.

www.penguin.co.uk   www.puffin.co.uk   www.ladybird.co.uk

First published 2019
001

Set in 12.5/17pt Bembo Book Mt Std
Printed in Great Britain by Clays Ltd, Elcograf S.p.A.

A CIP catalogue record for this book is available from the British Library

ISBN: 978–0–241–34474–3

All correspondence to:
Puffin Books, Penguin Random House Children's
80 Strand, London WC2R 0RL

PUFFIN BOOKS

THE LITTLE TOWN OF MARROWVILLE

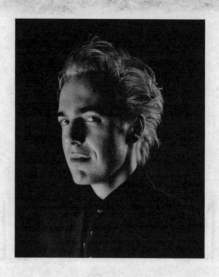

John Robertson is an award-winning stand-up comedian who has travelled the planet making children and adults laugh with fear since 2003. He presented over 100 episodes of Challenge TV's *Videogame Nation*, but is perhaps best known as the creator of the smash-hit interactive live show *The Dark Room,* as well as the video game of the same name. His darkly comic children's story, *The Little Town of Marrowville*, is his debut novel.

To my mother, Lynne, who survived

Contents

CITIZENS of
THE LITTLE TOWN of MARROWVILLE

AUBREY & AUBREY'S SISTER

HOWARD HOWARD

BONELESS CHARLIE

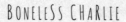
CALO

RIALTO GRANDE

BARNEY THE DOG
(RIALTO'S DOG)

CHIEF
SUPERINTENDENT
SERGEANT LORENZO
PLUG

GORGO

BOSS SMASHER

RODNEY PASTE

THE GRINDERS

PROLOGUE

Night had fallen on the little town of Marrowville, and soon the darkness would be joined by everybody's wet friend, rain.

And the rain would bring friends of its own.

Thunder boomed across the misty sea. Crooked bolts of lightning crackled through the blackened clouds. Water splashed off cobblestones and gurgled down long, twisted drainpipes, and – when he fell into a puddle – soaked the trousers of a running man.

Yes, tonight, in the little town of Marrowville, there would be a storm. Which, as everybody in the little town of Marrowville knows, is rain but with the ability to kill you.

The man cursed. His trousers were expensive, and his business was urgent. He got to his feet and dashed off as fast as he could, his slender legs propelling him past shuttered houses and shops in a blur of silk and finery. If you knew the layout of Marrowville, you'd know he was heading for the middle of town, where the buildings get tall and the people get rich.

Again, the thunder roared. Lightning cut the sky.

At least one person would perish tonight, and they would perish because of something brought by the storm, but it wouldn't be the running man. No, his part in this story would be much stranger.

The man pulled the brim of his hat low over his face, droplets of water sliding down his fine leather gloves. And he kept running.

His legs carried him down an alley. It wasn't a normal place to run, if you were running to enjoy yourself, but it was a very good place to go if you were trying to avoid trouble – unless, of course, there was more trouble waiting for you in the alley.

But trouble wasn't waiting for the running man: it was *hunting* him. And this particular trouble didn't care if he was on a street, or in an alley, or hiding behind a rubbish bin, or desperately slapping his hands against a door and screaming, 'Open up! Open up! This is very important, and so am I!' – which is exactly what the man was doing when the trouble found him.

The man looked up. A bolt of lightning blasted from the clouds and struck him in the head.

His leather gloves fell apart. His beautiful clothes

turned to smoking rags. His hair became the nest for a small fire. And he stood there, smiling the stupidest grin you can imagine.

Most people, when hit by lightning, don't survive. Or, if they do, they're changed forever. Their ears fall off. Or they lose the ability to eat celery because they're dead.

The running man had survived – and been changed. He said just one word:

'Fish!'

1
THE CRUEL MAN

Aubrey's father was a cruel man.

You knew he was cruel because he'd named his son Aubrey.

Aubrey's father had two names, or, because he was cheap, one name – twice. His first name was Howard. His second name was Howard. His full name was Howard Howard. Aubrey was Aubrey Howard.

Aubrey's sister didn't have a name, since Howard Howard liked to pretend she didn't exist, which, to his extreme alarm, was a game his daughter absolutely adored. He would open the cupboard for his breakfast and she'd burst out, screaming, 'I'm not here, Howard! I'm not here!'

But his daughter was there, and so, it turned out, were the heart attacks this game so frequently gave him. Howard Howard had spent a lot of mornings clutching his chest and thrashing around in a crunchy

puddle of spilled cornflakes.

His daughter would then be forced to spend a lot of time in the cellar, or 'no time at all' since, as Howard Howard said, 'She doesn't exist, Aubrey. The cellar is empty.'

Because Howard Howard was a cruel man.

And never be a cruel man, because eventually a crueller man will come along and deal with you.*

---

* And they may be a crueller woman. Or a crueller person. Or a crueller kid. Trust me, if you act like enough of a jerk, people will line up for the chance to fix you. And some of them will bring hammers.

Everyone in town knew Howard Howard's name was Howard Howard because it was a stupid name, and because he'd had it tattooed on both his fists. He also had six fingers on each hand, which people mostly noticed when they realized they could read the entire name of the man who was punching them.

Half the population of Marrowville had been thumped into unconsciousness by those six-fingered hands, and each shaken brain had gone to sleep with a memory of loose teeth and Howard Howard's leering features. He was a bruiser and a loser and a drunkard and a slob; as fat as a wheel of angry cheese, and as stumpy as an incomplete leg. Neckless and feckless and ruthless and thuggish; piggy, tattooed and cruel. He was Howard Howard, Six-Fingered Howard, How'Ard Howard. Too many fingers, too few names, too many scars and father of two (and that was two too many, as the neighbours agreed).

But soon Howard Howard would be dead, with both his names and all his fingers forgotten forever.

'Good,' said Howard's daughter, who wasn't there when he died.

(She was there, of course. She was there even after her father's head wasn't.)

This little family lived in a three-room house, each room

stacked on top of the other. At the bottom of the house was a ladder; at the top of the house was the same ladder. How they accomplished this miracle, we'll never know.

Aubrey slept in a cot in the top room. The cot had been the right size for him when he was a baby, and ten years later it was still the right size for a baby. His arms and legs dangled over the sides as he dreamed his little-boy dreams beneath a big bay window. At night, he could see the lights of the little town of Marrowville. During the day, he could see the little town of Marrowville. Like a lot of things in life, it was better with the lights off.

Aubrey's sister didn't sleep in the cellar where she wasn't.

Howard Howard slept wherever he wanted, usually flopping down on any of the old junk that littered the rest of the house. The whole place was less of a dwelling and more like a clogged bum – providing the bum was clogged with rusted engine parts and slabs of old concrete, and a ladder. And a man. And two children.

Howard Howard was a Wrecker: a government-sanctioned thug. His job was to work with the police to keep the crime rate up. He'd break into people's homes and smash the place apart. He could take anything he liked. Sadly, he only liked rusted engine parts and slabs of old concrete, which left him a lot of things to smash.

He once punched a painting that had looked at him funny. He thumped a horse until it became a donkey, and then he thumped the donkey, then the donkey died. All this happened in a pet shop that didn't sell horses or donkeys or paintings, so who knows where he got them from. He may have brought them himself, just to have something to punch.

'Oh dear, madam,' the police would say, filling out their notebooks in the middle of an obliterated living room. 'It seems your house and husband have been smashed by the Wreckers. Nothing else we can do here.'

Wives would cry, knowing the police had done all they could. After all, they'd filled out their notebooks – which was their job.

The little town of Marrowville had too many notebooks ever since an enormous ship carrying a cargo of stationery had crashed offshore. The police were sent to collect the cargo, and the Wreckers went down to drown anyone who didn't like the police collecting the cargo.

Decades later, the ship lay rotting beneath the water, a fact each new police recruit was obliged to write in their notebook. Once each police officer had filled a thousand notebooks with observations and crime reports, the notebooks would be burned, and the officer would be promoted. Usually to the rank of Wrecker.

And Howard Howard – Wrecker, decker, batterer and splatterer, lover of none, father of one (two) – was kicking a door with his heavy fight-boots.

'Open this damned door, Aubrey!' shouted Howard Howard, shrieking a din and reeking of gin. His boots thudded against the door of Aubrey's room, each blow so hard it was as though the thunder outside had come in.

Aubrey had climbed on to a pile of junk beneath the big window. His sister held him in her arms. He was only ten. She was only fourteen.

And that was twenty-four years too much of dealing with Howard Howard. The lights of stormy Marrowville framed the children in a halo of flickering amber, the street lights and house lights and lightning and rain the only things too far away to be shaken by their father's kicking.

There was a clattering of metal. Aubrey's sister had propped bits of engine up against the door. Stopping their father getting in was the only way to get some sleep.

But Howard Howard was in a terrible rage. His boots crashed against the wood. His deep voice boomed, 'Open the door, son! Or soon we won't have a door! And then we won't have a son!'

Aubrey's sister squeezed her brother tight. 'Shut up, Howard!' she yelled.

'I didn't hear that last bit, Aubrey!' said Howard Howard, his shoulder splintering the bedroom door. 'I definitely didn't hear that! Whatever it was, I didn't hear it! And I definitely don't want to hear it again . . . whatever it was.'

'It was me, you thick-headed goon!' said Aubrey's sister.

'Whatever I didn't just hear definitely didn't just call me a thick-headed goon, Aubrey,' said Howard Howard. 'Oh no, that definitely didn't just happen, not to proud old Howard Howard!'

He cracked his knuckles. That extra *crack* on each hand was enough to chill the bravest human mind. It meant that what was coming wasn't just cruel but *unusual*.

Twelve fingers tapped one by one against the door.

Howard Howard was thinking.

Whenever Howard Howard tapped his fingers, it sounded like the creeping footsteps of a massive spider. If the fingers tapped faster, it meant the spider was running. And, if the spider ran, it was running at you.

'He's going to kill us,' said Aubrey, who had said this so many times before falling asleep it had practically become a lullaby. There was no point counting sheep when you could count the seconds before your father reached you.

The tapping stopped.

Howard Howard's bald, bullet-shaped head smashed through the door.

Aubrey screamed. His sister didn't.

Now, let's you and me take a moment together. If you weren't upstairs with the children, you wouldn't have heard Aubrey's scream. Or the roar that left Howard Howard's lungs as he tore through the barrier of rusted engine bits. You wouldn't have heard him crack his knuckles as he lurched towards his kids.

If, say, you were outside, and standing in the darkness of the crooked road, and you were exceptionally quiet, you might, just possibly, have heard something very different. Not the spattering of rain. Not the rumble of thunder.

You might have heard music.

It was soft music – slow and tinny, its rhythm uncertain and faltering . . . a curious melody. Not curious in that it sounded strange, but curious in that if you heard it, you'd swear it was looking for something.

And it was.

The music rose into the house. It snaked up through floorboards and paper and engines and terror and fear. It rose in height, but not volume. It reached only the ears it was meant to reach – any extra ears were ears it would cut off. It curled itself into the middle of Howard Howard's brain.

It had a message for the man, and that message was, 'Come here, boy.'

Now, let's you and me talk again. If you really were

outside Howard Howard's house while the music played and Howard preyed, you wouldn't have been alone.

In the road stood two people with an enormous pram.

The music was coming from the pram, since the pram had a hand crank on the side, and a hand to crank the crank. The hand belonged to a pale man. He was definitely pale; he was a skeleton. He also was nine feet tall and wearing a top hat. Some people scream 'style' – but nothing about this man screamed anything, since he was too old to scream. He was a kindly corpse in funeral dress, with skinny bone-lips like a dried-up old fish. On his left hand, he wore a wedding ring – the simple loop of silver interlocking with the golden wedding band that hugged his wife's finger. And it really hugged her finger, since her digits were so wide and soft it was like someone had tried to put a collar on a tube of whipped cream.

Together, they marched forward. His long legs striding towards the house while she waddled alongside, short and fat and toddling backwards.

He cranked the organ and she hummed along – a gleeful old woman in harmony with a creaking old machine. He was dry; she was joyous. He was bent double; she was double his weight.

And from the pram their music played.

In Aubrey's room, Howard Howard suddenly stopped

13

roaring. He blinked. And then, quietly, he backed out of the ruined door.

Soon he was slowly climbing down the ladder.

He didn't know why he wanted to go downstairs, but he felt a sense of calm that was unfamiliar in his violent life. His heartbeat slowed into something that just pushed his blood around, instead of firing up his muscles to squeeze someone else's blood out. He reached the ground floor and walked to the front door.

The music was louder now. Pipes played a chattering tune, its rhythm made faster and faster by the whirling of the old man's hand. Howard Howard opened the door.

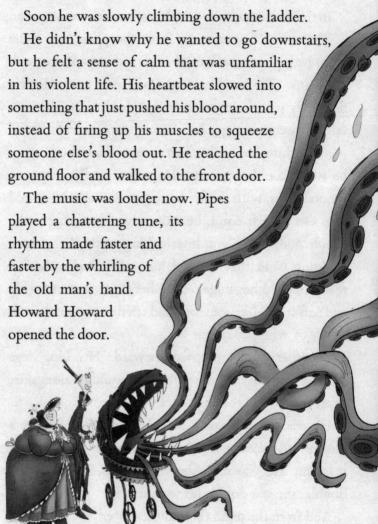

He saw
a nine-foot
tall skeleton
undertaker feverishly
turning a crank on a pram.
He saw shadows where eyes
should've been. He saw a fat
woman with her back to him.
He saw her shoulders shake with laughter.

'What's your name, lovely?' asked the
woman.

'Howard Howard,' said Howard Howard.

She tilted her head to the sky. 'In you go.'

He saw the black pram open. Black tentacles shot out.

Great dark snakes of slimy muscle wrapped round Howard Howard's throat and dragged him into the pram's body. The tall skeleton cranked harder, reeling Howard Howard in deeper as music flooded the neighbourhood. It was beautiful music – and it had a percussion section now. Under all the piping and tooting was a noise that sounded a bit like a big deep drum. It only sounded a little bit like that; it really sounded much more like a bully being chomped by an unseen mouth full of very, very large teeth.

The undertaker's bulbous wife unhooked her wedding ring from his and spun round. Where her eyes should've been there was nothing but two empty, shadowy holes.

However, she wore an exceptionally friendly grin.

These people were the Grinders. Their pram contained a machine that turned average friction into delightful music and horrible parents into delicious food. With a whoop and a song, they ground Howard Howard into a fine, fatherly mince.

The Lady Grinder giggled and jumped into the air to deliver a portly heel-click, before shoving plastic containers under the pram to collect the mince. She laughed a laugh like sherry glugging into an enormous mug. Her husband hissed with satisfaction. He rolled up his sleeves, revealing forearms of bone with veins wrapped round them, then pulled out the crank. The music faded as the mince slowly slopped into the tubs.

From his pocket, the Gentleman Grinder drew an ornate golden key, and, inserting it into the pram, he twisted it clockwise. The music returned, but loud and jolly – an invitation for all to come and see.

The Lady Grinder's friendly smile shone in the light. She trilled a rhyme, clutching several tubs in her arms.

'Come out, children . . . do not cry:
Every brute must one day die.
Monster breathing, Monster Dead,
either way, you Must Be fed.

Grinders Calling, Grinders here,
Now Suppertime will last all year.'

She stood on the doormat, a jolly lady wedded to a dead man and laden with tubs of mince.

Aubrey's sister made it downstairs first: a life of dodging Howard had made her quick and capable. She pulled the front door wide open.

'Hello, lovely,' said the Lady Grinder. 'I'm terribly sorry, but it seems your father is dead.'

'Good,' said Aubrey's sister.

Aubrey had sneaked downstairs. He hid behind his sister's leg. The Lady Grinder chuckled.

'Oh, you don't have to be afraid, lovely! Our baby only eats the bad people. And you're not a bad person, are you, Aubrey?'

Aubrey shook his head.

The Gentleman Grinder hissed. It might have been a laugh. It might have been several bees telling a secret all at once. It was a hiss.

'Yes, dear,' replied the Lady Grinder. 'His name is Aubrey. I'm glad we took his father. Imagine giving a boy a name like that.' She held out the containers to the children.

'These are for you. Howard Howard may as well be of some use to you in the next few weeks.'

'Thank you,' said Aubrey's sister.

'Do either of you have any questions?' asked the Lady Grinder. 'Normally, children have questions when we do this.'

'Are we orphans now?' asked Aubrey's sister.

'Yes, lovely,' said the Lady Grinder.

'Oh, thank goodness,' said Aubrey's sister.

The Gentleman Grinder hissed.

'I like her, too,' said the Lady Grinder. 'What's your name, lovely?'

But Aubrey's sister had gone back inside.

Aubrey watched the man smile, or at least grimace with dry gusto. The woman sighed. They locked their wedding rings back together and made their way down the street. The woman wobbled backwards; the man creaked forwards. They stepped into the shadow of a crooked house and – even though Aubrey could hear their footsteps echoing from further down the road – they didn't reappear. The Grinders were just noise now.

Aubrey looked up. The first rays of morning sun were starting to peek through the clouds.

He closed the front door.

Minutes later, inside the house, meat began to sizzle. And a cruel man became a very fine breakfast.

2
BREAKFAST

Aubrey's sister stood in front of the stove, carefully studying the hideously dented pan in which her father was frying. The pan was hideously dented from years of Howard Howard beating people with it until they were hideously dented, too.

The bumps and bends meant she had to be careful he didn't cook unevenly. After all, what's the point in being saved from a cruel man if he just gives you food poisoning afterwards?

She scooped up a dollop of Howard. To really cook a father, you need to know what he's going to taste like. Most dads taste of body odour and bad breath, and they smell of really big old socks. Some get infused with the taste of the food that gets trapped in their beards and stays there for decades.

When we cooked my dad, he tasted of dog. No further questions, please.

If your father was a good man, chances are he'd taste cosy and familiar. Then again, if he really was a good man, almost nobody would want to kill and eat him, so however would you find out?

Aubrey's sister put her finger in her mouth and nibbled a bit of warm mince. Coincidentally, it was a bit that had once been one of her dad's twelve fingers. It wasn't the fanciest finger food, but then he hadn't had the fanciest fingers.

She grimaced. Howard Howard didn't taste cosy and familiar, probably because he'd never been either of those things. His was not the flavour of warm coffee and large hugs, or even hot slugs and cold sick. He tasted of scum and ash.

'Argh!' she coughed. 'He tastes like someone who set fire to a pub, then peed on the flames.'

'He did,' said Aubrey, who was doing a handstand on the kitchen floor.

And why not do handstands? You only get one chance at being ten and eating your dad.

Aubrey's sister realized her father was going to need some pepper.

21

Quite a lot of pepper, in fact. She reached for the grinder, and then paused. The act of picking up a grinder was enough to put the previous night's music back in her head. A smile arrived on her face.

'Are you hungry, Aubrey?' she asked, cracking the pepper into the pan. 'I'm starving. I've been starving for *years*.'

She really was starving. They both were. Howard Howard had never fed his children. He had a daughter he pretended didn't exist and a son who he said existed, but didn't like, so the children had had to make do with the scraps of meat left over from their father's appalling meals.

They'd dined on squirrel heads and gecko tails, and the thin debris of whole raw ducks that had been cracked open and smashed by a twelve-fingered man. Howard Howard had never left enough food for his kids to get healthy – the spoils of his hunts were always tiny. He'd been a hyena masquerading as a lion – a vicious predator, yes, but his prey had never been particularly strong.

Both the children were skinny. In fact, skinny was too nice a word. Aubrey and his sister were as skinny as you think the word skinny is, and then half as skinny again. Aubrey's sister was thin like a beanpole, which is only thin because a pole can't eat beans. If a pole could eat, it would cease to be a pole. It would be a snake. And snakes don't eat beans. If they did, they'd fart and shoot into the sky like slimy missiles.

She was as long and skinny as the hairs on her head, while Aubrey was as short and messy as the ones on his. Aubrey wore a faded grey jumper that was whole bodies too large for him; Aubrey's sister wore trousers and a shirt she'd rescued from a bin.

'Do you know the last time I ate mince?' asked Aubrey's sister.

'Was it when Mum died?' said Aubrey, who was still upside down, but was pretty sure he always saw the world the right way up. 'Did she get minced, too?'

Aubrey's sister gently kicked Aubrey in the gentle way that older sisters do – the way that isn't gentle.

'Ouch!' said Aubrey, who was suddenly the right way up in a world that would always be the wrong way round.

'Don't talk about Mum like that,' said Aubrey's sister. Her face had suddenly darkened. Barely controlled sadness intruded into a voice much more used to strength.

She trembled, but not from fear, or the cold. It was

grief, half restrained. She put her hands by her sides, balling them into fists.

'Sorry, sis,' said Aubrey, wiping his nose. He was genuinely sorry. He knew jokes about their mother never worked with her.

Aubrey's sister sighed. She looked out of the window. The tears that she would maintain had never been there vanished. They were the tears of a girl whose father had said she never existed, and who hadn't even bothered to give her a name.

She was a girl with four years of extra memories her brother would never have, of a time when there had been more than Howard Howard and his two names and his broken junk and six-fingered hands.

A time when there had been a person called Mum.

Aubrey's sister sighed again. Then her grin reappeared. Once again, she was as tough as all older sisters are – and have to be.

She looked down at her brother. 'I'm sorry I kicked you.' She gave him an apology kick. Aubrey gave her a hug.

Aubrey's sister put one arm round the little boy's shoulder and flipped meat with the tool in her free hand. It was a huge knife Howard Howard had cut with another knife until it was rounded at the top. He called it the Vicious Spoon.

'The last time I had mince was before you were born,'

said Aubrey's sister, prodding their breakfast with the Vicious Spoon. 'Howard brought home a deer he'd shot. He said he'd shot it, but it turned out he'd headbutted it – as usual. Then the deer had walked into the road and been hit by a car. So he headbutted the car. Then he stole the car. Then he crashed the car into our front wall because he was concussed, you know?'

She smirked at her little brother. He nodded vigorously. Howard Howard had always been angry, concussed, drunk or all three at once. The trouble was, even if he was wobbly from drink or blood loss, it had just made him angrier. And wobbly anger is hard to escape because nobody knows where the punches are going to land.

'He'd stuffed the deer in the back seat of the car. He'd managed to knock its antlers off, but it turned out the deer *still wasn't dead*. And it was *fuming*! Mum opened the door and it jumped out – she didn't know deers could growl.*

'And she thought, *I'm not getting attacked by this feral thing*. So she let out her own feral thing – she opened the door for Howard – and he fell out flat on the ground! He stood up, looked at the deer – and the deer kicked him in the head. Then he kicked the deer in the head. Then he fell down. Then the deer fell on him . . .'

---

* They can't, but this one did. That's how angry it was.

35

'What did Mum do?' asked Aubrey.

'Oh, she just laughed! She took me inside and cooked breakfast on this stove. It was the only time she ever used it, Aubrey. Howard wouldn't let her feed me – but there he was, unconscious and pinned down by a bald deer!'

She looked out of the window again. 'It was the only time he couldn't stop her helping me.'

A silence fell on the children. It was heavier than a dead deer. That said, since it was just silence, even though it was heavy, a shout would've broken it. You can't break a deer just by shouting at it. Try it – the deer will break *you*.

The silence came with a realization: Howard Howard would never stop them doing anything ever again.

Aubrey looked out of the window, too. The sun was shining – a rare occurrence in the little town of Marrowville. The air was usually so filled with dust and fog that the sun was never yellow but a far-off ball that glowed brown, as though the sky had its own dirty, radioactive bumhole. But today beams of stained sunlight bounced off the young girl and her little brother as the stove was turned off and meat slopped on to two steel plates.

'Can we eat outside?' asked Aubrey, eager for a rare opportunity to get out to where the sun shone gloriously (and, let's be accurate, brownly).

Holding their plates above their heads, to avoid sharing their food with the stacks of filth in Howard's house, the children embarked on the adventure that was getting to the back door and out into the garden. You had to climb over mouldy piles of rubbish, slide past stacks of rusty engine parts and sometimes play a game of Is That Rat Dead?

The rules for Is That Rat Dead? were simple. If a rat was in your way, you had to poke it. If it was dead, you got a point, and the plague. If it was alive, you got bitten, and the plague. It was a good game if you liked dying. And rats.

Giggling (and with the plague), the children arrived at the back door, a big black slab of steel bolted shut with the bones of a man who had, presumably, lost too many games of Is That Rat Dead? Aubrey's sister slid the bones back in their holes, and the door scraped open.

The back yard was a mess of rust and weeds that rose up into a small mountain of scorched junk. At its top was a cracked, upturned bathtub, smeared with dreck and oozing suspiciously. If you sat on the bathtub, it would give you a fantastic view of the utter filth below.

The kids scampered up the junk, sat cross-legged and began to wolf down their food. Aubrey laughed, grey meat slopping down his chin. Aubrey's sister laughed, too. They laughed at how hungry they were. They laughed at the strangeness of the last few hours. They laughed because the monster in their lives was gone, dispatched by other stranger monsters.

And they laughed at the horrible taste of their freedom.

Now let's you and me have a chat about food. We'll start up in the sky, where most of Marrowville's food comes from. Far, far above the children's heads, a duck was flying. Ducks are able to fly, although flies, sadly, aren't able to duck. I know this because I used to hunt them. I've passed many days sharpening toothpicks into tiny spears and stalking the little buzzy-boys round my kitchen. Why, I used to leave a plate of rotting steak out on the worktop as bait. But this isn't, I suppose, particularly important right now.

What was important was that the duck was flying through a patch of mist and this mist was important. It hung down from the sky and clung to the ground, a shroud of endless damp as moist as a bosun's* pocket and as thick and grey as a despised elderly relative. To go to the edge of Marrowville was to see every road slowly fade away into a water-blurred nothing.

The mist had surrounded Marrowville for as long as anyone could remember, and at least as far as anyone could see, and, most importantly, as far as anyone could

* A bosun is a type of sailor. The traditional greeting for a sailor is 'Hello'.

go. Which brings us back to the duck.

The duck could fly, and, if it hadn't been flying, it could also have ducked. This would've been useful for the duck, because the mist that had always surrounded Marrowville had also always been filled with deadly flying razors. A cluster of them whizzed by, and the flying duck that didn't duck *wasn't missed*.

Moments like this had fed a lot of people in Marrowville. Sometimes whole families would stand outside, holding their plates up to the sky and praying for the sound of a startled quack. But, if you had a father as selfish as Howard Howard, who couldn't even be bothered giving you something as simple as a name, why would you expect food?

The children wheezed. They chuckled. They guffawed. They cackled. They crowed. The happy siblings laughed and ate until the laughter died like their father had. And when they had finished eating and laughing they lay on the bathtub, too happy and full to do anything but be happy and full.

'Don't talk to her,' a little whisper came from down the yard.

Aubrey's sister sat up.

Three other children had popped their heads over the back fence. They had the squinty, mean little faces of kids who had always been treated well, but who loved to treat others badly.

'What is it?' she called.

Two of the three faces whispered to each other.

'Don't talk to her.'

'She's not really there.'

The biggest of the kids smirked. He yelled, 'Hey, freaks!'

Aubrey's sister didn't even bother looking at him; she just picked up her fork and started eating again. Everyone in Marrowville was a freak. It wasn't the insult he thought it was. But to hear other people say she didn't *exist* . . .

'What are you eating, freaks?' the boy shouted.

Aubrey's sister looked at her plate, then glanced over at him.

'Deep-fried idiot!' she called.

At this, Aubrey bugged his eyes out wide. He stood up on the bathtub, stuffed his face with two fistfuls of mince, crossed his eyes and grinned, scraggly bits of chewed dude dropping out of his mouth and down his chest.

'And I'm still hungry!' he cried.

'Yeah, I reckon I could eat at least three more idiots,' agreed Aubrey's sister, lazily pointing her fork at the three little staring faces.

Quickly, quietly and with no intention of ever returning, the other children disappeared back behind the fence.

'Now, what would you like to do today, Aubrey?' asked Aubrey's sister, resuming her meal and calmly enjoying a forkful of father.

The little boy smiled. He'd never been asked that question, or at least not when the fun on offer was anything more enjoyable than poking a dead rat. He thought about it for exactly half of zero seconds. 'Could we . . . go into town?'

'Yes! That's the first thing we'll do!'

Aubrey's sister was full of pride. She could finally take her brother somewhere! Oh, she'd sometimes managed to sneak off into town when Howard Howard was out, and she'd come back to Aubrey with funny stories and little scraps of stolen food – but to finally share it all with him! To show her brother the great stone Victory Finger! The colourful shops selling colourful slop! The murky gutters where people fished for noses!*

She stood up. 'Let's go into town! I'll take you! We'll –'

Images flashed in Aubrey's sister's brain. Her thoughts were a dream of cars, roads, feasts, laughter, mist and,

---

* This was a popular game in Marrowville, where adults would see how many extra noses they could fit on their face. The first-ever winner was Two-Nose Jim, with three.

finally, escape. It was delightful, until her mind settled on a memory she absolutely didn't want to think about, especially not today. Fortunately for her sanity, she was interrupted. Unfortunately for her temper, the interruption was severely annoying.

Another head had popped over the rusty tin fence. Mrs Dalrymple was the elderly person who lived in a ramshackle cottage next to Howard Howard's apocalyptic splat of a home. She looked at both children, remembered she was meant to only be able to see one of them and then called out, 'Aubrey! You get down from there! You'll cut yourself.'

'Hello, Mrs Dalrymple!' said Aubrey. 'You can say hello to my sister – Dad's not around.'

Aubrey's sister was pleasantly surprised. Thirteen words! That was the longest sentence she'd ever heard Aubrey say. It was good to hear him.

Mrs Dalrymple shouted back, 'I don't know what you're talking about, Aubrey! You're all by yourself in Howard's garden!'

However, that . . . that wasn't good to hear. At all.

'Oh, I'm not here, am I?' said Aubrey's sister. 'You're going to do that thing where you pretend I'm not here because Howard told you to, and you were scared of him.' She stood up and shouted, 'Well, I'm here, Mrs Dalrymple! Look how here I am!' She picked up her plate and began waving it in the air. She jumped up and down. 'HELLOOOOOOOOOOOOO, MRS DALRYMPLE! HELLLOOOOOO!' She took some fried meat and pressed it to her upper lip. 'HELLOOOOOOOO! MRS DALRYMPLE! I HAVE A MEAT MOUSTACHE! YOU CANNOT IGNORE MY MEAT MOUSTACHE!'

Aubrey nearly wet himself laughing. Spurred on by this, Aubrey's sister tossed the steel plate high into the sky. For a moment, the spinning disc glinted beautifully in the sunlight, before, with the usual poor luck possessed by Aubrey's sister, it made a sudden and accidental journey over Mrs Dalrymple's head and straight into the wall behind her. Leftover bits of Howard Howard dripped on to his neighbour.

'I'm sorry, Mrs Dalrymple!' called Aubrey's sister, apologizing through the meat moustache.

The old lady glared at Aubrey's sister, then corrected herself and settled for glaring at the air *next* to Aubrey's sister.

'You'll want to go inside, Aubrey,' said Mrs Dalrymple, picking meat out of her hair. 'It's raining.'

She went back into her house. Anyone else would have called the police because a young girl had just pelted them with steel and meat, but there was no point calling the police in Marrowville. Firstly: there were no phones; you had to find the police and ask them for help, which they might give if they felt like it. And secondly: you can't arrest someone who doesn't exist. Or you can, but, if you do, whatever do you tell people when they escape?*

The children ambled back into the house.

'How do we get to town?' asked Aubrey, all grins. He'd had breakfast and a game and hadn't been yelled at by anyone. It had thus far been the best day of his entire little life.

'Well, before we do that, we plan for the future,' said Aubrey's sister, her head full of ideas about transport and travel, and possessions and what to do for money (their food being so nicely covered by another six tubs of premium-grade Howard Howard).

Those plans didn't escape her brain, however, since her speech was cut short by a sudden thud at the front door.

The children rushed into the front room.

The thud gave way to a crash. The crash was the door giving way to an enormous black boot. The door flew clean across the room and splintered. The boot was fine.

The children stared at the gap where the front door

---

* It was well known in town that Howard Howard didn't have a daughter. And that, even if he did have one, she didn't have a name, so didn't officially exist. This, ironically, made her one of the most famous people in town since she was, of course, the only one who wasn't there.

used to be. A tiny, wet, rat-like dog padded, shivering, into the front room. It sneezed.

The children stared at the sneezing dog – and it nearly took their minds off the six enormous men that were standing in front of the house.

The future had come to them.

3
WrecKerS

'WAKE UP, BROTHER HOWARD!' screeched the voice that belonged to the man who belonged to the foot that belonged in the boot that had kicked down the door. 'NOW EEEES THE TEEM FOR *VIOLENCE*!'

The man was huge; the door was splinters. The man thought, *VIOLENCE!* The door thought nothing – it was a door. Or it had been a door. Now it was pulp. And pulp doesn't think much, which is why you should always try to avoid getting kicked in the head.

In one hand, the man carried two large blood-stained boots. His voice, however, carried news, along with an accent of variable origin and quality: 'I KNOW YOU ARE HERE, HOWARD. I FEND

YOURRRR FIGHT-BOOTS* OUTSIDE!'

Aubrey and Aubrey's sister saw the man, then saw their father's shoes, then contemplated the idea that they were, once again, *about to die*.

It seemed that, when the Grinders minced Howard Howard, their pram had, perhaps sensibly, spat out his footwear. He'd been a rotten person, but his boots were the rottenest part of him. His six fingers could brand you with his name, but his boots were so dirty that, if he kicked you, fungus would grow in your skull.

The tiny dog sneezed again. The man, bred for combat and sensitive to all noise, booted the tiny dog. The tiny dog bounced all over the room, spraying everything with doggy snot and poochie widdle.

'Yuck!' said Aubrey, who had just received a morning shower that was sudden and unexpected – and not with water.

'HOWARD!' the man called, barrelling past the children. His voice whistled out of a crescent-shaped mouth on a crescent-shaped head. His curved chin jutted out the same distance as the bleached pompadour† that stretched beyond his forehead like a horrible yellow cliff.

He thundered up the stairs. Then he thundered down

---

* All Wreckers wear fight-boots. Fight-boots – they're boots for fighting.

† A pompadour is a haircut that sounds like a dog and looks like a mistake.

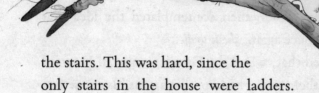

the stairs. This was hard, since the
only stairs in the house were ladders.
But he was so powerful the ladders would gladly
pretend to be stairs if he wanted. He thundered into the
kitchen. He thundered into the back yard. He thundered
back into the lounge. He farted. It thundered. The force
of the blast sent Aubrey flying face-first into the couch.

'Yuck!' said Aubrey, who, having already been
showered, wasn't expecting to be blow-dried as well.

The man looked at the ceiling, as though thinking.
He wasn't thinking. He never thought – he just looked
at things and sometimes killed them. 'Heeemmmm,' he
said. It was a 'hmmmm' with three extra 'e's. Always be
wary of people who can afford to add letters to words.
They might be very smart, or just very used to being
understood.

The man snapped his head down towards the
children. Aubrey's sister stared up at his chin. Aubrey,
face smooshed into the couch cushions, could only
stare at stains.

'Cheldreen, where *is* Howard Howard?' The man's
crooked teeth jangled in a mouth that reeked of wet

dog. Above the teeth, a crooked nose twisted like the broken back of a desert snake. His eyes were a brilliant green, and they stared Aubrey right in the toes, the little boy's feet still sticking up from the couch after the bum explosion that had knocked him over.

The man laughed. First it was shrill, then it was deep, then shrill again, as though he was actually a little girl, then an enormous hulk, then a little girl again.

Of course, he wasn't really a little girl. He was six feet nine inches tall. His muscles were barely covered by an outfit of jagged metal and cracked leather, and his boots alone required more skin than you could find on a reasonably-sized child. Nothing about him suggested he was a man to be left alone with children, least of all his arm tattoo of a sailor being boiled in oil, and his boots made from the skin of four reasonably-sized children. He wore a white cape with red streaks on it, which was clearly a shower curtain he had liberated from a crime scene.

'Good morning, Mr Grande,' said Aubrey's sister.

'Mr Grande' was Rialto Grande, Howard Howard's boss. Unlike most Wreckers, he had never been a police officer; he was just a criminal who the town paid to try to stop him being an even worse criminal. It didn't work.

'Barneeeey, heeeeel!' said Rialto Grande, picking up the tiny wet dog in his free hand. The dog licked his face, terror in its eyes. Rialto licked the dog back with a tongue larger than it was. The mystery of why the dog was permanently wet had been solved.

Aubrey scurried over to his sister. The dog sneezed. Rialto licked the dog again. The children shuddered.

Aubrey and Aubrey's sister had met Mr Rialto Grande many times. This was, however, the first after participating in a crime of their own. Every other meeting had involved them getting bruised, and that was just for existing.* As lawless as Marrowville sometimes seemed to be, you probably couldn't eat your father without getting at least some kind of punishment.

Probably something mild, like death.

They silently checked their brains for a plan, and simultaneously arrived at that old refuge of the desperate: smiling.

---

* Or, in Aubrey's sister's case, not existing, but still being within reach.

The children beamed at the hulking mass of flamboyance that had broken down their door. They smiled like they loved it when their door was kicked down. They smiled like they had absolutely no idea why Howard Howard wasn't currently standing in the boots the large man was holding. They smiled like their burps wouldn't smell suspiciously like their father.

They smiled like they knew what they were doing.

They smiled until they knew what they were doing.

(They didn't know what they were doing.)

'Hullo, Mr Grande!' said Aubrey, with the forced cheerfulness indicated by putting a 'u' in the word 'Hello'. He went to shake the giant's hand.

'The boy-one!' said Rialto Grande. 'The leetle boy-one! Howard Howard's very-own-boy-boy.' Rialto dropped Howard Howard's fight-boots and flipped Aubrey into the air. The little boy tumbled skywards, then stopped with a jerk. The jerk was Rialto Grande, who'd stretched out his muscled arm to catch the boy's ankle. Which is how, half a second before his journey back from the ceiling ended at the floor, Aubrey found himself dangling from the hand of a man who was 25% moron and 75% professional killer.

Rialto looked the boy right in his upside-down eyes. He held the dog to the boy's face. The dog sneezed again.

'Whereeee is your father?' asked Rialto. 'We are due to go *outtttt* and smash many things.' He dropped the dog, which went snuffling towards the kitchen, as though something of great interest was in there. Luckily for its doggy curiosity, there was something of *tremendous* interest in there. It was occupying six plastic tubs and a frying pan, and it used to be called Howard Howard.

Unwatched, Aubrey's sister picked up her father's fight-boots and slid her hands inside. It was too late to hide the blasted things, but if she could just find the right thing to press, she was pretty sure she could make the fight-boots do the incredible thing that fight-boots do.

Rialto Grande continued prattling.

'There are chandelieeeers to smash and walls to *crumble*! There are bones to boil and widows to make-make-make! But *where* eees Howard Howard?' Rialto Grande was getting carried away, which meant Aubrey was getting carried away, too; his tiny body was being flung round the room with every excited gesture.

Aubrey's sister saw three needs:

1. The need to get Aubrey out of Rialto's hand.
2. The need to cover up a crime.
3. The need to not appear to be doing either of those things.

She swallowed her reluctance and her pride, and then spat out a word she hated to use.

'*Dad* is . . .' she began.

Rialto Grande tossed her brother across the room and jammed a meaty finger right between Aubrey's sister's eyes.

'You've spoken to me twice, parasite.' Rialto's accent had disappeared. The extra letters were gone. The words cut. 'That is too many times.'

Unlike everyone else in Marrowville, Rialto Grande had decided he could see Aubrey's sister. And he hated what he saw.

Behind Rialto, the other five Wreckers strolled into the house. The Morton Twins were huge and fat, and had to smash the door frame until it was wide enough for them to squeeze through. The two overgrown hulks were connected by an enormous belly-button cord. It made walking difficult, but it gave them a handy place to hang their favourite hammers and clubs.

Rodney Paste came slinking behind. The artist of the group, his backpack was stuffed with the human skulls he polished and sold to people like Rialto Grande. Boss Smasher followed, his forearms large enough to be mistaken for two extra men, and his legs so narrow he had to use his arms to pull himself forward, like a gorilla.

Bringing up the rear was the hardskin,★ Gorgo, a mossy behemoth who had the look of a pet rock gone rogue.

'Genteeelmen, find Howard Howard and rustle him from his slumberwumbus, yes?' Rialto called over his shoulder, his eyes full of hate and mind full of murder. 'We neeeeed our very best puncho, for today

★ A 'hardskin' is a person whose father was a rock, and who shaves with a combination of a chisel and centuries of erosion. 'Erosion' is what happens to your parents' spirit every time you don't let them sleep in.

we flatten the church and the army.'*

Rodney Paste slunk over to his side. 'Terribly sorry, Mr Grande, but if he's not here, perhaps the storm . . .?'

Rialto raised an eyebrow. Unfortunately for Rodney Paste, it was one of his. The big man's hand had snatched his brow between finger and thumb, then lifted. Rodney's whole body dangled from Rialto's fingers.

'Areeeee you saying, Rodneeey, that we lost Brother Howard in last night's tiny sterm?'

Rodney Paste tried to nod. Or nod as well as he could, given he was being held in the air by his eyebrow.

'WE DOOOOOOO *NOT* LOOOOOOOOSE WRECKERS TO THE WEATHERRRRR, RODNEEEY. We are the strongest men in Marrowville, and we do not vanish when there is a little bit of rain!'†

---

* The Marrowville Church was a place where people went on Sunday mornings to get warm and feel bad about themselves but still better than they felt about the people who didn't go. It was very big and very old and had survived countless natural disasters, though it had never seen a hurricane as destructive as Rialto Grande. The army of Marrowville, meanwhile, consisted of four men whose dream had been to die somewhere that wasn't Marrowville. They wore uniforms and waited for the day Marrowville would be at war with somewhere else. Since there wasn't anywhere else, they mostly tried to avoid thinking, which is very easy to do if you join the army.

† This was, as Rialto knew quite well, a total lie. Oh, the Wreckers were absolutely the strongest men in Marrowville, but he'd been bursting into Wreckers' homes after every storm for ages. Heaps of his troops had gone missing under cover of dampness. It all meant he was now a large, violent man who was suspicious of raindrops and had a loathing for clouds.

He dropped the smaller man. 'Now – *hunt!*'

The Wreckers swarmed through the house, bellowing for Howard Howard and knocking over any stray garbage in their way. Since the whole house was garbage, every surface echoed with clattering and shouting.

The house was a cacophony of crashing and swearing – up in the bedrooms, down in the cellar, everywhere but the kitchen, where a very hungry Barney the dog had just found six tubs and a frying pan full of mince.

'Are your boys vanishing, Rialto?' asked Aubrey's sister, a smirk on her lips.

Her fingers had finally reached the hidden switches inside her father's fight-boots. Rialto was ranting. He screeched a secret. 'NO, MY WRECKER BROTHERS ABSOLUTELY DO NOT GO MISSING EVERY

SINGLE TIME
THERE'S A
THUNDERSTORM!
NO! NO! NO!'

The 25% of Rialto Grande
that was a moron seemed to
mostly live in his mouth. Still,
the 75% of him that was a
professional killer had ways of
making up for it.

Rialto Grande grabbed Aubrey's sister by the hair and
knocked the fight-boots from her hands. He lifted her
off the ground, a terrible yellow smile across his face.

Unfortunately for him, this meant Aubrey's sister's
feet were free to travel to places they previously
couldn't. She kicked him in both armpits.

He grunted. She did it again. This time with an insult.

'Your troops are deserting you! It's probably because you're such a revolting dog-licker.' Wreckers going missing during thunderstorms? Oh, this was *very* interesting news . . . I mean, Howard Howard hadn't gone missing, exactly – but he was definitely missing a few things now.

Rialto stopped smiling. 'I have hated you since your mother brought you home.' He raised his enormous hand to strike. She kicked him again. Every time she kicked, she spoke a new word, like a talking doll built for violence.

'SHUT.

'UP.

'RIALTO.

'NOBODY.

'LIKES.

'YOUR.

'HORRIBLE.

'HAIR.

'AND.

'STOP.

'LICKING.

'DOGS.

'IT'S.

'WEIRD.'

At the other end of the room, Aubrey's journey through the air had ended with a thud into the far wall. Pain overwhelmed his tiny head, and panic overwhelmed his tiny heart. Love meant he wanted to help his sister, but fear and logic meant he probably couldn't.

She'd always protected him when his father was on the warpath – and he'd never been able to help her. So what would change now?

And then he remembered – *everything*.

He began to crawl, a small boy on his own little mission to grab his father's fight-boots.

Upstairs, the skinny, skulking Rodney Paste had found a lot of junk, but no Howard Howard. Still, Howard Howard had always been trash, so maybe he was in there somewhere.

Even further upstairs, Boss Smasher picked up an old fridge and hurled it out of the window. It wasn't helping him look; it was just fun to do.

In the kitchen, Barney the dog barked. It was a bark that said, *I am a dog and I have found something and it is excellent.*

'Barneeeey!' cooed Rialto in the half-amazed manner of all humans who love their pets more than they love people. He dropped Aubrey's sister and sauntered into the kitchen, adoration removing every pause between his words. 'Whathaveyoufoundwho'sagoodboyyouare-agoodboywhathaveyoufound?'

Aubrey forgot the boots, ran across the room and hugged his sister. She pushed him away and sucked air into her winded lungs. Then she hugged him. It's a practical love that first fixes the problem, and then still goes in for the hug.

'*BOOOOYS!*' called Rialto. On every floor of the house, the clattering stopped. Rodney Paste, shoving engine bits into his backpack, hopped into the kitchen. Gorgo, eating engine bits, dragged his way in there. The children dashed towards the broken front door, but the Morton Twins blocked their path, like two human mountains carved entirely out of anger and fat.

'You don't go out there,' said Left Morton.

'Because we're here,' said Right Morton, who was a little smarter than his brother.

Everyone walked into the kitchen. Rialto was standing over the tubs of mince. He spun round and glared at the children.

'What eees theees?' he asked.

Aubrey's eyes widened. Aubrey's sister, sensing an opportunity, grinned. She whispered to her brother, 'Be hungry and adorable.' She nudged him. It was a nudge that said, *Start talking*.

'That, Mr Grande, is food,' said Aubrey, flexing his

acting glands. 'Oh, *please* don't eat it . . .'

Aubrey's sister joined in. '*Father* brought it back *especially*.'

Aubrey turned on the puppy-dog eyes, then immediately stopped in case Rialto started licking him.

Rialto Grande's grin widened, revealing teeth where teeth shouldn't be. His whole mouth was as bent and rotten as the skyline of Marrowville. He folded his massive arms.

'Weeeell, boy-boy, since your father is not heeeere, Wrecker Law★ says everything that's his is ourrrrrrs. And the stomachs of theeeese very large gentlemen probably say . . .'

Gorgo rumbled.

'Are you hungry, boyyyyyys?'

The Wreckers bared their teeth and roared.

'Howard Howard is veeerrrrry naughtyyyyy not to share this wondrous feast with his Wrecker brothers!' shouted Rialto. He cuffed both children on the back of the head.

'Cook for us!' he screamed. He picked up Barney. They began licking each other's faces in disgusting celebration. Yes, Rialto had been brain-throbbingly aggravated about Howard Howard, but free food? That would fix everything.

★ There's no such thing as Wrecker Law, but you try telling them.

The children hurried to the stove. An hour before, it had just been a symbol of their newfound freedom. Now it was literally the thing that could save their lives.

Aubrey's sister heated the frying pan with the secret joy of someone who knows they're about to destroy the evidence. Some garlic, onion and a pinch of spice would soon leave no trace of Howard Howard except his fight-boots – and that'd be fine: he'd just be another Wrecker mysteriously missing in a storm. Soon the men would eat. The crime would dissolve in bloated stomachs. Rialto Grande would go find something to hit. Freedom was just a series of contented belches away.

Aubrey chopped onions, but he didn't cry. He'd been seconds away from being hurt for as long as he'd been alive; onions weren't going to do any emotional damage.

Rialto licked raw mince out of Barney's fur. The Wreckers tussled and guffawed, pleased by their impending meaty feast.

Howard Howard, for his part, sizzled deliciously, and, when the spools of yummy meat changed from red to half-grey, the Wreckers descended. Six huge men flung themselves at the pan. They gorged on what they found, six colossal, slobbering, gurgling brutes gulping down protein like pelicans swallowing whole fish.

Rialto grabbed the hot pan in his inhuman hands. Steam whistled between his fingers. A normal person would've been burned – but Rialto wasn't normal.

Rodney Paste, who was slightly more normal than his boss, was so ravenous that he forgot just how invincible his leader was. Disastrously, he assumed Rialto was holding a nice, cool, non-superheated plate. He licked grease from the boiling pan. His tongue stuck to the scalding metal and went from raw to medium rare in about twenty seconds.

Rialto swooped his jagged teeth into the meat and gobbled down mince, onion and an unexpected delicacy: Rodney's tongue.

'YEEEEES!' said Rialto.

'. . . !' said Rodney, who may have sworn, not that anyone would ever know.

The meal was tremendous. Gorgo and the Morton Twins opened up the uncooked tubs and crammed handfuls of Howard into their meaty maws. Again, they slobbered, gurgled and gorged.

'WHAT A WONDERFUL MORNING, BROTHERS!' Rialto was practically singing now. Why, he was so happy he'd almost completely forgotten about Howard Howard, and the storm, and his not-so-secret worry that Wreckers seemed to go missing almost every time it rained.

Gorgo hoisted Aubrey up and wiped his mouth on the boy's hair. The Mortons slammed their bellies together and forced out a belch from both of their mouths. The twin belches slammed into each other, with the weaker burp going back into one of the twin's mouths, which just made him burp again.

Boss Smasher twisted the frying pan in his jaws, grease leaking down his chin. The men were all big grins and bloated tummies. The tubs of meat were empty.

Aubrey's sister was having the most wonderful day. 'Are you enjoying your food, gentlemen?' she asked.

Rialto laughed. The joy at finding a free meal had removed the homicidal rush he always felt when Aubrey's sister started talking. Because Rialto laughed, Gorgo laughed.

The Mortons laughed. Boss Smasher laughed. Rodney tried to laugh and failed. Barney barked.

Then Rialto coughed and fell forward.

The laughing stopped.

Now, let's you and me have a chat about table manners. The Wreckers' mothers had never taught them any. Most table manners are there so everyone can eat without noticing how disgusting the people they're eating with really are. But there's one particular instruction that's actually practical – and that is *chew your food*. Because, if you don't chew your food, it can lodge in your throat and choke you. And only mothers who didn't love their children would let them grow up never knowing they were one gobbled dinner away from the graveyard.

The Wreckers' mothers hadn't loved them. Consider this lack of instruction their little day-to-day attempt at assassination.

Rialto Grande was turning blue. He clawed at his enormous throat. Gorgo began to choke, too. The Morton Twins were coughing. Rodney Paste was choking (but not on his tongue). Barney the dog tried to bark and failed.

Boss Smasher lifted his enormous arm and smacked Barney.

Barney the dog coughed up a finger. The thick digit flopped wetly on to the floor. It pointed accusingly at the children. (It also pointed half digestedly, but let's not be gross.)

Quickly, quietly and certain this was the best time to be leaving, Aubrey's sister took her brother by the shoulders and steered him back into the front room.

Aubrey leaned over and grabbed his father's boots, which was a sensible use of half a second. If you're going to commit a crime, control as much of the evidence as you can – and, if you're going to be chased by someone like Rialto Grande, it's better to have a weapon, regardless of the smell.

The men kept choking. Boss Smasher whacked

Gorgo. The mossy rock-man coughed up long, thin black rags, the remnants of a shirt that had been passed violently through a mincer.

Gorgo smashed the nearest Morton. Left Morton coughed up a finger. It was calloused and rough and had the letter 'H' tattooed just above the knuckle. He smashed his brother. Right Morton coughed up a second finger. Its tattoo said 'O'. They both punched Rialto in the back.

Rialto Grande's face took an unscheduled flight to the kitchen floor. He groaned and squinted – he was eye-to-joint with another mangled digit. It had the letter 'W' on it.

The other men stared down at the scraps of fingers and shirt.

Painfully, Boss Smasher revealed a secret. He knew how to read. (Or at least read fingers.)

'H . . . O . . . W,' he said. 'It says HOW?' He tried to think, but he was mostly arms, not brains. He came up with, 'Hurgh, tha's prety philopobgical.'

Always be wary of a man who talks in misspellings. He's an idiot.

'We've never been asked a question by our lunch before,' said the Morton Twins in unison.

'Except maybe, "Why are you doing this?"' said Left Morton.

'Yeah. And, "Argh, my legs. Argh,"' said Right Morton.

'But that's not a question.'

'Nah. Didn't give 'em time for the squiggly bit at the end.' Right Morton was always a little smarter than his brother, which didn't mean much.

'It's clearly Howard Howard's fingers, you morons,' said Rialto, his outrageous accent forgotten. He coughed again. A half-chewed tongue flew out of his mouth and hit the kitchen floor.*

Aubrey and Aubrey's sister dashed through the hole where their front door had been and out on to the street. They had nothing but fear, youth, speed and a grubby old pair of fight-boots.

They smacked into their father's old car. Aubrey jumped inside the second his sister prised open the door of the rusty, antler-covered murdermobile.

Back in the kitchen, Rialto Grande stood over the remains of Howard Howard. The big man's eyes were wide and blazing. His head nodded uncontrollably, like he was answering an unheard question. Some of the remains of his warrior brother were in front of him, and his left hand spread out over his stomach as

---

* Where it was promptly picked up and chomped on by the furry face of Barney. Rodney would've liked to have done something about that, but nobody but Rialto was allowed to touch the animal – and what's the point of getting your tongue back if you won't have a head to put it in?

he consciously processed where some of the rest had
ended up.

His mouth twitched – the jagged yellow teeth flashing. When he spoke, his voice was quiet. 'Wreck them.'

The Wreckers poured out of the front door, hooting
for blood.

The car spluttered. Five men descended on it. The car
started, Aubrey's sister slammed her foot on the pedal
and five men splattered and scattered, scratched and

battered and swore that this wasn't the blood they'd been hooting for.

In the kitchen, Barney the dog bit one of Howard Howard's regurgitated fingers. Rialto, aggrieved and aggressive, kicked him. Barney sailed out of the kitchen window and over the back fence.

Which is how Mrs Dalrymple, having returned to her back garden, was unexpectedly hit on the head by a flying dog.

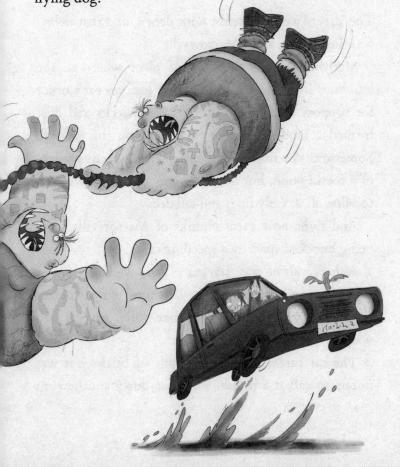

4
DRIVING WITH AUBREY'S SISTER

The streets were cluttered with debris, and that debris was the little town of Marrowville.

Marrowville was the kind of place where all the buildings look old and drunk, and lean on each other for support as they flake apart. Paint flecks and dust formed a kind of masonry dandruff on the ground. Sometimes you might get lucky and see a weedy garden, or a foetid pond, but mostly it was a town drawn by a toddler, all wobbly lines and tall decay.

And right now great chunks of Marrowville were being knocked apart by a speeding car.

Aubrey's sister was driving – and, while she was a gifted motorist, panic at the Wreckers' pursuit meant she lacked respect for things like rules, objects and walls.

The car careened through a pile of bricks – it was unfair to call it a house, since the dusty smithereens that remained afterwards resembled more a sandstorm than any trace of an actual building.

'Sorry! Being chased by murderers!' she called out of the window.

Oh, but she was happy.

A couple of hours before, she'd heard her brother speak the longest sentence she'd ever heard from him. She supposed it meant he was happy that Howard Howard wasn't around to ruin everything.

Now, zooming along in the dead Wrecker's car, Aubrey's sister heard her brother say what was, up to that point, his second-longest sentence.

'Are you sure you know how to drive, sis?' asked Aubrey, bouncing in his seat as Howard Howard's antler-covered murdermobile hurtled down the cobbled road, across the footpath, into someone's front garden, back across the footpath, into the road and back to the footpath, through a street sign, over a hill and into an ornately crafted iron park bench. 'It's just that lots of people are jumping out of our way.'

'It's a valid strategy!' said Aubrey's sister. The antlers on the front of the car had caught the bench, and now the car had a new, massive hood ornament. Sparks hit the windscreen as mangled metal scraped the pavement. 'The Wreckers won't expect us to drive on the footpath!'

Aubrey didn't know what a strategy was, but he

agreed. 'I don't think anyone would expect that, sis! I think that's why it's called a footpath!'

Four pedestrians dived out of the way of their car. Five pedestrians had tried. The fifth was now sitting on a park bench that was going on an unexpected journey.

But Aubrey's sister didn't care – her little brother was talking!

'That was sixteen words, Aubrey! A new record!'

The man on the park bench had realized he wasn't getting off the front of the car anytime soon, so was now happily eating his lunch as the machine rocketed along.

Aubrey's sister called to him. 'Excuse me, sir! My brother just spoke for a really long time!'

'What?' called the man.

'Excuse me, sir! My brother, who doesn't talk much, just spoke for a really long time and I'm so proud of him!'

The man looked at Aubrey through the windscreen. 'Young fellow! I keep hearing this voice, but there's nobody there! Aren't you clever, driving a car all by yourself and from the wrong seat?'

Aubrey's sister swerved the car. The man and his lunch and the bench made an unexpected detour straight over the road and head-first into a large inconvenient statue.

'He talked too much,' said Aubrey.

5
THE DOG & FIST

It was late in the afternoon, the sun was nearly down and the mothers, workers and assorted urchins strolling around Marrowville's Night Market were doing everything they could to avoid the Fishflinger. It would be dark soon, and it paid to get away from him before you couldn't see what he was doing.

'Fresh fish!' called the Fishflinger, a skinny, freckled nobody clad in naught but a brown sack filled with wriggling fish. 'Fresh fish for sale! Fresh, very popular fish!'

'No, thank you!' said Joanne Osprey, a tall person of no fixed personality. She and her friends were buying T-shirts of the One Tree, the only tree in Marrowville, from Mr Wuntree, the man who ran the shop where you could buy T-shirts of the One Tree, the only tree in Marrowville. Mr Wuntree was so old he looked like a gnarled tree stump in a suit, and he grinned his thanks from a mouth with Howard Howard stamped over it.

'Please ignore the man who throws fish,' said Mr Wuntree. 'His aim is bad and his odour is worse.'

'Fish!' shouted the Fishflinger, looking around for customers. There were, as always, none. He stood alone in front of Marrowville's finest drinkery, the Dog & Fist. Here citizens drank in the heart of town until they fell over and ended up in the gutters of town. But, since the Dog & Fist didn't open until all the kiddies had gone to bed, for most of the day its doorway was used by a deranged fish salesman.

'Popular fish!' called the Fishflinger, over and over, as the day slipped quietly into night.

Marrowville had its own charming preparations for when darkness fell, and these were a combination of fire-wires and freaks. A fire-wire was a string of lanterns slung between the town rooftops. A freak was, as I've told you, just about everyone in Marrowville.

Hunched over on the cobblestones, a pack of five Candleboys prepared to chase away the new evening's shadows. The Candleboys were tiny curled fellows born with fingers made of candles. And not small candles, either, but huge white waxen poles, each one the length of a tall person.

Their handler, Mr Flint, a bowler-hat-and-moustache

gruffleman,* rubbed a knife across a stone, tossing sparks at each of his boy's extended fingers until their nailwicks lit up. He grunted proudly as his Candleboys arched their backs and spread their hands wide, dragging their fiery fingers through hundreds of fire-wires. The square flickered red and white and green and blue as the line of five pulled illumination along the darkened street. A void filling up with magic.

The light revealed the passers-by who had been chattering away in the dusk. Not everyone was what they'd seemed. Two mothers pushing newborn babies turned out to be hardened criminals chained to steam-powered punishment prams – horrible whining machines that dragged them on an endless tour around town.

Both men were hardened brutes, but tonight they were hardened brutes dressed as something halfway between a princess and a whirl of fairy-floss; their pink, flouncy ruffles accessorized terribly with their dirty beards and murderous eyes. A mechanical baby listed their sins endlessly in a hideous, tinny cry: 'Arson, robbery, cake theft!'

'I never stole no cake!' said the taller one, clinging frantically to his disappearing street cred.

---

* A 'gruffleman' was a man whose job was to wear a bowler hat, have a moustache and look after Candleboys. They also tended to be gruff, since most of them didn't want this job, and also because the moustaches were nailed on.

A baker set out her stall of warm loaves and suspicious cheeses.

A donkey did whatever donkeys do.

A squadron of fourteen children chased a lizard up a wall, and then ran like mad when the lizard turned round and spat fire. It was a fire-lizard, and the children should have known better.

The Fishflinger, who had mistaken the children's rush towards him as a love of fishy produce, stayed where he was and ended up getting scorched. 'Fried fish!' he called. This happened every day.

The Fishflinger began to toss his blackened carp and haddock at anyone nearby. 'Fools!' he cried, shaking off the ashes of his scorched burlap sack. He was now not just a weirdo but a naked, grumpy weirdo in a sea of burning fish.

'Eat my popular fish! Everyone loves them!'

He chucked tails and fish heads at the sunset crowd: the double-spined acrobat deliverymen who climbed buildings like spiders to bring old people their shopping and pedalled off through the sky on tiny unicycles; Terry Patong, the divorced man who sold herbal soap; Harvey Patong (no relation), the divorced man who sold soapal herbs; Sherry Patong, the woman they'd both divorced who'd kept the Patong name and both their houses. Everyone was deluged in a rain of scorched scales, even Mr Wuntree, who added a new sign to his shop: THE ONE TREE – NOW WITH FISH!

Constable Thomas Squit leaned against the wooden front of the House of Needlessly Aggressive Sharp Things – the kind of shop where you might buy fight-boots or teeth-gloves* or a cigarette lighter that when you spark it up your liver falls out.

He wrote down everything he was seeing in his note-book. He'd filled 900 of them in the last year. Another 100 and he'd be allowed to burn all his notes and recollections, and finally start shopping for Needlessly Aggressive Sharp Things and kicking people like the Fishflinger was now doing.

'My fish are good fish! Shove them in your faces!' yelled the increasingly distraught haddock merchant. He yelled so loudly that he didn't notice the stomping sound coming from behind him.

Folk scattered to the other side of the street. It had nothing to do with the Fishflinger.

The door of the Dog & Fist clanged open. It was a heavy wooden door, made from heavy steel and painted to look like heavy wood. You knew it was steel because wood doesn't clang.

The door smooshed the Fishflinger into the wall.

---

* Teeth-gloves. They're gloves with teeth.

The wall was heavy brick painted to look like even heavier brick.

Calo, a muscular woman with a face that didn't pretend it had time for your nonsense, closed the door again. For the fleeting second she was visible from the street, white hair was apparent, as was a broom. And, if you'd spent that time looking at her white hair and broom, you'd have missed the long, thin string-sword dangling from her belt.

Now, let's ignore all that and take a walk down this alley. Look, everyone – a drainpipe. A rusty, dripping drain-pipe with a man in black climbing to the top. He's shinnied up the pipe – and now he's stretching his foot on to the cracked white window ledge at the side of the Dog & Fist.

(Have you ever read the word 'shinnied' before? It's only ever really used for people climbing up drainpipes. Isn't that strange? Some people think the word is 'shimmy', but that's a kind of dance. 'Shinnying' is pretty much a hug that takes you upward; shimmying is just something dancers do because they're too fancy for walking.)

The man on the drainpipe was so fast and nimble that he had already opened the window, climbed into his bedroom, closed the window and was now putting on his slippers. That all happened in the time it took you to read that bit about shinnying. You should pay more attention!

The man was a slender fellow, ancient and wizened,

with an upturned grey moustache and a black cloth wrapped round the top of his perfectly round head. He had a neck that looked like stretched-out dough, and a body that was mostly bone, but bone comfortably clad in a long-sleeved shirt of black fabric, with trousers that clung to his ankles. His legs were so thin that he looked like a half-inflated balloon being held down by two long strings.

His blue eyes twinkled with mischief; his purse rattled with loot; his knees cracked with age.

'That you, Charlie?' called a woman's voice from downstairs.

'It is indeed, my delicious sultana!' said Charlie, massaging his shins, which were a bit worn out after a hard day's shinnying.

'How was work?' the woman's voice called out again. Clinking was heard, and the *whoosh* of either running water or a sudden jet of flame.

'Work was –' Charlie slowly bent his upper body backwards – 'particularly fine . . .' His head was level with his waist now, and his body was a party of cracks and pops. 'No Wreckers, no police . . .' Charlie's head touched the floor, his slippered feet and unslippered nose pointing in opposite directions. He kept talking, his voice gentle and relaxed. 'It was, all in all, about as simple a day of crime as you can have.'

He reached into his pocket for a particularly nifty piece of plunder. Then he reached down to his shoe and pulled out another. He arched his back as far as it would go, and the prize he'd had gripped between his ribs popped towards the ceiling. Charlie leaped up and snatched it from the air. By the time he hit the floor, he was already sitting cross-legged and humming quietly to himself.

Charlie counted his riches. Before him lay three small, silver boxes. They were pretty to look at, warm to the touch – and, to his joy, *remarkably dangerous*. And he had three of them.

He chuckled, which meant his moustache dropped what it had been carrying, too. Now he had four of them. He scooped them up into his velvet bag.

Footsteps echoed up the staircase. They were the heavy steps of someone with authority. No, better than authority – *clout*. It was the footfall of someone who had done a lot of things with their life, and you would cry bitter tears if they decided to do something to *you*.

Charlie bent his knees and whipped his entire body forward into a low, extravagant bow.

The owner of the heavy footsteps strode into the room. Calo's muscled frame did not necessarily suggest the ability to stomp without effort, but beneath her knees her legs were thick iron rods decorated with a lifetime of dents and nicks. She wore baggy shorts, and a waistcoat that rattled with dangling corkscrews and bottle openers. Her long, thin sword clinked against her metal calves.

To the patrons of her pub, she was Calo the Bartender; to strangers and enemies she was Calo Steel-Shins.

To one person, however, she was 'my adorable strudel'.

She smiled at her other half, the charming old duffer and notorious cat burglar known as Boneless Charlie. As a younger man, he had been named after his suppleness. Now, in old age, he stood as springy and spry as a stick of wet bamboo.

Stomping over, Calo slid the cloth off her love's head. The top of Charlie's bonce was a finely etched tattoo of seven enormous eyes. Six of them encircled his head in a perfect ring. The final eye lay atop his scalp, as though worshipped by the others. While the other eyes appeared human, the final one seemed to belong to a mysterious reptile – the skin around it covered with intricate lines of scales, and its pupil shaped like an 'x'.

It was a beautiful tattoo, all tight lines and dark blue ink. If you looked at it long enough, you'd think the eyes occasionally blinked, and you'd certainly believe the one at the top meant you nothing but harm.

Charlie's real eyes met Calo's. If you were there right now, you'd see two people, who were very likely much older than you, embracing. And maybe you'd feel warm inside because they obviously loved each other. And maybe you'd think they'd always been like that – and they had. It's just that their world hadn't always been the same.

You, for instance, would see two eccentric old people in love, but you wouldn't see their past. Charlie was kissing the woman he'd married despite all the gunfire on their wartime wedding day.*

'My sweetness, I have for you in my hand the spoils from a fine day's thievery.' Boneless Charlie popped the velvet bag in Calo's outstretched palm. 'Now, shall we go downstairs for a chat and a fine sherry? Perhaps a pie?'

Calo peeked inside the bag. She was very impressed by all the silver, but confused by the fact that the bits of silver were square, and not a more useful shape, like, say, a whole bunch of coins.

And she was even more confused about something else.

Calo slid her sword through the pocket of Boneless Charlie's trousers and pulled it back. Three silver

---

* They'd met during a war. It didn't matter which war. They'd both spent a lot of time being where they weren't meant to be during events that weren't meant to happen. The finest thing about still being alive was that if anyone asked where they'd been or what they'd been doing, they could say they hadn't been anywhere and they hadn't done anything. After all, most of their friends couldn't say anything, what with being dead from doing things they weren't meant to be doing during events that weren't officially happening.

wedding rings dangled off the thin blade. She arched an eyebrow.

'Yes, my lovely pecan. I was hiding those from you.'

'Silly old Walrus-Head,' said Calo, hugging him tight. 'You don't hide loot from me or I'll stab you.'

'Ah, just like our wedding day.' He kissed her hand.

Calo fastened the rings to clasps on her waistcoat — three more bits of ill-gotten metal to jangle while she and Charlie tended the bar.

'And what did you do today, O fire of my furnace, O stoker of my soul?' Boneless Charlie kissed her shoulder as they walked downstairs. It's actually quite hard to do that to someone walking downstairs. He's lucky he didn't lose any teeth.

'Today I squashed the Fishflinger . . . again,' said Calo as she walked behind the bar. The bar was a beautiful slab of wood with a horde of snarling faces carved into its front. 'The poor man. I don't know why he doesn't just stand somewhere else. I get him every time. I miss the days when I had targets who knew how to dodge.'

Calo spied a fire-lizard on the far wall of the pub. There was no building in Marrowville that really wanted these little green intruders: one burp and you didn't own a pub any more, just a fire where the pub used to be. But they were very cute, and could keep a fireplace roaring for months.

A quick flick of the wrist and Calo's string-sword sailed through the air, a thin sliver of metal death out on a mission of slivery metal deathing. Up close, the sword was a column of steel that was only sharp at the tip. Fine etchings decorated its sides.

It struck home just under the fire-lizard, which gripped it with its tiny feet.

'Oh, my dolorous turnip! If you'd hit his gasoline gland, we could've eaten that. Or sold it as charred scratchings, I suppose.' Boneless Charlie's long legs tottered him noiselessly over to the lizard, which was blinking happily on his wife's weapon. He looked back at her, his moustache drooping downwards in concern. 'Is your aim off, my love?'

'No, it's just bored,' said Calo.

Now, Calo's string-sword. You and I know that it's called a string-sword because I just told you it was. Not everybody who encountered the string-sword knew it had a name. Most people, after all, called it 'Put that down!' and 'Aaaah!'

(And, since nobody knew it was called a string-sword, it follows that they'd have no reason to know why it had the name that they didn't know it had, now wouldn't it?)

Unbeknown to most, because most hadn't angered her, Calo's string-sword was attached at its base to an almost invisible line of razor-thin wire. The sharp bit went into the target, and the wire stayed in her hands, as though she was flying a dangerous kite. And a flick of her wrist meant that, once the blade was in, her targets didn't just perish – they danced. And the kite flyer became a puppeteer.

Calo flicked her wrist. The blade shot out of the wall and brought the lizard with it. For a moment, Calo had the kind of yo-yo that causes third-degree burns. It whipped towards her so quickly it seemed to cut the air.

Half a second before it hit her face, she struck the blade with an open palm. The fire-lizard sailed into the coals of the fireplace, where it burped happily. The fire roared to life. The string-sword twisted over Calo's back and found its home on the chain at her hip.

The fireplace was hot and, as long as the lizard stayed there, the pub would be safe. (And her husband wouldn't wake up in the night with an inferno where his moustache used to be.)

Boneless Charlie smiled at the fire, and the lizard scuttling around its warm new home. He tied his apron strings behind his back. The apron was a piece of clean white cloth with two pockets: one for change, and one, predictably, for loot.

'Ah, what a wonderful thing it is to be bored,' said Charlie.

'Bored and happy,' Calo agreed.

They were veterans of countless skirmishes. They'd crouched in shadows and taken down kings. They'd left loved ones behind – though, depending on the size of the explosion, it was sometimes fractions of loved ones, and not just behind, but everywhere.

It all meant they knew the luxury of just doing nothing.

Calo set to polishing mugs. Charlie wiped down the round wooden tables that took up most of the floor.

'So, nothing went wrong today?' Calo called from over the bar, fixing herself a tasty draught of Slugwater, the drink that goes down smooth, like a slug.

'Nothing even remotely out of the ordinary! No irksome police, no jerksome Wreckers . . .' Charlie's brow furrowed in thought, an activity that stretched the tattoos on his forehead downwards, turning staring eyes into half-runny eggs. 'Although I did stop by the One Tree.'

He had, too. He'd spent part of the afternoon jauntily clambering up the best and only tree in Marrowville. It was a very pleasant thing to do, especially since the One Tree was utterly colossal – its metal frame was a hulking skeleton for the huge warped chunks of bark nailed to its every surface, and thick clumps of leaves had been stapled to the end of every branch. It had been a part of

Marrowville for as long as anyone could remember, and it stood proud, tall and dead on a cliff right on the outskirts of town.

If you climbed the tree, you had the best view anywhere in Marrowville:* of a rolling, churning sea that crashed white into the cliff, and a view of the city that let you really drink in the decay.

And, if you were a thief like Charlie, well, all those leaves were a great place to hide.

'I climbed up and looked at the city. And then, well, I heard the most peculiar hissing noise.'

'Snake?' asked Calo.

'As it turns out, no. I got down and the whole tree was hissing. Every part of it was.'

Calo looked concerned. 'The tree was hissing . . .' Her mind was running through a hundred memories of battle and deceit.

Thoughtfully, Charlie ran the flat of his hand over his bald head. 'Oddest thing. Of course, I couldn't explore any further –' He stopped. For a half-second, he could've sworn his tattoos had just felt cold beneath his palm.

---

* The view really was terrific. On a clear day, you could see straight through to the amber cube at the top of Skyline's Ruin, where the mayor lived. Or had lived. Nobody was really certain any more. Skyline's Ruin was so tall and old it seemed like the fossilized husk of an invading beast, with bridges and smaller buildings growing into and through it over hundreds of years. The cube was the great beast's eye, and to see the town reflected in it was to see all of Marrowville upside down, and transformed into a golden memory. Gosh, the mayor was lucky, whoever he or she was.

Still, he supposed it could've just been a little stab of guilt – and there was no point being too troubled about a mystery, especially since he knew he was definitely about to be in trouble for something else.

'What went wrong, Walrus-Head?' asked Calo. She folded her arms, a half-smile on her lips.

Charlie smirked. 'Well, my beloved bricklayer . . . ah . . . about a minute after I started nosing around, three rather muscular Wreckers decided they'd like to quiz me on the origins of all the lovely things I stole today. So obviously I ran like hell.'

Calo's eyes glared a wifely glare. The look that says, *I am only playfully angry because I have become resigned to this familiar, mild problem.*

'Walrus-Head, you told me there were no police or Wreckers today.'

Charlie rubbed his moustache. 'Walrus-Head, am I?' He rounded the bar and picked up the glass of Slugwater Calo had poured for him. He gulped it down, his cheeks bulging with liquid.

'*Wahwuh-Hud?*' said Charlie, pressing his lips together.

'Walrus-Head!' giggled Calo.

Charlie slapped his cheeks. Slugwater sprayed through his moustache, the fine mist covering the love of his life. The bar would have to be wiped down a second time.

6
SERGEANT PLUG'S BIG DAY

It was lunchtime in the Marrowville town square, and the citizens were hungry for justice. An eager crowd of waistcoat-wearers, mutants, townsfolk and groundlings stood dandruff-to-lice in the shadow of the great stone Victory Finger, and waited for the Annual Chief Superintendent's Speech. Black smoke belched from chimneys; black teeth decayed in mouths; bystanders stood by and a juggler didn't juggle (so was just a jug).

Sergeant Lorenzo Plug, Chief Superintendent of the Marrowville Constabulary, sat on the marble stairs beneath the monument and sighed. He was actually the Chief Superintendent of Police, but his first name was literally Sergeant. His father had limited ambitions for his children, so had named them for the highest positions he thought they could achieve in the world. This was fine for Sergeant Plug, but terrible for his brother Toilet.

He stood up and stroked his bushy blond beard. Here

was a man of dignity, covered in badges of authority and trying very, very hard not to panic like a tiny child. He straightened his jacket: a magnificent confection of blue wool and shiny copper buttons. His medals gleamed, each a circle of jewels and precious metals that denoted bravery, determination and effort. His crisp white shirt was buttoned neatly at the throat, his white breeches swelled to contain thick thighs.

And his sparkly, feathered, skyscraper-tall cone hat ruined absolutely everything.

He sighed again. The hat had been given to him by Rialto Grande to mark his tenth year of not being promoted to the rank of Wrecker. He had to wear it on important occasions. It was Rialto's way of reminding Plug that *he* wasn't important. He could lead the police, but he was still unqualified to commit crimes. Plug didn't particularly want to commit crimes, but he thought that if there was just one person who had licence to commit crime, and they didn't do it, then maybe other people would do the same.

It was a lovely thought, and the kind of thinking that gets you written about in an encyclopaedia a few hundred years after the crowd flings you to the nearest lion.

Unfortunately, the Wreckers kept stealing his notebooks, and without them he couldn't be promoted. He couldn't arrest them for doing it, of course. Police officers in Marrowville could only write evidence in their notebooks, and Wreckers couldn't be arrested, especially since the evidence written in a police officer's notebook was really just a receipt for services rendered by the Wreckers.

Sergeant Plug stepped over to his horse, put one leg in a stirrup and hoisted his thick body up. With one swing of the leg, he was astride the enormous dreadnought: a great brown creature made of pure muscle and fed on oaty oats. The horse had a harness of steel all around his head and body, a fearsome tangle of barbs and biting spikes. He was, however, tragically unaware of this – and worryingly friendly. If he nuzzled you, you stayed nuzzled. Thirty police recruits had been severely injured because this beast thought they had a sugar lump somewhere about their person.

He was a terrible horse. His name was Terrible Horse. His friends called him Terry. (He had no friends. Or at least no friends who could still call him anything, on account of their appalling injuries. We'll be his friends, though, won't we? We should be pretty safe. After all, he's just a horse in a book.)

On top of Terry's head sat a raised lectern that had been designed to hold something tremendous. That tremendous thing was the Sacred Police Officer's

Charter, a 9,000-page book in a cover of swirling blue and gold metal. It glinted in the sunlight, a magnificent beacon of knowledge and authority.

It wasn't just 'a book'; it was, to the thousands in attendance, *the* Book, the most important object in all of Marrowville – the throbbing, beating heart of the town, from which came all wisdom and law. To see it was to be blinded by its brilliance, to honour it was to honour yourself and to disgrace it was to disgrace everybody.

Sweat broke out on Sergeant Plug's forehead. He knew he was going to get it wrong today. He always got it wrong. Oh, he read the Book to the people of Marrowville every year, and every year he successfully followed the rituals and nothing went *too* disastrously wrong. But everyone always treated him as if it was going to go so very, very badly!

'Don't forget, you can't touch it with your bare hands!' hissed a voice from below.

'I know,' fumed Sergeant Plug, with the tired tone of a man who had a big job to do and had to do it while wearing a stupid hat.

Everyone knew the rules for dealing with the Book – if you lived in Marrowville, you just knew them. If you didn't know them, you didn't live in Marrowville. And, since the only place anyone could live was Marrowville, everybody knew the rules:

1. Only very important people can open the Book.
2. Nobody is important enough to open the Book while touching the Book.
3. Wear gloves to open the Book so you don't touch it, but only if you're important enough.

4. The Chief of Police is important enough, but only if Rialto Grande says so.
5. If any of this goes wrong, blame Sergeant Plug.

(This last point had been in effect since before he became Chief of Police. Life is very unfair.)

And so, with white gloves on and with worries set to maximum, Sergeant Plug gripped both sides of the lectern and pulled himself upward until he stood ramrod straight on his horse's back. Here was a ten-tonne man on a terrible steed, an unwavering, unmoving mountain of iron and strength. The kind of person a town could, would and should depend upon.

Alas, his dangling stomach caught under the lectern as he stood up, which caused him to flop forward towards the Book. He clumsily shoved his gloved hands into its cover, as though trying to stop his thick cheeks smooshing into it.

His face flushed. He was shaking, and praying nobody had noticed. He stood back to attention. His fingers were sweaty in the gloves; his body was sweaty in the uniform. Great rivulets of anxiety ran from his massive forehead and dripped on to the leather of his saddle.

He shifted his foot nervously. He slipped on his own sweat and went from standing to sitting in the blink of an eye and an *ouch* of pain.

But nobody blinked. Everybody saw. The only thing still visible above the great lectern was his appalling hat, so it looked like a great feathery cone was about to address the town.

Giggles rippled through the crowd. Large events always benefit from someone official falling over.

Sergeant Plug straightened himself up as best he could, and then, when that didn't work, with the help of three police officers and a lot of grunting. Soon he was up again, and, when he began to speak, his voice was a blustery bellow that left his wobbly face hot and made his sandy moustache dance on the wind.

'Attention, Marrowville!' he said, thumping the lectern. Terry grunted. The laughter stopped.

Beneath the strings of unlit fire-wires, the citizens of Marrowville listened. There were enough of them out today for the square to be overcrowded. People's backs were jammed against the tall and bent things of wood and flaking plaster that Marrowville called buildings. There was a sea of people wearing Mr Wuntree's One Tree shirts. It was so crowded that the mist in the sky had lowered itself over everyone's heads, as though the clouds themselves had come down to hear the speech: a gloomy grey blanket blocked the sun with promises of exceptional dampness. (And razors.)

Sergeant Plug stretched his arms out as magnificently

as his poor self-esteem would allow. His foot trembled, and his underlings got ready to catch him if it all went wrong. Again.

'Justice,' said Sergeant Plug.

'Justice,' said the citizens of Marrowville, and each person put their fingers to the middle of their eyebrows in the traditional way of the town. It didn't make any sense, but traditions don't have to. A Candleboy singed himself trying to fit in.

Far above the ground, the Marrowvillian roofs of tin and shingle softly dinged under the single-wheel cycles of the double-spined deliverymen, baskets on their twin backs and silence on their tongues. A few rode their tiny copper unicycles along the fire-wires slung across the square, their amazing balancing act accompanied by nothing more than a slight creaking and squeaking in the air.

On the ground, which was, as normal, far below the sky, families hushed their smallest members with either threats or lollies. Every window in the square stood open as gentlemen and ladies leaned out for the yearly show.

Two small shapes-in-sacks tiptoed through the silent crowd. 'I'm hungry, sis,' whispered the shorter one. If you looked under the sack, you'd see its hair was very messy. If you looked further down, you'd see it was carrying a big pair of fight-boots, their top laces knotted together.

'Shhhh,' said the taller shape.

Sergeant Plug continued. 'My name is Chief Superintendent Sergeant Lorenzo Plug, and it is my honour and duty to welcome all of you to this year's Justice Week.'

At this, the crowd cheered. (Some goons hooted, as goons do.)

'This is an unfortunate Justice Week, as lately we have discovered that even our children commit heinous crimes against our town and its simple laws. I was informed earlier today that local legend and Wrecker Howard Howard was murdered . . .'

A small cheer rose from those who had at some point had the word Howard imprinted on their foreheads.

'. . . murdered by his son Aubrey, and his imaginary friend.'

At this, a giant picture of Aubrey was lowered from one side of the great stone Victory Finger. At the bottom of the picture was the name *Aubrey Howard*. On the other side of the Finger, another picture was lowered. It was a question mark with long hair.

The two shapes-in-sacks stood completely still. One pulled back his sackcloth hood and opened his mouth in astonishment; the other grabbed him and pulled his sackcloth hood back down over his head. The taller shape's face was invisible under her own hood, but, if you could've seen her mouth, you'd have seen a smirk become a grimace. And, if you'd been watching her very closely, you might even have noticed her stealing some fudge from a nearby stall.

'If any of you have any information, please bring it to the Wreckers. Or bring it to the police, so we can tell the Wreckers. We have two very small holes for them, so that justice may be done.' He pointed at two hollows that had been cut into the cobbles, each deep enough to lower a child into.

Sergeant Plug shuddered. He had asked if it was necessary to involve the whole town in a hunt for two children, especially when there was no evidence they'd done anything, or that one of them even existed. Plus, Howard Howard was a cruel man and everyone was probably better off without him. Rialto Grande had answered by thumping Sergeant Plug into a wall. And then Rialto Grande's dog had sneezed on him.

He moved on to happier topics: 'However, now that that's out of the way . . . may your pursuit of goodness be fun, and your shoes remain clean throughout.'

The crowd, knowing what that referred to, chuckled.

The taller shape-in-a-sack nicked some chunks of meat from the pockets of the laughing crowd. The shape didn't have time to be sad, or confused. It only had time to be practical, and then move on to emotions later. The shorter shape-in-a-sack was eating fudge, which had the advantage of being both practical *and* delicious.

'Let's go back to the car,' whispered the taller shape.

'Then *whut?*' asked the shorter shape, who'd have said more, but his mouth was full of fudge.

'We'll try to drive through the mist —' the taller shape was looking for the fastest way out of the square — 'and try not to die.'

Beneath his sack, Aubrey put another piece of fudge in his mouth. Wreckers, razor-mist . . . it was all the same. If he was going to die, he was going to do it after he'd finished his sweets.

Still safely atop his horse (for the time being), Sergeant Plug had reached the start of the most important part of the ceremony.

'I bring forth, at this time, the Sacred Police Officer's Charter!' With this, he raised the colossal tome above his head, then slammed it down on the lectern. The thud echoed through the minds of the thousands present. They were going to hear a reading from the single most important, beloved and respected object in Marrowville, a reading delivered by . . . well . . . a chap in a stupid hat.

Thousands of people bowed to the Sacred Police Officer's Charter and hoped the Chief of Police didn't think they were bowing to him.

An earless policeman saluted the Book with his one surviving arm. He glared at the horse with his one surviving eye. His name was Officer Jenkins and he had learned the hard way never to underestimate Terry's lust for sugar, or the horse's endless curiosity as to why people screamed whenever he touched them.

'I read to you now from the Sacred Police Officer's Charter,' said Sergeant Plug. A large white bird landed on top of his ridiculous hat, which now looked like an enormous Christmas tree that had been suddenly jammed up a swan's bum.

It was a miracle. The bird had flown safely through the razor-mist apparently just to ruin his dignity. Life definitely wasn't fair.

At the far end of the square, on the second floor of the Dog & Fist, Calo opened her bedroom window and popped her head out. Boneless Charlie lay snoring in their bed. (He was a cunning man, but a snooze is a snooze.) The Fishflinger, still stunned from the previous day's excitement, squinted in the direction of the crowd. He sat in the gutter and clutched a solitary, burnt, unflung fish.

'. . . this Sacred Police Officer's Charter . . . here . . . which was given to us by . . .' Sergeant Plug was trying to dislodge the bird without getting a fresh new medal on his chest or back.

Oh, how the bird reminded him of his father! Always present, always ruining things . . . always sitting on his hat. 'You will always fail!' Daddy Plug had said to him, sitting on his hat. 'Women! Sports! Career! Nothing will work! Why, you can't even get your own father to stop sitting on your hat!'

Sergeant Plug touched his hat and looked at a spotted teenager standing in the crowd, all poor posture and 'So what?' eyes. Oh, he wished he could've been like that when he was that age, but no, there was no slouching in the Plug household. Sergeant Plug had been born standing to attention. He had to stand. It was the only thing that stopped his father sitting on his hat.

The bird flapped its wings. Its legs were stuck in the ridiculous hat and it began to caw in distress. Sergeant Plug raised his voice. His deputies glared at the crowd, their eyes and uniforms daring anyone to look at the Chief of Police's accidental new pet bird.

'This Sacred Police Officer's Charter, which was given to us by –' he fumbled – 'given to us by . . .'

Sergeant Plug realized he didn't actually know who'd given Marrowville the Sacred Police Officer's Charter. It was strange: he'd made this speech many times, and he felt like he'd always known the answer before.

He turned to his right to see if the mayor knew. Too late he remembered that, while he knew Marrowville had a mayor, he wasn't entirely certain he knew exactly who that was.

He scanned the sea of faces in front of him. They didn't look like they cared who the mayor was, or who exactly had given them the Sacred Police Officer's Charter. They were here for the *justice*.

'Anyway, this Sacred Police Officer's Charter, which was given to us . . . was first given to –' he hit a bit he knew – 'the Sacred Police, who disbanded after some unfortunate business involving wine that turned out to be blood. Now, the first thing the Book wants is for everyone to shout out their name and address. Ready?'

Except for the two tiny shapes-in-sacks, every citizen of Marrowville bellowed out their name and address. If you wrote the noise down, it would look like this:

Fhueoagfouegrgst! Gfeujdjoag! 13jggodsgousbe82kadsdgj37!
MARROWVILLE!

That was always the best bit of Justice Week, because

Sergeant Plug knew something he was fairly certain nobody else did. When everybody shouted out their names and addresses, their names and addresses would suddenly appear, written down inside the Sacred Police Officer's Charter. No wonder nobody was allowed to touch it directly. This was a precious book that could do incredible things. And he had the only copy!

Well pleased, and almost at ease, Sergeant Plug continued: 'And now I say unto you: *You'll find yourself far less aloof when we've changed your mind with a horse's hoof.*'

Sergeant Plug addressed this last line not to the assembled public but to the miserable heads that stared up at him from far beneath his horse. Yes, at the level of Terry's hooves, a river of men and women were buried up to their chins in dry tar, each one a hairy, whining cobblestone in a footpath of wiggling and screams.

Some stared up from next to rubbish bins, some from next to potted plants. The ones that were literally beneath Terry didn't stare up at Sergeant Plug at all; they stared at a sky full of horse, and all the horrors that go with that.

'Each of you will be held in the ground for this next week, so that you may learn the price of minor infractions . . . like littering and piracy and murder. You unfortunate souls are to be stuck in the road and trodden upon by the good people of Marrowville,' said Sergeant

Plug, as the assembled good people of Marrowville began to unlace their normal footwear and put on their very heaviest boots.

A child picked up a bucketful of rocks. A nun pulled out a club.

'Your lack of feeling for your fellow citizens means you shall feel the clomp of their boots.'

The two shapes-in-sacks scurried through the crowd, praying they wouldn't have to feel the clomp of anything.

Just up from Sergeant Plug, Tom Inkling, Marrowville's best and only journalist, sat cross-legged on the window-ledge of the town's mostly empty bank. He wrote feverishly in his notepad:

Justice Week is here again! The vividly
vicious bash held once a year to the delight
of a population which likes its entertainment
interactive and, after a couple of tries, squishy.

Soon he would deliver his finished newspaper to Skyline's Ruin, and, by extension, the mayor. He'd never met the mayor, of course, but he was pretty sure there was one since they were the only person in town allowed to have a newspaper, whoever they were.

It had to be true: it was written in the Sacred Police Officer's Charter.

'You are to spend the next seven days as the street in the most popular part of town,' said Sergeant Plug. 'Here, beneath the beautiful Victory Finger, which commemorates Marrowville's victory over our enemies . . . or fingers . . . or our enemy's fingers . . . where you are to be trodden upon by your fellow citizens so as to teach you that, when a community walks, it walks only upon itself.'

'We walk upon ourselves!' came the chant of the throng as they got ready to walk on some people who definitely weren't them.

'Drop the words!' called Sergeant Plug, turning to shout at the officer on top of the Victory Finger. He turned at precisely the wrong moment and dislodged the bird, which rewarded him in the face with a fresh new medal for poor timing. His face turned red, except for the bit that was now obviously very white indeed.

'Ha!' said one of the heads in the road.

High above Sergeant Plug and his horse-borne lectern, a blue-uniformed constable unfastened the motto for a healthful and good Justice Week:

STOMP! STOMP! STOMP!

'All will now chant the Justice Week Creed,' said Sergeant Plug, wiping his eyes and bidding the crowd chant along. Together, they chanted the sacred words:

'IN MARROWVILLE, BATHED IN MIST,
WE STOMP! WE STOMP! WE STOMP!
ONCE A YEAR, WE TREAD ON CRIME!
WE STOMP! WE STOMP! WE STOMP!
WE STOMP OUT CRIME IN MARROWVILLE
BECAUSE OUR HEARTS ARE PURE
BUT OUR SOLES ARE FILTHY.
STOMPETTY-STOMPETTY-STOMP!'

'Stomp, citizens of Marrowville! Stomp until they've learned their lesson! We have shoe sellers at the ready if your feet get too messy!'

'STOMPETTY-STOMPETTY-STOMP!' cried the crowd. 'STOMPETTY-STOMPETTY-STOMP!'

People were getting rowdy. Some folk butted heads. (Some folk buttered heads, but they were weirdos and not worth talking about.)

The police band struck up a drumbeat. It was the kind of rhythm you could crush grapes to. (Or heads.)

'Oh hell,' said the head that had laughed only a few seconds before.

The crowd advanced on the submerged road people. Sergeant Plug looked at the man who had been laughing at him.

'Hello, Father,' said Sergeant Plug.

And as a sea of people began to dance, and redden their shoes a little, two shapes-in-sacks moved unseen as they squeezed their way through the deranged, cheering throng. If you looked under their hoods, you'd know that one was a skinny girl, her long black hair dirty and frizzy, her face set firm in careful concentration. The other was a tiny boy whose sticky-out, messy black hair was an enemy to combs everywhere, and whose mouth was currently making a huge dent in Marrowville's fudge supply.

If you were a citizen of Marrowville, you would have thrown them to the police, who would have thrown them to the Wreckers. Who would've thrown them, well, let's just say 'away'.

It had been a big day for Aubrey and Aubrey's sister. She had always wanted to show him the town, and on arrival they had discovered they had no friends, no home and no hope. But at least they had fudge.

Aubrey's sister saw a man's wallet on the ground. She considered it.

She was about to take her brother on a high-speed car ride towards almost absolutely certain destruction, and you don't need money to do that.

But, if the mist didn't take them, and the Wreckers didn't wreck them, they'd definitely need money to survive. Maybe they could buy something to celebrate not dying. Something like ice cream. Or medical attention, depending on how badly her plan went.

She moved towards the wallet, silently and subtly. Aubrey moved towards it, too. But too, too obviously.

And police officers, unfortunately, are very good at seeing what other people don't see. Especially if it's obvious. And especially if it's their big special day.

Sergeant Plug spotted a suspicious, small shape-in-a-sack about to pick up a wallet on the ground.

'THIEF!' he boomed.

He whipped his Terrible Horse into a gallop. There'd be no crime in Marrowville. Not during Justice Week. He and Terry bolted noisily towards the children.

But as loud as the horse's hooves were, and as much as Sergeant Plug bellowed, the sound of both were drowned out by the thunder of thousands of people stomping. Sergeant Plug was a policeman doing his duty, drowned out by the sickening sounds of justice.

7
Haven't You Always Wanted to Be Wanted?

Marrowville is the kind of town that has a lot of stories, and a lot of places to hide should you find yourself, regretfully, in one of those stories.

It has a lot of places to hide, unless, of course, you're in the busiest part of town, on the busiest day of the year, and the Chief of Police has just seen you stealing. Of course, you could hide among the crowds of people that make Marrowville Square the busiest part of town, but Chief Superintendent Sergeant Lorenzo Plug had a solution to that problem – and its name was Terry the Terrible Horse.

Sergeant Plug's armoured steed sliced through innocent people as he thundered towards Aubrey. Eager justice-doers got free haircuts as the barb-covered beast flew through the throng, his massive horsey hooves trampling citizens while his tiny horsey mind wondered, *Aw . . . how soon till sugar lumps?*

Aubrey's sister grabbed her brother. She spent a lot of time grabbing her brother. It's what younger brothers are for. Aubrey, for his part, chewed fudge.

The children ran. They ducked between legs and pushed between hips.

Sergeant Plug thundered, too, the bullied man now a terrifying figure sailing above the crowd. He clutched the pewter podium and scowled from atop the largest horse anyone had ever seen. He tore through the crowd. 'Thieves!' he shouted. His squad of running police officers wrote the word down, in case it was useful later.

'*Whuh thuh cuh?*' asked Aubrey, who saw getting chased by another mass of frightening people as no real reason to stop eating.

'The car is in front – excuse me!' said Aubrey's sister, sliding under the nun with the club. 'The car is in front of the laundrette, up Chicken Wringer's Lane.'

'*Whuh's ah lundurut?*' asked Aubrey.

'Aubrey, I love you –' she jumped over a lawyer – 'but we'll have to learn to cope with the fact that you don't know what a laundrette is another time –' she slid between two bankers – 'and another time we'll come back to town and I'll show you what it looks like at night – excuse me – it's really very pretty, but right now, if you could do me a favour . . .'

'Yuh?'

'Spit out your fudge!'

Aubrey, unaware that Terry the Terrible Horse was now but a bite's width from his own ear, turned and spat the fudge directly into the mighty steed's mouth.

The horse reared back, a look of dumb joy all over his face. Sergeant Plug fell to the ground, a look of dumb amazement all over his face. The Sacred Police Officer's Charter fell on the ground, a look of dumb anger all over its fa– What am I talking about? It's a book.

The crowd gasped, but not because of Sergeant Plug's terrible fall. They gasped because the Book had hit the ground. Sergeant Plug watched his appalling hat roll away, and groaned.

Aubrey's sister saw the Book. Its cover was pure gold. Two large slabs of pure gold. It was the kind of object that could be sold so two children would have food to eat and a safe place to sleep.

Aubrey saw the Book. He didn't see a cover of pure gold because it wasn't there. He didn't see what Sergeant Plug saw, either. In Aubrey's eyes, the Book had a picture of his mother on the front, and pages the colour of autumn leaves. It didn't matter that Aubrey had no idea what his mother had looked like, or what autumn leaves were – for a moment, he saw a face he desperately wanted.

Everyone who ever looked at the Book saw something they wanted, even if maybe they didn't all see the same thing.

Sergeant Plug saw something he didn't want. He saw two hooded urchins about to touch the Book. He got to his feet and reached for his truncheon. His thinning thatch of sandy hair was slick with sweat. He advanced on the children.

Aubrey's sister stared at the golden cover, but couldn't bring herself to move towards it.

Aubrey stared at the picture of his mother. His eyes watered as he reached out and touched the lines of her face, his right hand light against the Book's cover. If you'd listened closely, you might have heard music.

Sergeant Plug screamed, 'Don't touch it!' His eyes popped red. His truncheon knocked Aubrey away and into a gutter. The boy slept, and why not? A lullaby had been played, though entirely with percussion. The big policeman grabbed the Book.

Aubrey's sister saw her brother fly into the road.

Aubrey's sister heard Sergeant Plug screaming, 'You don't *touch* it! You never touch the Sacred Police Officer's Charter!' Aubrey's sister was restrained by police officers.

The townsfolk were aghast that someone had touched their Book. They formed a circle around Sergeant Plug and the two children. A police officer grabbed Aubrey's hood and pulled it back.

'We got him, Sergeant!' the officer called. 'We got Aubrey Howard!'

He became aware that Sergeant Plug wasn't paying attention.

Sergeant Plug was sitting on the ground, hunched over. He was crying. And not just crying: he was clutching the Book to his chest and wailing.

His huge body rocked back and forth. He began to stroke the Book's cover with his big gloves, the way you'd stroke a lost pet that had just come home, but to which you were extremely allergic. 'BOOK!' he wailed. 'BOOK!' People started to feel embarrassed. It was like their enormous Chief of Police had just learned the word 'book' and was disturbingly upset about it.

At the prodding of a junior officer, Sergeant Plug peered through tears at the unconscious boy. His eyes widened. Howard Howard's murderer had been found, and so quickly! He got to his feet and dusted himself off. Dignity had been restored.

Oblivious to a fugitive being discovered, and the hideous blasphemy committed against the Sacred Police Officer's Charter, Terry the Terrible Horse gnawed at his fudge and danced with glee. People ducked. Sergeant Plug didn't duck and got kicked in the noggin. Just like Aubrey, Sergeant Plug had a little sleep. Who knew horses could play lullabies, too?*

The Book flew through the air for the second time that day. Thirty police officers scrambled frantically to catch it. Thirty police officers didn't detect the little girl breaking free and picking up her groggy brother. Thirty police officers watched in amazement as the Book opened in mid-air and landed on Sergeant Plug's face.

Beneath the pages and beneath consciousness, Sergeant Plug appeared to scream.

'BLAME SERGEANT PLUG!' shouted the crowd, as tradition demanded.

Aubrey's sister hauled her unconscious brother down a convenient alley. He gurgled, which is a lot like talking

---

* Here is a classic horse lullaby:

> Go to sleep,
> Go to sleep,
> Ignore the horse in your bedroom.
> Go to sleep,
> Go to sleep,
> The horse has a gun.

and a lot like swallowing, though not quite either.

'Well, that was a great first trip to town, wasn't it?' Aubrey's sister muttered to herself, balancing the boy against her shoulder. 'See the sights, anger some police, watch your brother get knocked senseless . . .'

Aubrey's head rolled forward.

'I mean, why even go out? We could've been knocked senseless at home . . . Why are you so heavy, Aubrey? You've eaten exactly one proper meal ever.'

She stepped out of the alley and into the street and straight into a man. He looked down at the small shape-in-a-sack holding the smaller shape-in-a-sack.

Aubrey's sister glared up at the man from under her hood. Her eyes were sharp, like knives. Eye knives. Little eye-knives. Kn-eye-ves. Kneyves.

'I'm not here,' she said.

The man, who just wanted to live a quiet life, agreed, and walked home and out of this story.

Aubrey's sister trudged along the street. Her brother began to stir; his feet found purchase on the cobbles of Chicken Wringer's Lane. He opened his eyes and saw the laundrette where his sister had parked. There was the car, just where they'd left it. Only now it was on fire.

Aubrey's sister said something at this point, but I'm afraid you don't want to hear it.

8
THE WRECKERS ARE HUNTING

Rialto Grande looked at the upside-down old man and sighed.

'Havvvvvve yooooo seeeeeeen theeees leeetle boy?' he asked, one strong hand locked round the elderly fellow's left ankle. He shoved a photograph in the man's face. Then, realizing his mistake, he turned the photograph upside down, too.

The old man squinted. Barney sneezed on the photo.

'He looks justtt like theeees, but without the adorrrable dog's snoooooottt.'

The old man shook his head. This was a mistake, since it meant Rialto shook him. Rialto spun on one heel and flung the man over his shoulder. The frail gentleman sailed down the hall and head-first into a pile of similarly dizzy old duffers.

The Wreckers' search for Aubrey and Aubrey's sister had taken them out of Central Marrowville and all the way to the Billowy Lakes Rest Home for Discarded Oldsters. It was the only large building for miles, and the oppressive quiet of the countryside was making the Wreckers edgy.

All day, they had failed to find the children; but, worse, out here there were fields of sheep, and cows that stood and mooed at you. It was all far, far too healthy for a gang of violent city boys.

Rialto walked through the debris of a kicked-down wooden door and on to the rest home's un-kicked wooden veranda. He stared from the mown garden to the valley of wild grass beyond. He saw how the land dipped into the ground, then rose up into the tall cliff that was so gloriously crowned by the One Tree. Behind that tree was a sheer drop to the ocean, to a place called Wrecker Bay. Beneath the surface of Wrecker Bay lay the debris of a wrecked ship. Inside that ship floated the bodies of the first people to ever try stopping Wreckers from wrecking. Inside their bodies was . . . well, probably nothing — because sharks exist.

The sky was cloudy, and this far into the outskirts of Marrowville, there was no noise but the far-off rolling sea and the occasional 'Moo' or 'Baa'.★ The grey sky made it all too melancholy and dull to be serene. The

★ These noises didn't come from cows or sheep. Sometimes the pensioners would just get bored.

Billowy Lakes Rest Home's boundaries weren't walls, just miles of boredom and flatness. And, of course, the mist. The grey, depressing fog that kept Marrowville from the world (whatever world that might happen to be).

In frustration, Rialto Grande tossed a stray nurse into the sky. The sky must've been frustrated, too, because, after a few seconds, it threw her back. He tromped down to the gate.

'Heeeem,' he said. Doubt had arrived in his psychopathic mind, and he didn't know what to do with this horrible new feeling. He despised not being able to find the children, and he didn't like the look of those clouds, either. He remembered the hateful parasite girl screaming about his men deserting him. Half the day had already been spent digesting his best Wrecker – the last thing Rialto needed now was more of his soldiers disappearing under cover of thunder and lightning. He let his emotions out with another incomprehensible 'Heeeeem'.

The Wreckers were leaning on their truck. Where Howard Howard's car had been a tiny beetle covered with deer bones, this was a huge rust-red cockroach, its underside flanked by six segmented shafts of tangled metal that splayed sharp and wide from the sides of the car. These dragged on the ground and sparked wherever the Wreckers went, the scraping and squealing a warning that they were coming, the sparks a visual cue that it was already too late to run.

'What nummmmber house was theeeeet?'

'Forty-eight,' said Boss Smasher, who had been counting on his own fingers till he ran out of them, so had collected some more on the way.

'Fortyyyy-et. Forttty-et houses and nobody *knooooows* where the cheldreen arrrrre.'

'Mebbe they got eaten,' said Left Morton.

'Yeah, mebbe they got eaten,' said Right Morton.

Rialto squeezed the top of his nose between thumb and forefinger. The Mortons were obviously hungry. This would derail things for the next few hours.

'Howard Howard tasted good,' said Right Morton.

'Can we stop off and eat another friend?' asked Left Morton.

'I want to eat a free-range buddy – it's more ethical,' said Right Morton, who was smarter than his brother.

Left Morton guffawed. 'I want to eat Rodney. Any complaints, Rodney?'

Rodney Paste hissed. It was somewhere between anger and fear, and nowhere near his tongue, which had, of course, last been seen giving Barney the dog a lovely morning snack.

Gorgo rumbled. It was somewhere between a gurgle and an avalanche.

'Gorgo's right – everywern beck in the Cockroachhh. We'll go beck into town.'

Gorgo rumbled a second time. He'd been trying to say he wanted to eat Rodney, too.

Rialto's crew piled into their rust bucket. It coughed black smoke as they tore their way back towards Central Marrowville.

⟨≡≡≡≡⟩

Seven hours later, the nurse regained consciousness to find a policeman standing over her.

'It looks as though your door has been kicked in and all your elderly patrons banged on the head,' said the constable.

'Yes, that's right.'

'Very good,' said Constable Thomas Squit, filling in the end of his 1,000th notebook. Once he'd taken his sacks of books to Sergeant Plug, he could finally leave the police force and be what he'd always wanted to be – a criminal.

'Can somebody help us?' asked one of the old people in the home.

'I'm terribly sorry, but that's not my job,' said the departing police constable.

9
WHERE DO HUNGRY CHILDREN GO?

With almost everyone in the town square, Chicken Wringer's Lane was deserted. Except, of course, for two small children dressed in sacks, and their new friend, a medium-sized fire.

Howard Howard's car was burning merrily. Its petrol tank had exploded, which meant the deer antlers had been smoked, the bonnet had blown off and the seats were aflame. A single wheel rolled by the children, a rubbery circle of red fire that picked up speed as the lane sloped down.

Aubrey, who was dazed, but not currently ablaze, cheered loudly. Aubrey's sister, who was neither on fire nor concussed, covered her brother's mouth and pulled his hood back over his head. She didn't bother putting her own hood back on. Her face had just been shown to the entire town and, even if everybody was going to try to kill her, they were apparently still going to pretend she wasn't real. According to the Wanted poster, she didn't have a name and she'd never even had a face, so what was the point in hiding? She didn't exist, and they were going to make sure of it. She had nothing, and she was nothing.

And she was sick of it.

'Of *course* the car's on fire!' Aubrey's sister shouted at the sky. 'Why wouldn't it be on fire? Our father was ground to mince by the world's tallest skeleton and a beanbag lady with a big black pram! That was wonderful! I liked that! Then a policeman with a ridiculous hat thumps my brother in the head! He had a horse made of spikes! There's a fog in the air that cuts off the whole town, and everyone in town wants to stomp on us until we've got less brains than the Morton Brothers!'

She was raving now. She was raving so much that she didn't see the man who'd walked out of this story walk back into this story. He wasn't anywhere near the children; he'd just strolled back to his house a few metres down Chicken Wringer's Lane, and then wandered out on to his roof, where an enormous hot-air balloon was tied to the chimney. The man climbed into the basket and untied the rope.

Man and balloon floated into the air. They rose up and up and up and up into the sky. Soon they'd disappeared into the mist. And the mist didn't like it.

'We're being chased by murderers and the police! *Who work for the murderers!*' Down below, Aubrey's sister was still shouting. She was shouting so loudly that she didn't see a small bit of the sky flash red, or hear the massive balloon bursting.

'If anything, it's fine that the car's on fire now. What's amazing is that the car wasn't *always* on fire!'

Aubrey staggered over to the blaze. His sister kept yelling at everything and nothing.

'What else have you got?' Aubrey's sister continued. 'We finally had food! We had a home! Now we're stealing things – of course we're stealing; we've got so much nothing that I don't even have a name! People think I don't have a face! Do I have feet, or are these just two squids that got lost one day? Do I even have a brother, or is Aubrey just some kind of giraffe in disguise? Is he a secret giraffe? Oh, you know what – I bet that if he was a giraffe . . . oh, I bet that giraffe would be on fire, too, *just to be inconvenient.*'

Aubrey stood by the fire, apparently warming his hands. Aubrey's sister stood away from the fire, clenching hers.

The man who'd been in the balloon fell out of the sky and smacked into the ground in front of Aubrey's sister.

'ARRRRRGH!' said Aubrey's sister, who'd had enough of today, and that was before it started raining people.

Aubrey didn't notice – he was busy grinning stupidly at the burning car.

The girl looked helplessly at her brother, whose lopsided smile was fluctuating between 'happy idiot' and 'I need serious medical attention'.

She forced herself to calm down, or as calm as she could get. After all, she had a little brother to keep safe. It was time to get back to business.

'C'mon, Aubrey,' she said. 'Let's go somewhere else.' She stepped over the man who'd fallen from the sky. Of course he had. What was another dead man on a day like today?

Aubrey's sister had once again resigned herself to things going wrong, which meant she'd do what she usually did when that happened: fix it, then cry later – and alone.

She started dragging her brother away from the car. Her brain was in the process of improvising a new plan, especially since her original one was now an inferno in the street.

Grinning, Aubrey flopped his head back and smiled up at his sister. 'Do you want a marshmallow?'

In the time she had been shouting, and a man had fallen from the sky, Aubrey had somehow managed to toast two fluffy marshmallows on the wreckage of Howard Howard's burning car. They were as soft as his brain felt, and only slightly less singed than their father's vehicle.

Aubrey's sister popped one in her mouth. She giggled; it was a little bit of stress leaving her like the first peep of steam from a kettle. 'If we don't get out of here, we'll be thrown to the Wreckers. Then the Wreckers will tear us apart. Then they'll throw the bits into the sea. Then the bits will be eaten by fish. Do you want your bits to be eaten by fish, Aubrey?' With that, she pulled his hood back up, and slung the fight-boots back over his shoulders.

Aubrey burrowed his head in his sister's arms. 'I don't want to be eaten by fish. It'd take them too long to eat me.' He narrowed his eyes. 'I'm a Secret Giraffe.'

'Yes, you are,' Aubrey's sister agreed. 'A giraffe so secret that it's actually a very short young boy.'

'A boy that doesn't eat leaves.'

'It's almost like you're not a giraffe at all.'

Aubrey whispered, 'I am the Most Secret Giraffe.'

Aubrey's sister laughed and hugged her brother. A burning car, threats to life and limb and a man who'd fallen from the sky, and the bit he'd noticed was that she'd called him a secret giraffe.

'*Mwish*,' said Aubrey.

'What's that?' asked Aubrey's sister.

'It's . . . not the noise a Secret Giraffe makes,' said

116

Aubrey, keeping a secret known only to Secret Giraffes.

Further down the lane, a black van with no doors began to rumble up the road. One of the young Wreckers inside leaned out of the window and smashed a rubbish bin with a metal pole. Then he saw the fire. Then he saw the children.

'MURDERER! TINY MURDERER!'

The van sped towards Aubrey and Aubrey's sister. Other men leaned out, foaming at the mouth like the rabid dogs they'd just had for lunch.

The children ran round a corner. One of the fight-boots on Aubrey's shoulder came loose and swung out. It hit Aubrey's sister in the face. She fell down. Aubrey turned to see what had happened, which meant it spun round and hit him in the face, too.

'Great, Aubrey – it's just like Howard's home,' said Aubrey's sister. She picked up her dazed giraffe brother and steered him down the nearest alley, which was harder than you might think. His concussion made it like pushing a shopping trolley with a wonky wheel.

The alley was dark, but the further they went, the safer it would be. The children marched on. Soon the alley was nothing but an echoing series of thuds and apologies, as a woozy boy bumped into walls and his sister quietly said sorry (sometimes to him, sometimes to the bricks).

And then it started to rain.

'Of course it did,' said Aubrey's sister, who was starting to suspect her life might be part of a novel.

Frustration burned through Aubrey's sister's head. It had been such a simple idea: take the car, load up with food and money, and try as hard as you could to leave Marrowville. Take your brother somewhere nobody knows him and everyone could finally get to know you, to a place where you don't get hurt every single day. Somewhere without Wreckers . . . and maybe with a police force that did something other than chase little children. Somewhere the sun wasn't brown.

But nothing was ever that simple for Aubrey and Aubrey's sister. Nothing is ever simple. (Some people think mathematics is simple. If I could do mathematics, I wouldn't be writing this.)

The Wreckers were clearly hunting for them – and if Rialto was out hunting, then the countryside would be filled with trucks of wild men blocking every road that led away from Marrowville.

And, even if the children could somehow manage to get through the vicious blockades, the roads would only lead right back to Marrowville anyway. Anything that went outside Marrowville went straight into the permanent mist. Sometimes that mist was brown under the polluted sun. Sometimes it was grey under the angry clouds. And sometimes, if people walked into it, the mist turned red, and those people didn't come back.★

A memory arrived in Aubrey's sister's head. She pushed it away. This was not the time.

'Sis, my hand's burning,' said Aubrey, tripping over his twelfth bin.

'Did you put it in the fire?'

'No.'

'Really?'

Aubrey nodded.

'OK. Let's keep walking and hold that hand out in the rain.'

Aubrey stuck his right hand in the air, palm out. Aubrey's sister rubbed his back. It was better than nothing. They kept walking down the alley. It had turned out to be much longer than expected. Every time it seemed it was going to end, it would curve between yet more buildings. The children didn't even notice that the ground was gradually sloping downwards, or that a fine grey mist was rising up to meet them.

Aubrey's sister turned to see if anyone was following them, but the path they'd taken was gone, replaced by a wall of black concrete. She looked ahead. The alley was

★ I say 'sometimes' because sometimes people would come back. Just, you know, the way food sometimes comes back. You know it used to be food, but it sure doesn't look like it now.

sloping into a tunnel, dark and long, with no telltale light to say where it might end.

Softly, almost beyond her hearing, organ music played.

At the burning car, the team of Wreckers were confused, and, like all thugs, they were ready to turn that confusion into violence. There was only one problem – they couldn't find the alley the children had just run down. There was a simple reason for this: they couldn't see an alley because there wasn't one there, and the alley that wasn't there wasn't for them. It was just for the eyes it was meant for, and nobody else.

Back in the middle of town, human traffic was jammed from the Victory Finger all the way to the built-up district of the South Town Bridge. Justice Week had never known excitement like today. Even the folks getting trodden on were thrilled. The gossip had got around – the child and the question mark that had killed Howard Howard had knocked the Chief of Police off his mighty steed! Tom Inkling dashed home to write the daily edition of his newspaper. Soon he'd deliver that one edition to his one reader.

Terry the Terrible Horse nuzzled the fallen form of Sergeant Lorenzo Plug, the spikes on his muzzle ripping his master's beloved uniform.

'If we don't stop that horse, the Chief Superintendent won't have any clothes left,' said a constable.

'I've only got one arm from dealing with that horse, and even that arm ain't right,' said Officer Jenkins. 'Leave him be. I bet he feeds that thing with a nosebag full of actual noses.'

Nuzzled by a horse, and nicked by spikes, Sergeant Plug awoke beneath the Book. Nobody had moved it because nobody was allowed to touch it.

His face was enveloped in its thick gold pages, as though he was under a blanket of heavenly knowledge. He sighed contentedly, his head throbbed and his face felt like it was burning, but it didn't matter. He was so happy. He sat up and held the Book to his chest, hugging it like he would have his very own child.

The officers around him did not share his joy. This was yet more confusion to add to an abnormal day. Sergeant Plug had fallen off his horse, which was bad enough, but he'd also failed to capture two wanted criminals, in front of everyone in town – and now he was blissfully happy!

In fact, Sergeant Plug was so happy that he was still smiling when Terry nuzzled the side of his head and shaved off half his hair. He was still smiling when he stood up and all his clothes fell off.

Then he stopped smiling.

10
Mrs Dalrymple's Revenge

In Chicken Wringer's Lane, the rain had finally doused the blaze that had consumed Howard Howard's antler-covered murdermobile. Ignoring this entirely, the squad of young Wreckers were headbutting the wall they thought the children had walked through. They were making progress, but mostly towards brain damage.

Ignoring them entirely, an elderly woman stepped out of the laundrette. Mrs Dalrymple's posture was proud and her head was bandaged. She strutted triumphantly to Howard's car. Behind her, six silly boys' skulls smacked off cement. After all, if you can't find an alley, make one. With your face.

A black truck pulled up. Boss Smasher stuck his nugget-like head out of the driver's-side window.

'Boys! New rule – Mr Grande says every Wrecker goes inside when it rains. Everybody in the truck.'

As dizzy young dullards wobbled their way over to

the truck, Mrs Dalrymple spat on the blackened husk that had been her neighbour's vehicle, then turned on her heel and began walking home.

Sliding a hand into her handbag, she patted Beryl, her pet fire-lizard.

'Nobody throws a dog at Mrs Dalrymple,' she muttered.

In the alley, Aubrey and Aubrey's sister were no longer in an alley. It was more accurate to say that they weren't anywhere. They had walked into darkness. The mist that swirled up from beneath them cooled the burning in Aubrey's hand, but where their footsteps should've echoed off cobblestones and walls, there was no noise.

They moved forward, but where exactly forward was they didn't know. And they definitely didn't know where forward *went*.

Aubrey's sister spoke. No words arrived. She shouted. No sound came out. She may as well have screamed into black water.

And suddenly they were falling. The alley that had become a tunnel had become a hole. Their guts lurched as gravity pulled them down and down. They speeded up. They screamed, but sailed past where their voices should have been, as though their words had grabbed on to invisible ledges as their bodies dropped.

Far beneath the children, a single point of warm orange light shone upward. As they plummeted closer, it grew into four points of light split by a black cross.

Before impact, both children screamed for a final, silent time.

Boneless Charlie had a nightcap on his hairless head and two tiny nightcaps on the tips of his moustache. Calo was eating chocolates in bed, spearing them from the box with the tip of her sword. It was sleepy time at the Dog & Fist, and Charlie opened their bedroom window for some fresh air.

Instead of fresh air, Aubrey and Aubrey's sister (who was so good at bursting out of things) burst screaming through the window.

Boneless Charlie had never seen two children fly through a window before. He'd definitely never seen two children fly so quickly that the smaller one shot right across the room and banged into the wallpaper on the opposite wall.

Calo had also never seen two children fly through a window, but she wasn't particularly bothered. Her string-sword sailed through Aubrey's sister's hood and snatched her from the air. With a jerk of her wrist, Calo had the young lady pinned to the ceiling by her clothes.

Boneless Charlie peered at the boy. 'My love, did you order some unconscious children?'

Calo glared suspiciously at Aubrey's sister. The chocolate she'd been eating slid down off the blade.

Aubrey's sister opened her hand and caught it. She took a bite. 'Thank you,' she said.

11
THANKS FOR POPPING IN

'Charlie, there's a small girl hanging from the ceiling –'
Calo squinted at Aubrey's sister – 'and she's holding my
dessert.'

Calo was sitting up in bed, the line from her string-
sword held taut between two fingers. She was alert yet
curious. Children very rarely burst through her bedroom
window, and, when they did, they never, ever stole her
bedtime feast.

'I noticed that, my sweet truffle-piggle! And hello,
young lady!' Boneless Charlie bowed low and scooped
up Aubrey's unconscious body. 'I'm assuming this
conked-out waif is your brother?'

Aubrey's sister didn't answer. She didn't know what
was going on. How did she get from falling down a hole
to swinging from a bedroom ceiling? Who were these
people? Did they know who she and Aubrey were?
Had one of them just said 'Hello' to her?

With no other options, she decided to take a hostage. She opened her mouth again and popped the rest of the chocolate she'd grabbed straight between her teeth.

Calo was shocked. Her mouth went completely flat, like an earthworm that's gone under a car. She let the news of what the little girl had just done filter all the way through her brain.

She said one word. 'Brave.'

Boneless Charlie chuckled. He'd lived long enough to be charmed by tiny acts of defiance. He smiled up at Aubrey's sister.

'Fabulous move, my dangling darling! Now, this young fellow's had rather a bad bump on the head, so I'm going to wake him up and fetch some ice for the swelling.'

Aubrey's sister blinked.

'If you'd be so good as to have a word with my lovely wife, I'm sure she'll be more than pleased to withdraw her sword and unpin you from the rafter.'

Aubrey's sister tried to fathom what she was seeing and hearing. There was a skinny man with kind eyes and a luxurious moustache, and the moustache was wearing two hats. He grinned as he carried Aubrey to a chair that wasn't wearing a hat at all.

Aubrey half opened his eyes. What he saw was like nothing he'd ever known. There was a woman on a bed.

She was holding something he couldn't see, but it had something to do with a sword. And apparently that sword had shot through Aubrey's sister's hood, so now she was dangling above the nicest bedroom he'd ever seen. And all this seconds after falling down a hole neither he nor his sister had known was there.

There was a cough. The woman had a box of chocolates in her lap. Three fluffy pillows propped up her back and head, and her legs were curled up under a red-and-black patterned duvet. Aubrey's sister had never seen anyone look so dangerous and so comfortable at the same time. She quite liked it.

The man whose name was Charlie sat Aubrey up in the bedside chair. He began to hum a little tune. He went downstairs and came back with ice and a damp cloth. He wrapped the ice in the cloth, and gently pressed it to Aubrey's forehead.

Aubrey whispered some words. Unfortunately, they were, 'I'm a . . . Secret Giraffe.'

Boneless Charlie chuckled again. 'Well, I'm Charlie, and if you're a giraffe . . . well . . . I suppose that makes Calo and me secret zookeepers!' He turned to Calo. 'You know, my wonder, I've always thought of this place as a zoo.'

'We're more popular than the zoo, love,' said Calo, her eyes fixed on Aubrey's sister. 'All our animals are drunk.'

'Wouldn't it be lovely to see a drunken panda?' mused Charlie. 'It'd be cute, of course . . . but also *wobbly*. "Hello, Mr Panda," you could say, and it would fall over, and then sing an old song it used to know. What do pandas sing, do you think?'

He stroked his chin. 'Something about bamboo?' He began to sing. '*Oh, I'm bamboozled, which is oozled, but I guess with more bamboo. I'm bamboozled by you, baby, with your bam-bam-bam-bam-bam-boo.*'

Aubrey was more confused than his sister, and he wasn't dangling from the ceiling. He tried to focus on the singing old man, who crouched down until they were nose to nose. The man's eyes were blue and sparkly, and, when he smiled, the sides of his face crinkled up like old paper.

'Good day to you, young master Secret Giraffe! If you'd be so kind as to not eat our ceiling fan, or do your giraffey business on the floor, I don't think anyone will mind if you stay here until you feel better. Hold this to your head, there's a good chap.'

Aubrey held the flannel to his forehead. He was starting to feel better, even though he didn't know if pandas could sing or what a panda was.

He looked at his sister, who seemed to be standing a couple of metres above the ground.

'Sis, why are you flying?'

The woman on the bed coughed again.

There was a gap in the room that needed to be filled with explanations.

Aubrey's sister stared at the woman on the bed, who stared back, unblinking and stern. Then the woman's jaw moved a fraction, as though she didn't mean it to. Aubrey's sister realized that, when she hadn't been looking at her, the woman had sneakily put another chocolate in her mouth and was pretending she hadn't.

And, while Aubrey's sister didn't normally trust adults, at least this one didn't immediately seem to be trying to terminate her and her brother. Maybe she'd kill them both once she'd finished her chocolates, but maybe she had a lot of them and death would have to wait a while. Or maybe, just maybe, she just liked chocolate.

It was worth a shot.

'Hello,' said Aubrey's sister, pulling the chocolate treat out of her mouth.

'And hello to you,' said Calo. Her voice was rich and pleasant, like a chocolate river, or, in this case, a river that would like its chocolate back.

Since she was pinned to the ceiling like a butterfly that had angered an insane lepidopterist,* Aubrey's sister decided to go Full Polite.

---

* A lepidopterist is a person who collects butterflies or moths. Fun fact: they're all insane.

'I'm sorry to have intruded on your bedtime, but it seems my brother and I have somehow managed to fall through your window.'

'It does look like that, love.'

'Are you going to hurt us?'

At this, the woman shifted in bed. 'Well, that depends,' she started. 'Why are you here?'

Aubrey's sister slowly raised the chocolate back to her mouth. Pathetic as it may have been, at least she had a hostage.

'I don't know what happened,' she said. 'We were running from some Wreckers, so we ran down an alley – and then we fell down a hole that led to this window.'

Calo tilted her head towards Boneless Charlie. 'Well, only the best people run from Wreckers.'

'We are the best people! Except me, I'm –' Aubrey dropped his voice in case anyone else was listening – 'a *Secret Giraffe*.'

'Getting less secret about that by the second, Aubrey,' said Aubrey's sister, who wasn't being particularly careful with her secrets, since it was getting increasingly hard to tell what was real.

Hearing the boy's name, Boneless Charlie clicked his tongue. A suspicion had just been confirmed. Calo gave no sign she'd heard anything but nonsense.

'Fell in a hole, did you? That's a fun lie. You weren't just sneaking around outside and trying to rob us, were you, sweetheart?'

'Oh no.'

'I hope not. And you're not assassins?' Calo thought for a moment. 'Very, very small assassins?'

'No!'

'Well, that's good because we are regular-sized assassins.' Calo slid out of bed with a *thunk*, her metal legs turning her relaxed stride into slow-moving thunder.

'And these regular-sized assassins do get pretty ticked off if folks come into our bedroom, looking to turn the night into a place for screams and dark business.'

She advanced on Aubrey's sister. The girl popped the chocolate back in her mouth. Calo growled.

'You're getting slightly frightening, my love-dumpling!' said Boneless Charlie, his face a picture of joy regardless.

Calo waved him away. 'Oh hush, Walrus-Face.' She stood in front of Aubrey's sister and folded her arms.

Aubrey patted Boneless Charlie on the leg. 'It's OK. I'm an animal, too.'

'I don't know where you've come from,' said Calo, 'and I don't think you mean us any harm, but I do believe you're running from the Wreckers . . .'

She took Aubrey's sister by the shoe and slowly turned her round, her hood twisting on the sword's blade. The bedroom had a window that overlooked the town square. It was Calo's way of showing her something.

'. . . because we know who you are – and so does the rest of Marrowville.'

Aubrey's sister saw night-time. (Was it night already? What day was it? More importantly – what day *had it been*?) The square's tiny fire-wire lights were like glowing acne on the night's dark skin, and the towering Victory Finger stood as huge as a crusted cold sore. Its tip was lit with fiery torches. Electric spotlights flooded the length of its stone body.

Just below the inferno and bang in the middle of the light hung their por-
traits – Aubrey's a face, and Aubrey's sister's a question mark. Aubrey's name still written in full, while she got nothing. And new words had been added, too – a fresh pronouncement stamped in black ink fluttered below their pictures.

AUBREY HOWARD
WRECKER-KILLER
MURDERER OF NOBLE BROTHER HOWARD HOWARD
VIOLATOR OF THE JUSTICE WEEK PARADE
CANNIBAL, THIEF, BOOK-BOTHERER
ENEMY OF MARROWVILLE
(AND ACCOMPLICE)

Calo pointed at Aubrey. 'You are the Extremely Wanted Aubrey Howard.' Then she looked back up at Aubrey's sister. 'And you're . . . you're Howard's daughter, aren't you?'

Aubrey's sister's face screwed up in disgust. She hated that even though Howard Howard was dead she was still his child.

'I never knew Howard Howard had kids.' Calo's face darkened. The images that arrived in her head were not pleasant. 'You must've had a horrible time.'

Charlie's moustache drooped sadly. 'Howard Howard was a cruel man,' he said to no one in particular.

'Oh, we know,' said Aubrey. Charlie clasped the boy's shoulder.

For a moment, Calo remained still. She was thinking. Then she was done thinking, and jerked her sword hand back. The blade shot towards her. Aubrey's sister fell to the floor. To Calo's surprise, she landed on both feet.

'The police say you murdered your father, which just means the Wreckers say you did,' said Calo.

'But we didn't –' said Aubrey's sister. 'We –'

Calo snapped her sentence off. 'Don't worry, love – I never liked that twelve-fingered thug, and I'm glad he's dead.'

She slid her needle-thin weapon back into its scabbard, then leaned forward and took Aubrey's sister by the shoulders. Her voice was soft.

'We don't normally have too much time for criminals in this place, but we hate Wreckers. And your father wasn't just a Wrecker – he was, without a doubt, one of the biggest turds I've ever met.'

Aubrey's sister beamed. No adult she'd ever met had talked about Howard Howard like that. Or had talked to her. It was very satisfying.

'And even if you did kill him,' Calo continued, 'we don't need to know. We know exactly what kind of man your father was.' She glanced towards her husband. 'Charlie, I think these kids have had a rough night and a rough life.' She turned back to the children. 'How about we get you both something to eat, and then fix you up some beds?'

The children were stunned. Aubrey's sister because she hadn't experienced kindness since her mother, and Aubrey because of, well, continually getting hit really hard in the skull.

'Do you want this back?' asked Aubrey's sister, her mouth still full of her chocolate hostage.

'No, love, that's yours. You're a brave girl and, with the trouble you're in, trust me, you deserve chocolate.'

'Thank you.'

'Also, it's covered with your spit, which doesn't make the flavour any better.'

Boneless Charlie offered Aubrey a hazelnut caramel. The boy took it happily.

'We can have ourselves a midnight feast,' said the spry old man, his moustache pointing upward like a hairy smile. He began to sing again:

'*Oh, I'm bamboozled, which is oozled, but with more bamboo. I'm bamboozled by you, baby, with your bam-bam-bam-bam-bam-boooooo.*'

Aubrey joined in on the *bam-bams*.

Calo motioned for Aubrey's sister to follow them downstairs. It was very dangerous to take the children in, but that was OK. Given enough reason, she and Charlie could be very dangerous, too.

She smiled and asked the girl one question: 'Love, what's your name?'

12
BACON, TREES AND SCREAMING

Downstairs in the pub, Calo, Boneless Charlie, Aubrey and Aubrey's sister sat round a wooden table and noshed the bacon sandwiches Charlie had just fried up. They sat in the dark, a single candle flickering on four smiling faces and a lot of shimmering grease.

Calo and Boneless Charlie drank Slugwater. Aubrey and Aubrey's sister drank lemonade. They'd never had lemonade before bed. But then they'd never had a bed. Or lemonade.

'So, an old lady and a tall skeleton minced up Howard Howard?' Calo was grinning from ear to ear.

'Yes!' the children chimed in unison.

'He hissed when he talked, and he had a giant black pram, and then these tentacles dragged Howard into a mincer that they had hidden in there.' Aubrey's sister knew she was blurting out her story, but Calo and Charlie had asked, and seemed very keen to listen.

'Then they gave us the mince.' As his belly filled up, and his head stopped hurting, Aubrey had returned to knowing he was a human – and not a Secret Giraffe.

'You didn't eat it, did you?' asked Boneless Charlie.

'Oh yeah, we did,' said Aubrey's sister. 'We were starving.'

'Pshaw! How did old Howard taste?'

'Not as good as this bacon!' said Aubrey.

'That's surprising. He was a pig, too, after all.' Calo had a wry smile on her face. She'd never liked children, but child fugitives who could casually talk about eating their horrible dad were just fine.

'So, who are you two?' asked Aubrey's sister. She wasn't great on trust, but dealing with brutes had given her enough strength to be more confident when she met friendly people.

'My name is Calo, and you are inside the Dog & Fist, Marrowville's finest drinking establishment, home to some of the world's most inept barfighters and chunderous★ drunks. Mind the fire-lizards.'

Another gasoline-filled reptile had crawled up the wall. With a flick of her wrist, Calo had it surfing on top of her string-sword and rehomed it in the fireplace. It

---

★ 'Chunder' is a word from a faraway land. It means 'vomit'. To be 'chunderous' is to be like thunder – 'thunderous', but vomitty. Imagine a hailstorm with no hail, just plenty of noise and really big globs of sweetcorn.

frolicked happily, burping little flames.

'How do you do that?' asked Aubrey's sister, a sudden blast of heat the perfect accompaniment to her astonishment.

'A combination of practice and a blade,' said Calo. 'From my previous career as . . .' She looked helplessly at Boneless Charlie.

'A dentist,' he said.

'Yes, I was a dentist! I used to whip bad teeth out just like that. Used to flick bad molars at the wall. I was good at it, but my customers never came back, so I gave it up.'

Aubrey was suspicious. 'You already said you were assassins.'

Boneless Charlie laughed. 'Oh, little man! That was just some flimflam – my tin-legged tangerine was just trying to scare you, in case you'd been sent to kill us by . . .'

139

'. . . other dentists,' said Calo, who realized their lie had limits that were really easy to spot.

'So – you used to be dentists, and now you run a pub. And you have a sword you flick into the air . . . and you knew Howard Howard . . .' If Aubrey was suspicious, Aubrey's sister was downright cynical. 'There's no way Howard knew a *dentist*! I saw his teeth both in and out of his head. They were rotten brown stumps!'

'Oh, we wish we could've done something about his teeth,' said Calo, idly cracking a knuckle. 'Sadly, we just never got the chance.'

'You know, we really don't just run a bar,' said Charlie. Calo glared at him. 'Oh, come, my darling, it's a big world – let's give them a bit of truth.'

'Is it really a big world?' asked Aubrey. He knew he lived in a world, but he had no idea Marrowville wasn't all of it.

Boneless Charlie placed his long, thin fingers in the middle of the table, then lowered his face behind his hands. He lowered his voice, too, I suppose in order to reach where his face had gone.

'When we're not at the pub, I'm a burglar. In fact, I am the greatest burglar who has ever lived.' He wiggled his fingers in front of his mouth and he was no longer a walrus-head but a ten-fingered octopus-face.

'Charlie . . .' Aubrey's sister was musing on the name.

Suddenly Boneless Charlie clicked his fingers and the candle went out. Darkness descended.

He snapped his fingers again. The candle lit up. Both the children's knives and forks were twisted into his moustache.

He tilted his left hand over his shoulder and pointed behind him. 'Do you see that empty bottle on the bar?'

The children nodded.

Boneless Charlie grabbed the side of his chair and backflipped. Man and furniture spun together in the air, then split.

Charlie's long, lithe body sailed across the room as he dived head-first and backwards down the bottle's neck. His whole body stopped up the empty bottle with a satisfying *whump*. Charlie had jumped into a glass bottle that couldn't possibly contain a human body – and it didn't: his left foot stuck out.

Half a second later, the chair landed in front of the bar.

The bottle containing Charlie tipped over and rolled forward. It landed safely on the chair's cushion. Aubrey and Aubrey's sister rushed over. Charlie's foot was sticking out of the lip of the bottle, their knives and forks stuffed between his toes. Playfully, he wiggled his foot.

'Bring it over here!' said Calo excitedly. She'd seen Charlie do this hundreds of times, but it was always a joy.

The children picked up the bottle and carefully carried it over to her. Calo took it from them with one outstretched hand. She feverishly grabbed Charlie's ankle and tried to uncork her husband.

A wave of recognition hit Aubrey's sister.

'BONELESS CHARLIE!' she said. 'There's only one thief in the whole world who can do this trick!' She spoke into the bottle, her words echoing down the neck. 'Howard complained about you once. He said you'd stolen something. He said Rialto was going to . . . deal with you . . .'

Calo grimaced. 'Why do you think his foot's stuck outside the bottle? This is the most nimble acrobat who ever lived, and your father snapped his ankle.'

She uncorked him. Boneless Charlie sprang out of the bottle, backflipped and landed on one foot. He pushed the other one out to the children, knives and forks wiggling.

'I'm afraid, my darlings, I've got a bit of toe fungus. Do you like mushrooms?'

The children laughed and covered their faces the way you only can when someone you like says something delightfully revolting.

Smartly, Charlie planted both feet on the floor and fell forward on to the table. He spread his palms wide and landed like a gecko. He looked up at the children and grinned. And, when Boneless Charlie grinned, everything about him became a smile. His moustache twitched up and his eyes glimmered with mischief and fun. He raised his eyebrows and the children's hopes.

'We're going to help you, children. Calo and Boneless Charlie will help you. We know very well what it's like to be chased, don't we, my love?'

He looked down the table at his wife. Calo was sharpening her string-sword against her clanking leg.

'Oh yes. But trust me – we're a lot better at doing the chasing.'

While the children giggled with their two very strange new friends, Sergeant Lorenzo Plug sat alone, doing the opposite of laughing.

He had plonked his sizeable behind down on the

creaking chair in his office. A single light bulb buzzed pathetically above his head, like a dying insect coughing out orange electricity.

It was a bare room with cracked grey walls and bars on the windows. His office was a jail cell. Rialto Grande had thought it would be funny if the Chief of Police had to oversee Marrowville's law and order from inside a prison. Rialto thought a lot of things were funny.

Sergeant Plug's eyes stung with tears, and his entire face burned. At first, he'd thought it was from the previous day's embarrassment, but it hadn't stopped. He'd slathered his face with a thick white ointment, which didn't help with the burning, and made him look like a clown. The man who should have been the big brave Chief of Police was yet again a miserable buffoon sitting alone in long white underwear, his medals still pinned to the fabric on his chest. He'd sent the other officers home, and now, in the basement of Marrowville's prison, he sobbingly prepared to do something terrible.

He pulled the Sacred Police Officer's Charter out of a drawer in his desk. It shimmered in the dim light. He stroked the ornate cover with his bare hands.

Until he'd fallen off Terry the Terrible Horse in front of the whole town, Sergeant Plug had never touched the Book with his skin. Everyone knew that you never did that. And if you did do that – you blamed Sergeant Plug.

So now he blamed himself. The Book had fallen on his face — and he felt as though the words inside had seared themselves into his cheeks. Now he couldn't stop touching its cover. He opened it up, remembering to blame himself.

There, as usual, was the secret message that scarred the Book's inside cover. It was a single word rendered so harshly that the savage black letters looked like they'd been burned there. The word they spelled was:

STOMACH

He'd never understood that. He was so sensitive about his weight that he'd always thought someone had vandalized the Book just to mock him.

He turned to the second page. Normally, it contained a lovely guide about how to be a friendly police officer when nobody is your friend. Today it was blank.

He turned another page. Then another. All blank. He opened the Book to the middle — nothing. He flipped through to the end, but the pages of the most important book in history were all blank. It was impossible! Where were the instructions that had guided his life? Where were the names and addresses of the people of Marrowville? Was he such a terrible policeman that someone had stolen his *words*?

Sergeant Plug began to sob again. He'd barely noticed that the pages weren't even gold any more. Blank sheets of dirty beige paper stared up at him.

His thick tears dropped on to the pages. When they fell from his face, they were water. When they hit the Book, they splashed red. The tears began to slide down the page, streaking into red spiderwebs of misery. Soon the page was covered with red blotches and jagged crimson lines. Lines that became words:

I SEE YOU.
AND YOU ARE EMPTY.

Sergeant Plug slammed the Book shut. Its cover had changed. Where once there'd been a shimmering blue image of a police officer, there were now moving human eyes.

Hundreds of eyes staring at Sergeant Plug. And they hated him.

He tried to throw the Book down, but his hands were curled round its edges and wouldn't respond. His hands burned. His face burned. The Book laughed at him.

Boneless Charlie and Calo leaned by the open door of their guest bedroom. They had carried the two exhausted children upstairs to bed. Aubrey snored softly. His sister slept silently, curled up and comfy under sheets and a quilt. They were warm and safe, which might sound boring to some of you, but, if you ever live your life cold and frightened, you'll be amazed how grateful you are the day you're cosy.

'A tall skeleton and an old woman, and their pram,' whispered Calo.

'Yes, my sweet, it would appear that these children have encountered the Grinders.'

'We can't protect them from people like that,' said Calo as they made their way to their own bedroom.

'They fell through a hole that led to our window. That means the Grinders sent them here.'

Calo looked worried. Charlie hugged her and kissed the top of her head. 'I expect we'll see what they want, my darling.'

'It'll be blood, Charlie. It always is.'

They looked out of the window. Far beyond the flames of the Victory Finger, and far beyond anything they could hear, a lightning bolt hit the One Tree.

The tree hissed for a second time.

13
HAPPINESS AND THE FISHFLINGER

Aubrey and Aubrey's sister had been living at the Dog & Fist for about a week when Charlie first said he'd like to take them out for an adventure.

It had been a lovely few days. The kids had slept well, they'd had hot baths and hot food, and at night, after the pub had closed, everybody sat round the table and played games. For a week, nothing went especially wrong, except that Aubrey tried to do Charlie's backflip bottle trick, which meant Calo had to catch him before he hurt himself, so she'd lassoed his ankle with the string-sword's invisible line.

But even that was OK. With Aubrey swinging from the ceiling, Aubrey's sister had invented a new game called Aubrey Tennis, which was very popular with her, and not at all popular with Aubrey.

For the first time in their short, eventful lives, the children started to look healthy. They looked smart, too. Charlie had slid through the keyhole of a dressmaker's and stolen them some clothing. Unfortunately, his foot had got stuck, so he'd had to grab whatever he could reach. The kids weren't keen on the enormous turquoise pair of grandmotherly bloomers, and the wedding dress was completely useless, though they'd sometimes hold it up and drop it on Aubrey so he could do his impression of a bride who has transformed into a puppy and can't get out from under her great big dress.

Eventually, Calo went out and bought the kids some proper clothes. Aubrey's favourite outfit was black jeans and a grey jumper that did one thing better than his old one ever did – it fitted. Aubrey's sister went for black-and-white striped trousers and a long black shirt with silver buttons that closed at the throat. Aubrey looked friendly and messy; she looked like someone who'd always been told they didn't exist and had decided that was complete nonsense.

They were both given long navy-blue jackets in case they got cold. Calo and Charlie said they could decorate the jackets any way they wanted. Aubrey took some charcoal to his right lapel, drew a series of smudges and insisted he was a blue tiger.

Aubrey's sister took the charcoal and wrote three words down the back of her coat:

I'm Not Here

And both of them got a pair of solid leather boots.

'You can hide things in boots,' said Calo.

'Yes, indeed,' Boneless Charlie had agreed, jumping out of one of Aubrey's.

Oh yes, they'd all had great fun inside the pub, but Charlie still desperately wanted to take the children out somewhere. Aubrey had begun to make himself useful by cleaning the downstairs tables, and that was sign enough for Charlie that it was time to do something big.

'The poor things must be bored witless if they've started cleaning the place,' said Charlie.

'Let them,' said Calo. 'You're bad at it and I hate doing it.'

Aubrey really loved cleaning up downstairs. Calo insisted the windows stay shuttered, so nobody could peek in, but Aubrey enjoyed listening to the sounds of the market outside.

'FISH! Stop ducking, you fools! Eat my delicious fish!'

Especially the sounds of the Fishflinger.

His sister came downstairs. 'What are you up to?'

'Shhhh,' said Aubrey, waving her over. 'I think the Fishflinger's about to sell something.'

150

Through the door, the children heard a deep murmuring.

'Haddock. It's haddock.' The fish salesman's voice rang out clear and stern.

The murmuring continued. Then the sound of footsteps running away.

And then the inevitable sound of a human body being pelted with fish while a naked fish salesman yelled at them.

'Bad luck, Fishflinger,' said Aubrey's sister.

'Bad luck, whomever he was talking to,' said Aubrey.

'Whomever? Where'd you learn that?' Aubrey's sister had noticed her brother wasn't just saying more words but there were new ones in there, too.

'Charlie taught me!' He held two fingers under his nose to pantomime the thief's luxuriant moustache. 'Oh, my precious nutmeg! "Whom" and "whomever" are the words you employ when you want to convince people you're fancy and smart at the same time.'

He danced round the tables. 'Whom! Whom! Whom! I am Whomever, the Great Owl of Fanciness! Whom! Whom! Whom!'

Aubrey's sister laughed. 'Well, Great Fancy Owl, shall we give your friend the Fishflinger a treat?'

Aubrey agreed. 'Whom,' he said.

'Do you know what the word means, Aubrey?'

Aubrey giggled. 'Nah, sis, it's just really fun to say.'

So it happened that, one night, as the Fishflinger was sleeping on his mat, dreaming of the ocean, and fish – and, oddly, running – something brushed his arm. He stirred. It happened again.

He opened his eyes. There, in front of him, were two Marrowville banknotes. Money!

The thing in the world he loved best after fish, and his mat! His third favourite thing: money! The perfect thing with which to purchase more fish!

He peered at the notes. They each had a hook in them. And the hooks were attached to two fishing lines, and those lines went up the front of the Dog & Fist and into an open window on the second storey.

He laughed. 'Want to go fishing?' called the Fishflinger.

'Yes!' answered Calo, standing between two chuckling kids. 'Quiet, you two!'

The children were standing at the window, each with a fishing pole in their hands. Calo had said they could do this as long as they promised not to make too much noise, or fall out of the window.

'Are you ready?' asked the Fishflinger.

'We certainly are!' Charlie replied, twisting his moustache into two hairy fishhooks.

Carefully taking the money off both lines, the Fishflinger gently attached a fish to each hook. Then he wiggled the fish.

'I got a bite!' said Aubrey.

'So did I!' said Aubrey's sister.

'Reel them in, my loves!' said Charlie.

The Fishflinger held the tails of both fish and pulled.

'They're fighting!' said Aubrey's sister.

'Give 'em hell!' cried Calo, her warrior spirit arriving at the first sign of any struggle.

The kids backed away from the window to their beds, their fishing poles bending against the strain as they reeled and reeled and reeled . . .

. . . until the Fishflinger decided to let go.

Two trout flew up through the window and flopped on to their beds.

'Thank you, Fishflinger!' called Calo.

'Fish!' said the Fishflinger, waving up at the window.

'Pop them in the pot! Pop them in the pot!' Charlie scampered from bed to bed as the children unhooked their catch, a saucepan in one hand, smoking fire-lizard in the other.

And so, as they sat down to a meal of charred fish, everyone declared the evening a success, even if the kids' beds reeked of fish for another few days.

14
THE FINEST DAY

It was a lovely weekend morning: the pillows had been washed, the Fishflinger's produce had long since been eaten, and Boneless Charlie was finally convincing his wife to let him take the kids on a proper out-of-the-house excursion.

'What adventure do you want to take them on?' Calo was sharpening her sword on the armoured shin of her right leg. Sparks were flying as she dragged metal over metal. The screeching was unbearable.

'I. WAS. THINKING. THEY. MIGHT. LIKE. TO. GO. AND. SEE. THE. ONE. TREE.' Boneless Charlie was shouting as loudly as he could, but, over the scraping noise, his voice sounded quiet (which is why his words are big, but with no exclamation marks).

'Let's think about this, love. On the one hand, it's a dumb decision, and risky.' Calo was cool and thoughtful. Then she made up her mind. 'But, on the other, they haven't been outside all week.'

'And, my blackened rose petal, they are staying with the two most cunning minds in Marrowville.'

'Oh, Walrus-Face, they're staying with one of the most cunning minds in Marrowville – and the man with the prettiest moustache.'

Charlie and his facial hair grinned. You don't notice insults when you've got a really pretty moustache.

He called over to Aubrey, who was trying to fit his hand inside a bottle.

'Aubrey, get your sister – we're going outside!'

'We're going to see the One Tree!' Aubrey danced up to the room he and his sister had come to think of as theirs.

Aubrey's sister was sceptical. 'Aubrey, haven't you seen the Victory Finger? Haven't you seen the colossal pictures of us hanging in the town square? If we go outside, what's stopping a bunch of Wreckers from grabbing us? Or anyone grabbing us, for that matter? Remember how scared we were when we came here?'

'I don't remember getting here, sis. I just remember we fell, then Charlie put some ice on me and I felt less like my brain was kicking my head from the inside.'

Aubrey's sister was feeling so morose she didn't even notice her brother had said thirty-two words – absolutely a new record.

'It's an unnecessary risk. We should stay here and think about what we want to do next. I'm happy – and I know you're happy – but we can't go out, and we can't hide inside a bar for the rest of our lives, either.'

'Sis, when Dad was alive, did you think that we were even going to *have* a rest of our lives?'

'You raise a good point.' The girl's shoulders sank. 'I want to get us out of Marrowville, Aubrey. I just don't know how.'

'But we could have an adventure while you figure it out . . .?' Aubrey was hopeful.

'We can think about it here.' Aubrey's sister was hopeless.

Charlie's head slid round the doorjamb. 'Are you ready to go? I thought you'd like some sunshine, such as there is on another fine, polluted, misty day in Marrowville.'

'Charlie, we're the two most wanted criminals in town. How are we going to get anywhere without being – and I say this with respect – brutally executed?' asked Aubrey's sister.

Charlie spun and did a dance. 'Because you're living with the people who used to be the two most wanted criminals in Marrowville.'

'What happened?'

'The two most wanted criminals died.'

Aubrey's sister had more questions. Charlie had a smirk where an answer should've been.

Out the back of the pub, Calo had prepared a small cart with two wooden crates on top. Both crates were labelled.

'OK, loves – who wants to be inside DANGEROUS BEES and who wants LESS DANGEROUS BEES BUT ALSO STILL BEES SO DON'T TOUCH, PLEASE?'

Aubrey bolted into the second one. Aubrey's sister reluctantly climbed into the first. She thought this adventure was a stupid idea, but she figured that a stupid idea with her along would be about 30 per cent less stupid.

Boneless Charlie hitched his bicycle to the cart. 'And what do we say if someone tries to open a crate of bees?'

Aubrey said, 'We rock back and forth and go buzz until they're convinced they'll die from a thousand tiny stings.'

'Jolly good.'

Boneless Charlie shut the crates on the children. He stretched his shins and hopped on to his bicycle. What a glorious day it was! The sky was a rare blue, the sun was shining and the birds were singing. But they weren't birds and they weren't singing. They were fish the Fishflinger was tossing into the air.

'Fly! Why won't you fly?' he yelled. The fish splattered

on the ground. 'Oh, listen to my glorious symphony!'

'Morning, Fishy!' called Boneless Charlie, his knees bouncing along under his chin as he pedalled towards the town square. He beamed as he cycled through the sun-drenched market.

Stallholders called out to him: 'Hey, Charlie!'

'Charlie!'

'You got some bees there, Charlie?'

He cycled round the Victory Finger. Justice Week had finished, and all the holes that had once contained living criminals were now filled with the same criminals, except they were just a little bit deader.

The colossal portraits of Aubrey and Aubrey's sister still flapped in the breeze. Charlie's moustache turned up. He'd shinnied up the Victory Finger earlier in the week and written SECRET GIRAFFE on Aubrey's big forehead.

People were very confused by this Secret Giraffe message. Ever since it had appeared, the citizens of Marrowville had started worrying that their most notorious murderer might be an animal in disguise, and so had started doing everything they could to prove that they weren't also secretly giraffes.

Folk walked around with tin plates strapped to the tops of their heads to prove their necks couldn't go any higher. The Candleboys were worried people would think their long fingers were herds of giraffes, so started yelling, 'Fingers! Fingers!' when they lit the evening's lamps, which was the only thing that could make them creepier than they already were.*

It had been an eventful week in Marrowville unless you were Aubrey and Aubrey's sister, who had pretty much had a lovely holiday.

And, as Boneless Charlie took his knees and bees on a pedal around the town, Tom Inkling squeezed today's only newspaper into a metal box outside Skyline's Ruin. This was particularly hard to do, since the box was apparently packed with every newspaper he'd ever written. He didn't know whether the mayor read his newspapers, but his sacred orders were to always publish one.

And today's was a beauty – surely the mayor would enjoy today's feast of violence and gossip, even if the police and the Wreckers were no closer to finding what

---

* In fact, the confusion about the Secret Giraffe Mystery was such that Rialto Grande had gone to the zoo to harass some penguins. Tom Inkling had devoted an entire day's newspaper to it.

'Why are you bullying these penguins, Mr Grande?' he asked.

'Becauuuuse I do not lek to be taunted . . . and because I am anngrrrry. And also because these penguins owe me moneeeeey.'

How penguins owed anyone money was a mystery even more complicated than the Secret Giraffe. Where would they keep it if they got it? And, if they had it, what would they buy?

the townsfolk were calling the Secret Giraffe Murder Boy, and his accomplice, the Girl Who Isn't Here. With a strain, he ratcheted the box shut. Another edition had been delivered. He whistled at the crazy world of his masters.

Boneless Charlie whistled, too, since he was the master of his crazy world, and his crazy world was wonderful. He was biking halfway up the South Town Bridge with pulsing veins and two boxfuls of bees that were actually happy children. He waved cheerily at a stray police officer.

The police officer saw the crates and wrote the word 'Bees' in her notebook. It was the last page of her last book. Once she burned the pile of her work, she could finally be promoted to Wrecker but, since nobody had seen Sergeant Plug for a few days, she didn't know to whom to show the fire.

Outside the Dog & Fist, the Fishflinger slumped dejectedly. The penguins that were meant to be buying fish from him were late.

Boneless Charlie zoomed the bicycle into the grassy valley that led up to the One Tree. The children squealed in delight as the bike sped downwards, sunlight flashing through the gaps in their crates. As Charlie pedalled up the far side, they heard the waves crashing in Wrecker Bay, far below the cliff that held the structure everyone in Marrowville had agreed to pretend was really a magnificent plant. The only piece of nature that didn't kneel low to the ground, or cling helplessly to the sides of buildings – the One Tree.

'All right, my darlings – out you pop!'

Aubrey and Aubrey's sister opened their crates. They blinked and stretched.

The One Tree was colossal. Its steel beams reflected the brilliant sunlight, so the whole thing looked like a tree that was sparkling from the inside.

'Let's climb it,' said Aubrey.

The kids were up the One Tree in a flash. They hoisted with their arms and pushed with their legs and soon they'd plonked themselves on a bough at the very top. The tree groaned and clanked in the wind, but they could barely hear the metal shifting over their overwhelming laughter. They waved down at Boneless Charlie.

'Look over the cliff!' he called.

They did. The sun was blinding. Beneath them, the blue sea foamed, endless glorious ocean stretching out to the misty horizon. No ships, no buoys, just a clear view straight through the surface of the churning sea all the way down to the shipwreck after which the glorious Wrecker Bay had been named.

They giggled and swung their legs. Sunshine, an

ocean, a tree and a shipwreck. It was one of the finest days you could have.

They turned round and saw the silhouette of Marrowville. They saw a cloud of dust on the road. They saw something large emerge from the dust.

They saw a truck of Wreckers hurtling up out of the valley.

The finest day ended.

15
The Wreckers and the Tree

Aubrey screamed. His sister grabbed his face and muffled the sound. She pulled him down into a clump of leaves.

The Wreckers' truck skidded to a halt. At the foot of the tree, dust sprayed Boneless Charlie's kind eyes. The truck's side door opened. Boss Smasher's arms lurched out, accompanied by the rest of his body. His arms were so massive that he punched the ground instead of walking, each blow another step that drove him towards Charlie. Behind him, Left and Right Morton waddled their bulbous way along, implements of destruction clinking on their umbilical cord.

Boneless Charlie could have backflipped into the tree and hidden. Boneless Charlie could have slid into a knothole. Boneless Charlie could have done a lot of things.

Boneless Charlie crossed his legs and whistled.

'Boneless Charlie,' said Boss Smasher.

'Bonehead Charlie,' grunted Left Morton.

'Yeah, Bonehead Charlie,' grunted Right Morton.

'You have something that belongs to us. You ran last time.'

'Ah, my muscle-headed gentlemen! Are you enjoying the sunshine? I'm just taking my bees out for a walk.' Charlie gestured at the labelled crates.

'Bees don't walk,' said Boss Smasher.

'Yeah, Bonehead Charlie, bees don't walk,' said Left Morton.

'Yeah, they just bee,' said Right Morton, who was just a little bit smarter than his brother.

Boneless Charlie stood up and clapped his hands. 'Oh, you're always so right, Right Morton! Bees do be. I be, too, but I'm not a bee, too. Or a beetle. Or a beanstalk. Though I be alive. And being the kind of –'

Boss Smasher beaned Boneless Charlie. That doesn't mean he hit him with some beans. In some parts of the world, 'bean' means getting hit in the head. In the same parts of the world, it also means head. So Boss Smasher beaned Boneless Charlie with his bean.★

'You stole from us, thief,' grunted Boss Smasher. He was in no mood for games. Charlie groggily stood up. He was always in the mood for games.

★ I don't know why people say this. I suppose it means some people have beans for heads. I'm just saying that the next time you eat a cooked breakfast, be careful – you never know whom you're eating.

'That was a good whack, Boss Smasher. If I was a teacher of the noble art of thumping, why, I think I'd give it a . . .'

The goons' eyes widened during Charlie's pause. They prayed it wouldn't be another joke about bees.

In the tree, the children's eyes shone. They knew it would be another joke about bees.

'I'd give it a . . .'

On the ground, Rodney Paste covered his ears. He knew how angry Boss Smasher could get.

'. . . B.'

Boss Smasher grabbed Boneless Charlie by the head and shook him. He had the usual bully's intolerance of wordplay, wit and other people enjoying things for any reason, ever.

Left Morton said, 'Ask him.'

Right Morton said, 'Yeah, ask him.'

Boss Smasher said, 'You haven't seen them two children, have you, Boneless Charlie?'

'I fear, Boss Smasher, that after such a wonderful headbutt, while I am willing to answer your question, I'm now quite incapable of doing so.'

Boss Smasher thudded him into the tree. The tree clanged. Boneless Charlie dropped to the ground, which was nothing to an adventurer of his unparalleled bendiness, but the impact meant Aubrey's sister lost her grip on Aubrey. He slipped and grabbed the branch. His feet dangled under a thick clump of nailed-on leaves. If any of the Wreckers looked up, they'd see him.

Boss Smasher was shouting at Charlie. 'Give us what you took, tell us about the children, or I break whatever bones are left in you!'

Charlie just grinned. 'My brawny sweetheart, I have no idea where those children are.' He spied Aubrey's feet up in the tree and quickly changed the topic. 'Also, has something important gone missing? Because I'm rather certain, if it has, you're not sure who's taken it and are just hoping it was me.'

Boss Smasher shouted, 'Not true! You took it!'

'Then why don't you tell me what it is that I've stolen?' Charlie's moustache twisted into two question marks.

Boss Smasher's tiny brain whirred. He'd been ordered by Rialto not to tell Charlie what it was he was meant to have stolen because Rialto didn't want anyone to know he'd ever had the thing that had gone missing. It was very confusing.

Up in the tree, Aubrey whispered to his sister, 'Do you feel heavy?'

'What?'

'Do you feel heavy? If we dropped out of the tree, do you think you could knock out a Wrecker?'

Aubrey's sister was astonished. She'd never seen her brother make a plan before.

'When did you start coming up with strategies, Aubrey?'

Aubrey urgently checked his skin. 'Oh no! Do I have strategies?'

Aubrey's sister smiled. 'It's not an illness, Aubrey.'

Aubrey nodded. 'Ah, I've got a lot of strategies, sis.'

He farted. 'Was that a strategy?'

'No, Aubrey.'

'That's a shame – I've got heaps of those.'

At the foot of the tree, Rodney Paste heard the distant *parp* of a little boy's fart. He hissed and pointed. His Wrecker brothers ignored him. They were too busy bullying Charlie.

Left Morton's lips twisted into a sickening smile. 'That's a lovely pub you got, Bonehead Charlie. Be a shame if it was to burn down, Bonehead Charlie.'

His brother joined in. 'That's a lovely wife you got there, Bonehead Charlie. Be a shame if she was to burn down, too.' Right Morton was always just a little bit smarter than his brother. But not, perhaps, right now.

At the mention of Calo, Boneless Charlie stood up. His moustache had gone ramrod straight and the cheer had gone from his blue eyes. The face that crinkled up when he smiled was now stern. He clenched his jaw.

Unlike his usual garrulous self, he didn't dust himself off, or grin, or skip round his tormentors. He just slowly began to remove the cloth he always kept wrapped round the top of his bald head.

Quietly, he said to the Wreckers, 'Oh, that's unlucky, gentlemen. It seems I do have an answer to your queries, after all.'

Trying to pull her brother back up, Aubrey's sister spied Charlie's head tattoo for the first time. The cluster of eyes glared at her, and she was so spooked by the reptile eye's unblinking hatred that she nearly dropped her brother straight to the ground.

The Wreckers stared at Boneless Charlie. They'd never seen him with his head uncovered, and, while they were strong men with limited brainpower, they knew enough to know what danger looked like – and right now it looked like an unsmiling, skinny old man with a dark tattoo of eyes all over the top of his head.

Charlie spoke. 'Never threaten my wife, lads. For a start, she's much more frightening than me. Also, that's a nice set of faces you've got there. It'd be a shame if they were covered in a strange and alarming swarm of angry bees.'

Charlie skipped to the side and flipped open the crate labelled DANGEROUS BEES. He spun and kicked it at the Wreckers' feet. The men flinched and covered their faces, expecting a swarm of fuzzy death to barrel straight up their noses.

'Buzz! Buzz! Buzz! Buzz!' cried Boneless Charlie.

There were, of course, no bees, but in the second and a half it took Boss Smasher and both Mortons to realize that, Charlie had already run up the middle of Left Morton, bounced off his stomach and backflipped on to the side of the tree. He stood as comfortably on its vertical trunk as you or I might stand on horizontal land. He spread his arms wide in welcome.

'Gentlemen, I haven't taken anything from you (except your dignity, in about five seconds) and I won't be giving anyone any children, as I am too old and Calo doesn't want any.'

The Wreckers charged.

'But you're right – this doesn't seem the time to be talking about that since you all seem quite disgruntled.'

The Wreckers rushed Charlie, who skipped lightly up the tree's surface. All three of their heads smashed into the part of the trunk he'd been standing on. The One Tree rang like a gong. Charlie flipped over the now-groggy men. He grabbed the umbilical cord that held the Mortons together and pulled it taut.

Boneless Charlie had just turned two huge brothers into the world's largest bow and arrow.

'Boys, you are about to receive what we in the wars

used to call "the rough end of the pineapple".'

He let the cord go. Their clubs, axes, beating-sticks, in fact everything the Mortons had ever bought or stolen from the House of Needlessly Aggressive Sharp Things, sailed into Boss Smasher, who sailed into the tree. The One Tree gonged again, like a church calling its congregation to prayer.

Boneless Charlie dusted off his hands. Honour indicated that it had been a terrific scrap. The Wreckers had been humiliated, Charlie had shown them he was to be taken seriously, and Boss Smasher wouldn't be waking up for a fair spread of time.

Unfortunately, there was only one of him and four of them, and while the Mortons were impressed that Charlie had knocked down their strong friend, they were also terrific cowards who had a lot of weapons. The Morton Twins grabbed their clubs and advanced, while Rodney Paste continued hissing about the fart he'd heard.

Aubrey's sister was concerned. She racked her brains to come up with a way to help Charlie.

Aubrey turned to his sister. 'Do you want to see my Fatal Coconut?'

'What?'

In the next second, Aubrey did two things.

The first was jump out of the tree.

The second was shout, 'FATAL COCONUT!'

Aubrey landed right on Left Morton's skull.

Aubrey's sister could have stayed in the tree, but she went everywhere her brother went. She dropped from the branch on to Right Morton's head, screaming, 'FATAL COCONUT!'

Left Morton lost consciousness. Right Morton lost consciousness. Charlie whirled round and punched Rodney Paste on the nose.

'Acceptable Potato!' said Charlie.

For his part, Boss Smasher slept the sleep of the recently thumped.

Boneless Charlie went over to the children. 'Are you hurt, my heavy berries?'

'No,' said Aubrey's sister. 'It never hurts to fall on the Mortons.'

'They're like snoring trampolines!' said Aubrey, who was bouncing up and down on Left Morton's stomach.

The smile returned to Charlie's eyes. 'Shall we go home?'

'I think we'd better,' called Aubrey. 'I just jumped so hard on Left Morton he let out a strategy.'

Charlie padded over to the bike and slowly righted it. Ah, it had been a terrific day. Sunshine, a bike, a view, a tree, fake bees, the kids, a fight, some unexpected coconuts – what more could anybody want? He began to whistle.

But Aubrey's sister didn't share his jaunty mood. 'Why did you bring us here?' she demanded.

Charlie went quiet. He pulled his headcloth out of his pocket.

'You knew we'd be in danger! And you were in danger, too! If you'd upset the Wreckers, why would you bring the two people they're also hunting out with you?'

Boneless Charlie slowly wrapped the cloth back round his head. 'My love, I did it because it was a beautiful day – and you deserved to enjoy it.'

'But hiding in the pub was sensible!'

'And life is the freedom to sometimes be stupid. You'll understand this when you're older.'

'Oh, will I?'

'Oh yes. The older you get, the stupider you can be – and in a whole new set of exciting ways. Come on, we'd best go – they'll wake up eventually.'

Charlie helped the children back into the one crate that still stood on the cart. It had been a most eventful few hours. Quickly, he skipped back to the One Tree's trunk. It was as majestic as always, even though today the grass at its base was strewn with unconscious murderers.

He whispered into the dead wood. 'No hissing today, eh?'

He heard nothing but the roar of the distant ocean. He was relieved.

'Well, I suppose you two don't come out when it's sunny.'

The tree continued to ignore him. You can ignore pretty much everything when you're a tree. Except fire, and chainsaws, and the occasional koala.*

Boneless Charlie was delighted by the silence. He'd had a secret suspicion about the tree, but it had been for nothing. He danced his way back to the bike and nimbly swung his leg over the saddle. It was time to set off home with his little family, and his knobbly knees bobbed up and down as he pedalled. And then, on the wind, he heard three noises.

The first was a light hiss.

Then a distant clap of thunder.

Then a tiny stab of music.

'Please be kind to them,' he whispered.

His tattoos felt cold again.

Right Morton, who was just a little smarter than his brother, had not been knocked quite as unconscious as the other Wreckers. He'd opened his eyes. He'd seen Boneless Charlie hoisting a young girl into a crate. He'd seen the old man whisper something to the tree.

---

* Koalas are Australian animals. They eat eucalypyus leaves. The only reason they eat leaves is because trees are the only things on earth that move slower than koalas do.

But the girl was his focus. She wore a long blue jacket. On the back it had said, 'I'm Not Here'.

In that moment, Right Morton knew exactly where he could find Aubrey's sister. It was exactly where she wasn't right now, but would be in about half an hour, when Charlie had pedalled his bike there.

Then a bee landed on his open eye.

He regretted being a little smarter than his brother.

16
THE ARGUMENT THAT WASN'T

Upstairs at the Dog & Fist, the children were playing in their room. Downstairs, Calo wasn't yelling at Boneless Charlie.

Oh yes, she was exceptionally angry, but she was also fairly certain the kids had spent enough of their short lives listening to adults yell – and that included today's skirmish at the tree. So, even though she wasn't shouting at Charlie, she was very, very busy finding reasons to silently throw her string-sword at objects that Charlie was standing very, very close to.

'Three Wreckers showed up, and you didn't hide, and then . . . *You. Dropped. The. Kids. On. The. Wreckers.*' Calo hissed each word, trying to keep her anger as quiet as her weapon. Her sword sliced the air near Charlie's hand and embedded itself in his tea towel. She pulled the sword back and the tea towel went flying out of the window.

'Thanks!' shouted the Fishflinger as a tea towel he

hadn't seen softly hit him on the back of the head.

Charlie continued wiping the bar, but minus the cloth, which meant he was now a grown man who seemed to be massaging woodwork for no particular reason.

He made the easy excuse of a man who was literally made of excuses. 'Oh, there'd have been no point hiding, my delightful crab-stabber. They'd clearly seen me and decided they wanted something. If I'd hidden –' he fumbled for an ending – 'well . . . they might have climbed the tree and found the children.'

'So, instead, the children's bums found their heads.'

Calo's sword found a bottle of Madame Plonksy's Finest Fortified Grape Slop. With three flicks, it was uncorked, emptied into a mug, flung out of the window and smashed.

'Ouch!' said the Fishflinger as a bottle he hadn't seen forcefully hit him on the back of the head. He fell over. Luckily, the ground was there to break his fall, which it did, along with his nose.

'You've put us all in danger, Charlie, like some kind of stupid amateur.'

Amateur was a dirty word in their house. An amateur was someone who didn't even get paid. A criminal who didn't do it for the money was just insane. An assassin who didn't get paid was just a murderer.

'The only reason we've survived is because nobody's

tried a frontal assault,' said Calo. 'Now, you've almost certainly been seen with the kids, which means Rialto's going to bring his little army here.'

Calo was on the warpath, which is the path where war happens. If war happens and it's not on the path, tell it to get back on there before it steps on the flowers. Charlie and Calo had once fought in a war where two armies were stopped because a little old lady told them to stop fighting in her garden. Of course, since it was a secret war, this may never have happened, and, if it did, well, it's a secret.

'And you say you didn't want those idiots to climb up the tree?! Walrus-Head, who'd do that? Gorgo? Boss Smasher? Left and Right Moron? I've seen those boys get confused by stairs.' Calo would've crossed her arms, but having a sword in one hand meant, if she crossed them now, she'd never be able to cross them again if she tried.

Charlie raised his eyebrow – then, seeing that the string-sword was on its way to where he'd raised it, lowered it again. Then he ducked.

The string-sword's blade lodged herself in the black wood behind the bar. Its owner lodged herself in a black mood in front. She continued. 'I once saw the Mortons look at a staircase for ten minutes because they couldn't figure out if the stairs were going up or down. So they stood and waited another half-hour for the "up" staircase to arrive.'

Charlie thought about twanging the string of the string-sword like a guitar, and weighed up whether his trained, professional and deadly wife would find this funny.

'And when, as you'd expect, it didn't arrive, they said, "Dese stairs must be out of order." And do you know what they did then?'

Charlie's brain had moved into the gear that says, *I'm pretty sure she'll laugh . . .*

'THEY PUT THE STAIRS IN ORDER. THEY RIPPED THE STAIRCASE APART AND FILED THE STAIRS ALPHABETICALLY. STAIRS CAN'T *BE* FILED ALPHABETICALLY, CHARLIE. THEY ALL START WITH "S". By the time they were done, there were no stairs. Just a long, flat, wooden road where the stairs used to be.'

Charlie reached up and twanged the string. He sang, '*Oohhhhh, I'm just a long, flat wooden road where the stairs used to be.*'

Calo smirked. 'Careful, Walrus-Head. Once the stairs were gone, the people on the top floor couldn't get down, so they starved to death. The point I'm making is that those louts would never climb a tree – and I think you know this. You don't have to climb a tree to see what's in its branches since scientists invented this little activity called "looking".'

Charlie sauntered over to the fireplace, which meant Calo's flying string-sword hit smouldering coals. She yanked on the cord. A smoking black lump sailed between Boneless Charlie's legs.

'Careful, love, you nearly singed me familiars.'

Calo was so focused on being upset with Charlie that she didn't notice the fire had nearly gone out.

If she had, she'd have wondered where all the fire-lizards had gone. There weren't any around. There weren't even any crawling on the Dog & Fist's walls. Normally, when she was grumpy, she'd have caught one and dropped it down Charlie's trousers. It wasn't especially fun for him, but it really cheered her up. And the fire-lizards seemed to like it, too.

'What did you think you were doing, Charlie? You're a criminal – you know better than this!' Calo gave an exasperated sigh.

'Yes, my love, but I . . .'

'What?'

'I . . . I . . .'

Calo squinted. It was a squint that had made bandits squeal in fear. With her husband, it made him spit out truth.

'I didn't want to set a bad example to the children.'

Calo's bark of laughter just about knocked her over. Soon she was bent double and red in the face. She slapped her knee, which hurt her hand, but it didn't stop the absolute torrent of guffaws. 'You didn't want . . . you didn't want to set . . . YOU STEAL THINGS FOR MONEY! Not even money; mostly you steal for FUN! We're TERRIBLE examples to children! Don't you remember the war? We used to go into villages and –'

Aubrey popped his head round the corner of the stairs. 'What are you two talking about?'

'DENTISTRY!' Calo and Charlie shouted in unison. Aubrey went back to playing with his sister.

'My love,' said Charlie, 'these children are heroes and, as we agreed, they deserve to be happy.'

'And alive, Charlie. They deserve to be happy and alive and not torn apart by that homicidal mutilator Rialto Grande.'

'What's a mutilator?' Aubrey was back.

'It's a type of dentist who's not very good at their job,' said Calo.

'OK.' Aubrey went back to playing with his sister.

'The Wreckers are going to come here, Walrus-Head! And we've got the children! I like them – don't get me wrong – but they're the most wanted kids in town –'

'. . . which wouldn't normally be a problem . . .'

'Not even a little one! But – somehow – the Grinders have brought them here. Old Boneface and Big Beanbag Head have some great plan and those kids and us are trapped in it. So that's a cosmic disaster. And now the Wreckers are probably on their way.'

'Well, my yummy rum plum, I didn't want to make you even angrier . . .'

'Oh, there's more?' It was Calo's turn to raise her eyebrows.

'. . . but I'm fairly certain the Grinders are using the One Tree to get into Marrowville.'

Calo's military brain ticked over. 'There was a storm the night they took Howard Howard . . . and then lightning struck the tree the night the children arrived . . . and that hissing – you think that hissing is the skeleton undertaker saying he's on his way, don't you? Did your tattoos go cold?'

Boneless Charlie was flabbergasted. He'd never told Calo about his tattoos going cold.

'How did you . . .?'

'I'm an assassin, a bartender and your wife. I know everything you've ever done, thought, or intend to do or think, Walrus-Head.'

She threw her arms up in the air. 'Well, this is just *ideal*.'

'Well, my love, you did say you were bored.'

'Dammit, Charlie, has it ever occurred to you just how secure you have to be to even get bored? It usually means you're not starving, or on fire.'

Charlie sang, '*I was bored and on fire once. Ohhhhh, I'm just a long, flat wooden road . . .*'

'Don't test me, Walrus-Head.' Calo's mind was racing. Why would the Grinders be using the One Tree? Everyone liked the One Tree, but a picturesque view of the ocean hardly seemed the ideal requirement for a pair of immortal murderers.

'At least the Wreckers won't be any trouble.' Charlie patted the bar again. He really liked massaging that woodwork. Suspiciously so, in fact.

Calo's face went dark. 'No, they won't be trouble. They'll just be like a rock falling into a pond.'

'What do you mean, my love?'

'First, there'll be a splash, then ripples on the surface, and then the further the rock drops, the greater the chances it'll hit something big in the dark water.'

Charlie looked concerned. Calo wasn't big on metaphors. Metaphors are for people with the time and inclination to not say what they mean.

Calo smirked. 'Also, rocks are stupid. And they can't swim.'

THAT was the Calo he knew. It was much better.

'Um . . .' Aubrey was at the top of the stairs again.

'WHAT?' asked Calo and Boneless Charlie simultaneously.

'What's a dentist?'

17
Just Between Us Girls

A few hours later, Calo swung open the door of the Dog & Fist. The sun was setting and the street's lanterns were lit. A team of four Candleboys slunk back to their enclosure to sleep and grow more wax. The Fishflinger was sitting on a tea towel, the final rays of light hitting a face too glum for sunshine.

'You all right, Fishflinger?' asked Calo, sweeping aside fish scales, glass and assorted fish guts.

The Fishflinger stared into the distance. He sighed. 'They'll never find the Secret Giraffe Murder Boy, you know. They'll never find the Girl Who Isn't Here. Law and order is being destroyed by children who might be animals and children who might not exist at all.'

'What?'

He held up a rotting fish. 'The penguins I was meant to sell these haddock to never arrived. I kept these haddock fresh in my pants for days, but the penguins never came. Who punches a penguin?'

'What?'

'FISH! FRESH, POPULAR FISH!' The Fishflinger sprang off his towel. He'd spotted some people who looked like they'd never had a fish thrown at them. He ran over to make sure they didn't miss out, and that he didn't miss them.

Calo had never known the Fishflinger to do anything but fling fish. His sudden interest in current affairs was worrying.

She went back inside. Soon it would be opening time, and the pub would be filled with the citizens of Marrowville. They would drink and talk about nothing until the drink made nothing seem like everything and she had to throw them out (which was really something). But that didn't mean she couldn't have even more fun beforehand.

It also didn't mean the Wreckers wouldn't turn up any time they wanted.

Calo's life had once again hit a level of tension she recognized from her past. It wasn't an old friend. She patted the clanking string-sword at her leg. Now, *that* was an old friend.

She went upstairs to the children's room. Aubrey's sister was sitting on her bed, reading a book. It was Calo's dog-eared copy of *Psychological Warfare for Fun and Profit*.

Calo leaned on the doorjamb. 'Who taught you to read? Not Howard.'

Aubrey's sister looked up. She smiled. 'Definitely not Howard. I don't think he could read anything but his own name.'

She thought a moment. 'Of course, with the faces he punched, he had plenty of chances to do that. He hit people so hard the tattoos on his hand would get printed on their faces. He might have been called Howard Howard, but, if he didn't like you, it'd look like your name was Howard Howard Howard Howard Howard Howard Howard Howard.'

Calo laughed. 'Did your mother teach you to read?'

The girl's smile faded slightly. 'Yes.'

'Do you mind me asking where she is?'

Aubrey's sister didn't mind, but her smile had been replaced by half-sad thoughtfulness. 'The lady Grinder said we were orphans, so I'm pretty sure she's dead.' She sighed. 'I'd always hoped she was somewhere outside Marrowville.'

It was Calo's turn to sigh. 'Ah, love. I'm glad she taught you to read. You're a smart girl, and it's a hard life.'

'What's outside Marrowville? I've only ever seen the mist.'

Calo sat on the bed. 'If your mother is outside

Marrowville, then that's the same as being dead.'

'So there *are* places outside? Dangerous places?'

'There used to be places that were dangerous *and* lovely outside. But nobody leaves Marrowville, petal. They haven't for years now. Not with the razors in the mist. You'd leave Marrowville a person and ten seconds later –' she made a throat-slitting gesture – '*that*, but all over.' She groaned. 'There's no point even armouring yourself – I've seen it shear through the biggest trucks you can imagine. Chopped up everyone inside.'

Aubrey's sister thought about it. She said two words: 'I'll escape.'

Calo smiled. This was a remarkable young woman.

'I'm going to bundle my brother into the biggest car I can find and drive so fast through the mist we crash straight into somewhere better. And then I'm going to keep going. I'm going to keep going until we find our mother.'

Aubrey's sister was feeling determined. She was so matter-of-fact, even when she talked about her dreams. Some cynical people might say there's no point being matter-of-fact when you're pouring out your dreams, since, while your dreams matter, they might never become fact.

'And I'm going to keep Aubrey safe, and I'm going to . . .'

She paused. A memory had appeared in her brain. She fought to keep it out.

'. . . and then we're going to . . .'

The memory had won the fight. She saw her mother.

Howard Howard's car had pulled up at the limits of Marrowville. The tiny vehicle's motor was a muted pitter-patter as it gradually came to a stop, slowing down and down like the heartbeat of a dying man.

But, while it was Howard Howard's car, Howard Howard was nowhere to be found. Aubrey's sister's mother had stolen the car.

The road had trailed off into the swirling grey nothing that stretched out beyond the town. Aubrey's sister sat alone in the passenger seat. There was no Aubrey – he was still a baby, then. He was sleeping in his cot, back at the house and back when the cot still fitted him.

Her mother had leaned over and kissed her on the forehead.

Her mother had got out of the car.

Her mother had dashed into the mist.

Aubrey's sister had sat in the car until Rialto's gang of Wreckers turned up. Howard Howard had leaped out of their van and run frantically to his car door. His eyes were wide with panic.

His wife was gone. He scrambled round to the mist's edge. His six-fingered hands had balled up into those dangerous fists. He slammed them into the roof of the car. The other Wreckers were shouting at him now. Mocking him.

He drummed his fingers on the metal roof. He was thinking. He opened the car door.

Howard Howard pulled Aubrey's sister out of the car and hurled her head-first into the razor-mist.

'Are you all right, love?'

Aubrey's sister had forgotten where she was. And she'd definitely forgotten what she was talking about.

'Sorry,' she began. 'It's just, when I was little . . .'

She wasn't certain she could trust anyone enough to tell them this.

She looked at Calo. If she was going to tell anyone, she decided it was going to be her.

'When I was little, our mum drove me to the edge of the mist, and left me there. She didn't say goodbye – she just left me in the car and ran straight in.'

Calo listened.

'I don't know when he got there, but eventually Howard showed up. He picked me up and hurled me into the mist after her.' She was struggling to make sense of it all. 'I don't know why she did it . . . I don't know how I got back . . .'

Calo raised an eyebrow. She'd disliked Howard
Howard before she met the children, but that was when
he was just another Wrecker. Now that she knew more of
the real harm he'd done, she despised him. And she wasn't
feeling great about their mother, either.

'All I remember is shadows. There were huge shadows
in the mist.' The girl was rambling now. 'And I survived
. . . but, if I survived, maybe Mum did, too!'

Aubrey's sister was bunching up her long hair in her
fists. 'But why did she leave us with Howard? And why
didn't the razors come? Was I just lucky?'

Silently, Calo weighed up the word 'lucky' and how it
related to the little warrior in front of her. Aubrey's sister
was lucky to be alive, but her life was brutally unfair.

And then Calo, her military brain going over all the
information she'd been given, asked the wrong question.
'Did the shadows say anything?'

Aubrey's sister stood up. Surely she was being mocked.
She'd shared too much and was now being made fun of.
Once again, she pushed all her passion and pain far, far
down into herself. She aimed for politeness: 'You and
Charlie have been so good to Aubrey and me.'

Calo was surprised. 'You don't have to get up, love.'

Aubrey's sister laughed – the quiet little laugh you give
when everything is too sad and it's all become ridiculous.

Calo didn't laugh. She was trying to cheer up a girl

whom she couldn't ever take anywhere safe because there wasn't anywhere safe to go. At any moment, a gang of armed thugs could burst in and kill all of them. Anywhere they went, those thugs could find and kill them. And, if they went out into the mist, well, she imagined it'd try doubly hard to kill someone it had failed to before, especially if she'd seen the shadows.

And then, of course, there were the Grinders.

The girl deserved to know the facts, but she also didn't need to worry about problems bigger than what she was about to face.

'Love, can you sit down, please?'

No adult had ever actually said please to Aubrey's sister before. She sat down next to Calo.

Carefully, the ex-assassin put her arm round the girl. Unaccustomed to the contact, Aubrey's sister flinched, then settled.★

'I need to let you know a few things, love. Not all of them are good.'

Calo spoke carefully. 'Thanks to Charlie's . . . whimsy,' she said, 'there's a chance the Wreckers know that you're here, which means the police do, too.' She

---

★ Aubrey's sister had an internal classification for adults – it went Possibly Dangerous, Dangerous and Very Dangerous. It didn't go any higher because, if it did, she couldn't defeat them, and where would be the fun in that? Charlie and Calo had been so tremendously nice that they had been downgraded to Possibly Dangerous.

looked straight at Aubrey's sister. 'I don't want you to worry. I think you know there's no such thing as being completely safe — but even in blood-curdling peril you've got the best insurance anyone has.'

'What's that?'

'As long as me and Charlie are with you, we're going to try to keep you safe.'

Aubrey's sister was touched. 'Thank you.'

'I'm sorry Charlie mucked up. I don't know why he didn't just run away from them.' Calo looked up at the ceiling.

'That's OK. It was a stupid idea, but it was a lovely bike ride.' Aubrey's sister's smile had returned. 'And I've waited years to thump one of the Mortons.'

Calo decided it was a good time to ask Aubrey's sister the question she'd come in to ask in the first place. She looked down at her.

'Young lady, would you like to learn how to use a sword?'

Aubrey's sister's eyes flashed.

'Calo, that is the only thing I've ever wanted to learn.'

18
CRUEL MEN

'Whoosh!'

'Ting!'

'Whoosh!'

'Ting!'

Aubrey and Charlie sat on the stairs and watched as Calo gave Aubrey's sister her first lesson in the fine art of bladed combat. Whip-thin needles scratched the air as the sparring partners ducked and weaved between the tables and stools of the Dog & Fist. Opening time was half an hour away, and the boys were amusing themselves by adding sound effects to the fight.

'Whoosh!'

'Ting!'

'Whoosh!'

'Thud!'

Metal hit metal. Some metal missed metal. Some metal hit wood. Some chairs would need replacing.

Boneless Charlie spoke softly to Aubrey. 'Little man, we think a spot of danger is on its way.'

'Oh.'

'But don't worry. They're just a gang of armed ruffians, and, well . . . we won't let anything happen to you now, will we?'

He turned his attention back to the fight, cupped his hand to his mouth and shouted: 'Ting!'

Aubrey watched his sister. She was blazing with excitement. She was picking up the basics of the string-sword very quickly, and was backing up her newfound skills with wild enthusiasm.

Calo was also backing up – properly trained, the young girl would already be a formidable opponent against a healthy barfighter. Or maybe an injured Wrecker.

'Thud!'

She was definitely a great opponent for the bar stools.

Aubrey turned to Charlie. 'Can I practise something, too?'

Charlie's eyes twinkled. 'Of course! Go and fetch those big boots you had around your neck when you first came through the window.'

Aubrey scampered off and returned with his arms full of Howard Howard's spiked fight-boots. Charlie held out his hands and took the footwear. He peered closely into one filthy shoe. What he saw inside put a twinkle in his eyes, and a stain on his face.

'Aubrey, do you know how these work?'

'You put your feet in them?'

'Always a good start with a shoe, but there's a little more to these ones . . .' Charlie tinkered with the sole of the left boot. 'You see, first you twist off the heel like this . . . and then, if you're very lucky, this pouch at the tip of the toes pops out.'

He handed the pouch to Aubrey. It was a leather sack with a patch of the shoe's sole at the bottom. He'd never known it was there. He'd only ever seen his father's boots from the outside, and usually thundering towards him at speed.

Charlie spoke with the patient voice of someone genuinely happy. 'Now, these are fight-boots, so they're bigger than normal boots. See? The part you put your foot in stops here, behind a shield of reinforced iron, but, to the naked eye, there's more shoe – oh, don't touch the spikes, Aubrey! They're spikes – they're for spiking –'

'Ouch!'

'– and that, my darling, is why we don't do that. Now these little leather bags . . . do you see? They slot in the hole behind the false toecap. And this shield that houses your real toes needs to be iron because if you half fill this pouch with gunpowder –' Charlie carefully tipped black granules into the tiny pocket – 'then slot it back in . . .' He tapped the pouch back into place and twisted the heel. A firm click suggested it was locked back in its secret home.

Aubrey peered at the shoes in fascination.

'What happens now?'

'Well, my tiny warrior, usually now a chap would catch a fire-lizard.'

'Why?'

'Fire-lizards love gunpowder and tiny spaces. You catch a fire-lizard, stuff it in with the gunpowder and then, every time you kick someone, jets of fire shoot out of the spikes on the end of your feet.'

'That doesn't sound good for the fire-lizard.' Aubrey thought for a moment. 'Or anyone.'

'Oh, it isn't! But these are the shoes of a cruel man, Aubrey. Howard Howard didn't care about you or your sister, so I doubt he'd have minded crushing a few reptiles.'

Aubrey was confused. 'How'd you know they were his?'

'Well, for a start, when the son of a noted thug shows up with boots bigger than he is, you presume those boots belong to someone else and –' Charlie leaned back – 'your father stomped me with these boots a good few times. He'd knocked me to the ground and was going to fry my face off – or at least sizzle my moustache. But something stopped him.'

'What was that?'

Charlie chuckled. 'Well, dear boy, he didn't secure his lizard! Overconfidence leads to sloppiness, which leads to the bottom of your shoe falling out and your lizard escaping. It was a cute little fellow – and angry, too. And it did not seem pleased to have been trapped near Howard Howard's stinking feet. It turned round, opened its mouth –'

'And spat fire at him?'

'No, it was the oddest thing. A deer with no antlers came out of nowhere and kicked him in the head. *Then* the fire-lizard spat fire at him. Strangest thing I've ever seen.' Charlie chuckled at the memory. Then, his mind on the subject, he glanced at the fireplace. Where *were* the fire-lizards that normally lived in there? He hadn't seen one in weeks. Not at the market, not anywhere.

Aubrey looked excited. 'I'll burn Rialto's hair off! I'll make a Morton casserole!' He was starting to jump around. 'I'll keep my sister safe! I'll . . .' He paused. 'I don't want to hurt the fire-lizards.'

Charlie calmed the boy. 'Oh, little man, judging by her ferocity with that blade, I suspect your sister will keep both of you safe for the foreseeable future. These, however, will help in an emergency. And worry not about the lizards.' He ruffled Aubrey's hair. 'You don't have to be a cruel man to deal with cruel men, Aubrey. Sometimes you just have to be a bit firm –' Boneless Charlie pulled something from his pocket – 'and a bit clever. You can do that, can't you?'

Aubrey nodded. He was sure he could be clever: he'd been told for ten years that he was stupid, but, of course, the fellow who'd said that to him had ended up as several tubs of mince.

Boneless Charlie held a silver box in the middle of his palm. Delicately, he opened its lid. Inside was a compartment stuffed with tiny pipes and clear glass bulbs. And inside each bulb was a purple liquid, and in the middle of that liquid . . . a tiny fire.

'This, Aubrey, is an artificial fire-lizard. It was made so that Wreckers would always be able to burn anything or anyone they wanted, all the time, with every step, and without the inconvenience of having to catch a fresh lizard.' He closed the box's lid. 'Only four were ever made, and it just so happens that, well, I have all of them.'

Charlie spun the box on one finger. 'The blast this little doodah produces is much stronger than what you'll get in a normal fight-boot, and –' he tossed it in the air absent-mindedly – 'while I suppose a more responsible person wouldn't give them to a boy your age, you're a good chap, Aubrey – and you can have two of them.'

Charlie caught the box in one hand and pulled another from his pocket. 'One artificial fire-lizard, one sister of an artificial fire-lizard.'

He twisted the heels on the boots and slid the metal siblings into the secret compartments. There was a bubbling and a sizzling.

'Put your shoes on.'

Aubrey slid into his father's enormous boots. They were heavy, and his little feet came nowhere near to filling them. Charlie busied himself with knotting the laces as tightly as he could.

Sensing that some new information had entered the room, Calo held up one hand and called a halt to Aubrey's sister's training session.

'Walrus-Head, what have you given the boy?'

Charlie giggled. 'Now, Aubrey, jump!'

Aubrey leaped into the air. His little bones and muscles pushed him upward, gravity pulled him downward and the ground stopped his fall. But it was enough to start up his artificial fire-lizards. The bubbling got louder. The sizzling became a scream of hot metal. Steam came off the top of Aubrey's boots. Inside, the flames engulfed the purple liquid and became columns of scorching heat that rushed down the pipes to the waiting gunpowder, which had no purpose but to explode, and no desire to do anything else.

'AUBREY!' said Aubrey's sister in the silence that sometimes descends just before an accident happens.

The jet of fire was so massive that it blasted Aubrey into the air like a rocket, then through the ceiling like a ceiling-seeking rocket, then through the roof like a rocket that used to love ceilings but had always dreamed of flying into space.

'Hmm . . . There's a *slight* chance I overdid the gunpowder,' said Boneless Charlie.

Aubrey blasted through the air above the Dog & Fist. Night had fallen on Marrowville, and soon, he realized, would he.

In the twinkling light below, he could see a crowd of people waiting in the street for the pub to open. They didn't seem to notice the boy with flaming shoes shooting ever higher into the air.

'Have you noticed that boy with flaming shoes shooting ever higher into the air?' one man asked another.

'I haven't noticed anything since my wife left. She used to do all my noticing for me. Now I don't know if she's taken the kids or if I've sat on them and they're dead.'

His friend said, ''Ere, you've got something on the back of your trousers.'

The man pulled off some matted grey fur with a collar attached. 'Oh well, that explains where the cat went.'

In the pub, Calo kicked a chair under the hole in the ceiling that had just been made by Aubrey's sudden trip into the night sky.

She wheeled on her husband. 'Charlie, I've only seen fight-boots do that once before.' Then she remembered that Aubrey's sister was there.

Have you ever seen parents try to hide that they're angry, or that they're talking about something they don't want their kids to know about? What happened next was a bit like that.

'Why is it that they've just done it again . . . now . . . in our bar, miles from where we used to do those . . . things that we don't do any more . . . and years after we stopped doing the . . . other things that meant I saw what those things just did . . . that thing with . . . those things on the day that *thing* did the thing and I lost a couple of things and the sky went . . . thing and everybody died?'

Luckily, Calo knew her husband well enough to be sure he'd understood all that, even if you and I are currently very confused.

'Well, my splendiferous . . .'

She also knew her husband well enough to know when he was just mucking around, which was *all the time*. 'What have you done, Walrus-Head?'

'Well, my ponderous . . .'

Like Calo, Aubrey's sister was curious, and dangerously quiet. She put her hands on her hips. One hand was there to show the importance of the question she was about to ask, and the second pinned her stringsword to her side (because otherwise it was going to pin Charlie).

'Charlie,' she began, 'what have you done with my brother?'

Charlie stretched. The pub was about to open, and the time had come for a bit of tactical confessing. He straightened his bandanna and moustache.

'Well, before you and your brother arrived, I went out for a fine day's thieving. I took some rings; I took some money; I stole some fruit – my wifey-poo loves her fruit.'

'You'll never be able to comfortably wifey-poo again if you don't tell me what you've done,' said Calo.

'My vicious sweetheart, I was purloining* a delightfully plump tangerine when I saw Rialto Grande lumbering through the square, guffawing to his *cheldreeeeen* that he'd had the boys at the House of Needlessly Aggressive Sharp Things "wheeeeeep up a

---

* If you don't know the word 'purloining', it's just a fancy word for 'stealing'. Other fancy words for stealing include 'homage', 'booking fee' and 'baggage allowance'.

leeeeetle sometheeeeng for heeem". So, having nothing better to do, I followed.

'They lurched their way into the shop, and ordered a look at their "special presents". So the shopkeeper brought out these four metal squares. Rialto thumped them – and they shot out jets of fire so massive they even spooked the big rock-man, Gorgo. It was amazing. He really went mad. Started squeaking and shaking and covering his big chest. Odd for a hardskin to do that, especially –'

'Get on with it,' said Calo.

'Indeed, indeed – look, Rialto said he was going to have these little blighters made for all the Wreckers, so they could torch whole buildings with a few kicks. Now obviously we couldn't have that, so a few hours later I went back. Now I have them.'

'Is this why the Wreckers have been chasing you?' Aubrey's sister asked, choosing this line of questioning over 'Do you think my brother will land anytime soon?'

'No. The Wreckers have no idea. Isn't it lovely?' Charlie made eye contact with Calo, who pointed her sword back towards the fireplace. Charlie felt a familiar singeing coming on. He turned back to Aubrey's sister.

'Of course, they *suspect* I took them, but suspecting I took them hasn't been reason enough to come in here and face dealing with –'

'Me.' Calo grinned. All three of them were smiling. It would be a mistake to say that Calo intimidated everyone in Marrowville, but she did have a particular way of looking at people. It was the sort of look that suggested you were at risk of waking up in a place you didn't recognize, and wondering where exactly your thumbs had gone.

Charlie sighed. 'But now they're hunting children – and a shot at grabbing these two might be worth dealing with you, my pretty poison pancake.'

There was a scream. Aubrey had landed in the chair. 'The Wreckers are coming! I saw them marching!'

Calo beamed at her husband, faith restored. 'There's a point to everything you do, isn't there?'

Charlie walked to the front door. 'Oh, I don't know about that. But I suppose we'd better open up.'

19
FIESTA

Rialto Grande gave Barney the dog a good-luck lick, and then closed the visor on Barney's tiny suit of doggy armour. 'Who'smyleetleknightknight? Who'sRialto's-leetleinveeenceeebleBarneyknightknight?' He licked the armour. It was time for a raid, and nobody was allowed to hurt little Barney (except for, well, Rialto Grande).

There was a distant *boom*. Rialto blinked at the streak of fire that was suddenly interrupting the darkening sky. It had burst from the roof of the Dog & Fist. Even though he was streets away from there, Rialto could swear he heard a little boy screaming. It was a sound he was very good at recognizing, having heard it so very, very many times.

He dropped the dog and yanked a spyglass from Rodney Paste's backpack. It was a handcrafted tube of plated brass pasted together from teeth fillings and old church glass. Barney, for his part, hit the cobblestones.

He clanged. His bark echoed in the armour.

'Brother Smasher, do those flames look familiarrr to youuuuu?'

Boss Smasher gurgled a laugh. 'They look like the fire what you frightened Gorgo with.'

Gorgo squeaked. The others laughed as the huge rock-man curled into a mossy ball. He hated fire, and they all knew it. But then they all hated *weakness*.

Rialto glanced over his shoulder. 'Brother Gorgo! Get uuuup, you weak fool!'

Gorgo showed no signs of getting up. He squeaked again and his whole body shook.

How you act when someone is panicking is a terrific test of what kind of person you are. Of course, Rialto Grande had never wanted or needed to calm down a panicking person since he was usually the reason they were panicking in the first place.

'Thees cowardeece sickens meeeee, rock-man!' Rialto spat as he turned his back on the men. Again, he trained the spyglass on the streak of flame rocketing wildly through the sky above the Dog & Fist.

He cooed an order. 'Boooooooys, hurt Brother Gorgo till he feels ready to fight.'

The other Wreckers grunted with pleasure.

Rodney Paste skipped over and slapped the miserable hardskin on the back of his flinty head. Oh, this would be a fun game! Gorgo was big like a mountain, but he was squeaking like a small mouse-like . . . mountain.

The Mortons waddled over and parked themselves in front of the man who'd once been an unbeatable skull-cracker, but who was currently just a big squeaking lump.

Rodney winked at Boss Smasher, who fist-walked up to Gorgo, his massive Smasher arms driving his rough knuckles into the road while his tiny Smasher legs dangled in the air.

Without even looking behind him, Rialto extended his arm. It was a signal.

Boss Smasher, whose body mass was almost entirely those strong arms and the broad shoulders and chest you get when you have to walk on your hands all the time,★ howled. He forced his arms up under Gorgo's armpits, and locked his fingers together across the back of the bigger man's neck. He flexed his muscles. The pressure jammed Gorgo's head down and forced his arms to his sides, leaving his rocky chest open.

'COWARD!' screamed Boss Smasher, the word blasting into Gorgo's ear.

Rodney Paste narrowed his eyes and tilted his head. There was something growing on Gorgo's chest. It was

---

★ Of course you do. If you only walk on your hands, every step you take is technically a press-up.

tiny, and almost totally hidden by a scrappy patch of moss, but not so hidden that a practised bully couldn't find it.

Rodney pointed and hissed. He doubled over, his spindly body rocking with delirious mirth.

Left Morton saw it, too. His flabby face curled into a bloated mask of cruelty. He was thrilled about the raid, but this was a special treat before battle. He scraped the bottom of his boot on the cowering giant's flinty face. 'What's that little thing, big man? Is that why you're scared of fire?'

'Reckon he's scared of fire? He's a rock – you should see how scared he is of paper,'★ said Right Morton, who was smarter than his brother (and still smarting from a bee sting to the eye). Then he looked closer, and saw what the other Wreckers had already discovered.

'GORGO'S GOT A FLOWER GROWING ON HIM!'

Right Morton grabbed the hammer from his umbilical cord and struck Gorgo in the forehead. Gorgo squeaked again.

The Mortons laughed in unison. It was a horrible,

★ This is a reference to the game Rock, Paper, Scissors, which works like this – paper beats rock, scissors beats paper, and anyone who gets sick of the game can pick up a real rock and then we'll see how tough you are with your little bit of paper. Don't actually do this, though, otherwise the game becomes Rock, Paper, Scissors, Jail, and jail beats *everything* . . .

throaty line of gluggy belches, two throats croaking like a dozen angry toads drowning in a bog.

Gorgo looked away. He was ashamed. It wasn't that he didn't want the flower growing on him – it had just shown up in his moss one day. He liked it. He'd watered it with sweat and tried to keep it safe. It was so little.

The Wreckers howled at his misery. It didn't matter that he was one of their brothers: all kindness was weakness and weakness deserved torment.

Rialto marched over, a scowl across his feral face. He fixed his eyes on the tiny white plant.

'Is this eeeet, Brother Gorgo?' he asked. 'Theese is why you cannot stand the *flame*? You are protecteeeeng theees leeetle *blossommm*?'

Gorgo said nothing. His trusted brothers had turned on him, and the embarrassment of their laughter had drained his body of all its strength.

'Weellll, I must do *sometheng* about your discom-foooort.' Rialto pulled on the first of a pair of very heavy leather gloves. He nudged the Mortons out of the way and crouched in front of Gorgo. He pulled on the second glove. He raised his hand to his frightened underling's eyes.

'You knooooowww what these cen dooooo, don't you?'

Gorgo nodded.

Rialto lowered his hand to Gorgo's chest, extended his

index finger and slowly pressed its tip against the flower.

Gorgo's eyes widened; he shook his head madly. Trembling and squeaking, he tried to squirm away from Rialto's hand.

'Firrrrre is our business, Brother Gorgo. A Wrecker who cennot destrooooy will beeee destroooooyed. Are you a Wreckerrrr?'

Gorgo squeaked.

'Are you a Wreckerrrrr?'

Gorgo fought to keep his voice low and deep. He growled.

'*Much* betterrrrrr.'

Rialto leaned forward and crushed the flower between his finger and thumb. He pulled it into his fist.

'Now get up.'

Gorgo got up. Rialto Grande opened his hand. A wisp of black smoke escaped his fingers. Ash fell to the ground.

Twenty pairs of feet pounded up the road. A voice called out, 'We're here, Mr Grande!'

Rialto leered with pleasure. Finally, the raid could start. Not only had order been restored among his main boys, but his extra squadron of troops had just arrived. Twenty extra Wreckers he'd enlisted for the occasion stood to attention behind his usual shambling band of mutants.

These were new Wreckers, all fresh-faced ex-police officers, ready to roar with rage and keen to crash and crush. They were fit, they were capable, they were muscular, but they were young – their leathers weren't yet ragged or torn, though a couple had rubbed strawberries into their shirts, hoping their new leader would think the stains were blood, and be suitably impressed.

Rialto had picked them especially for this little task. He'd long been of the opinion that young people he didn't care about could be very useful. (And, best of all, disposable.)

The new recruits were very excited to be on this mission. Some of them had only filled out 500 notebooks, but had been promoted anyway. They felt very special. They felt so special Rialto was pretty sure they'd probably barely notice if they were killed.

He took one last look through the spyglass and spotted the thing that had been streaking through the sky plummeting back into the Dog & Fist.

'Booooooooooys, Boneless Charlie and Calo Steel-Shins know we're coming.' The twisted war machine that was Rialto Grande's brain had become focused. 'They jusssssst told me where sometheng I want *went*, and showed me where the cheldreen are. Let's go to their house and show them how gentle we can be.'

'Not even a little bit,' said Boss Smasher. He smirked. He'd successfully made a joke. It was the cleverest thing he'd ever done.

Rialto turned his broad back on his band of goons, his shower-curtain cape providing a satisfyingly authoritative *whoosh* as it went. The smile on his lips

was poisonous, the yellow teeth like a series of rusty daggers in the gloom.

'But . . .'

Someone was unexpectedly talking.

'. . . I was the one who saw the kids,' whispered Right Morton, who was usually smarter than his brother. He was whispering to Left Morton, who at this particular moment was being very smart. He had, after all, shut up.

Rialto spun back round, which meant the cape whooshed in reverse.

'Did somewern say sometheeeeng?' he asked, tilting his head to one side like a curious dog, if the dog was curious about why you thought it wasn't about to tear your throat out.

'I saw the girl get in the box, back at the One Tree,' said Right Morton. He didn't notice that his brother was tugging nervously on their umbilical cord.

The veins on Rialto's forehead were starting to pulsate. Why couldn't a gang of trained murderers just shut up and murder? First there was the flower, now this.

'So you *deeed*,' cooed Rialto, suddenly looming over both men, 'and, without your valuable contreeebution, we wouldn't beee hereee nowwww.'

He curled his right hand round the Mortons' umbilical cord and wrenched the bulbous boys forward. Their bellies bounced against each other as they struggled to get free.

'What do you neeeeed, Brother Right Morton?'

'I . . . I was just thinking a little bit of credit,' said Right Morton, nodding at his brother for support, 'a little bit of praise . . .' Left Morton was shaking his head. They shared a lot of things, did the Brothers Morton, but Left Morton wanted no part of Rialto's attention.

'. . . a bit of attention. That's all, Mr Grande.'

Rialto's eyes flashed. He unslung the Mortons' favourite mallet from their cord and held it between their skulls.

'Pants chocolate,' said Rialto Grande.

'No, no, no, no,' moaned Left Morton, less a stone-cold killer now and more a blubbery man blubbering.

'PANTS CHOCOLATE!' shouted Rialto Grande, raising the hammer.

'Please not pants chocolate,' moaned Right Morton.

'PANTS CHOCOLATE FOR RIGHT MORTON!'

Rialto chomped his monstrous yellow teeth down on Left Morton's blimp-like nose. The fat man squealed.

There's nothing so sad as a thug who belongs to another more vicious thug. The Mortons were a pair of criminals too stupid to be trusted with simple tasks, and too violent to be trusted in general – so they'd given themselves up to a smarter, deadlier man.

And that deadlier man knew everything about them. Like how their bodies were so connected that if you told Left Morton to poop in his pants, then Right Morton would be the one who did it.

On schedule, a mound of 'pants chocolate' arrived in Right Morton's trousers.

The other Wreckers, new, old, massive, mostly arms or skinny and tongueless, laughed. Nobody noticed that Gorgo didn't.

'Is that enough attentiooooon for youuuuu?' asked Rialto. He turned back to his troops. 'Shall we get back to murdering now?'

They cheered. The platoon of Wreckers tromped forward. They were well armed, and they had secured their lizards. Their loaded fight-boots breathed orange flame in the darkness of the street. If you were to put your ear to their toes, you'd be able to hear fire-lizards getting squished. But then you'd also be very badly burned, so you may just want to take my word for it.

The Mortons followed. They were bullies who had been humiliated, but, like all bullies, they'd feel a lot better once they'd made someone else suffer.

In a few minutes, the Wreckers would be at the Dog &

Fist. In the few minutes before that, the little family of two orphans and two former assassi– DENTISTS had a brief chat. And served a *lot* of drinks.

'You see,' said Boneless Charlie, 'now the Wreckers know that we know they're coming, and that we know they know you're here, and they know that we know that they know you're here and they know that we know who you are, and they know that we have their souped-up fight-boots, and they know that we know that they know we have them.' He was flipping between the bar and the tables, doling out Slugwater and Grape Slop to masses of Marrowvillian ne'er-do-wells.

People cheered, glasses clinked, the fire roared and Charlie defied gravity. The pub was full and a small war was on its way, but, when Boneless Charlie felt like a chat, nothing could stop him.

Calo leaned behind the bar and pretended to look for something as three skinny ladies ordered themselves forty-five pints of Red Rosie's Blackout Juice. She spoke quietly to two sets of hidden ears. 'And since the Wreckers know we know they know we know and so on – now they'll be just a teensy bit scared.'

Aubrey and Aubrey's sister sat crouched under the sink. They heard their friend's words, but mostly watched her manner change. As cool and tough as Calo could be, right now she was exhilarated. She'd missed her *actual* work. And her work, as far as anyone could tell, was the devil's business.

The children huddled. They'd huddled together many times before, but this was different. Aubrey's sister held a string-sword tightly in her left hand, the invisible string twirled round her fingers in two loops, as Calo had shown her. Aubrey still had his fight-boots on, and was being very careful not to stamp on them too hard, lest he suddenly found himself orbiting another planet.

Aubrey's sister whispered to Aubrey, 'The Wreckers should be scared.'

'Yeah.'

'You're not scared, are you, Aubrey?'

'I am. I'm pretty sure if I kick something in these boots, I'll explode.'

Aubrey's sister put one arm round him. 'If you explode, I'll explode, too.'

Aubrey should have laughed, but didn't. He could have screamed, but didn't. He could have farted, but didn't, since there was no telling what kind of havoc gas would unleash with those explosive boots. Instead, he was quietly studying his right hand.

He realized, numbly, that it was burning again. It had burned when they'd run down that mysterious alley, and then nothing for weeks. Now, at the worst possible time, it really hurt.

20
POOR OLD PUT-UPON PLUG

Sergeant Lorenzo Plug hurt, too. His face hadn't stopped burning since his public embarrassment, and his mockery by the Sacred Police Officer's Charter had twisted his soul. He was miserable before that, but now he was a tear-sodden tissue trapped in the soft body of a very large man. He was, at least, back in uniform, the uniform he wore when out on street duty. It was blue, it had buttons on it . . . and it featured, as Rialto had demanded, another massive and ridiculous hat.

He fought to keep the tears out of his eyes as he sized up his troops. He had brought his own squadron of police officers to the Dog & Fist. They stood in the street, notebooks at the ready. Some were so excited they had three notebooks open at once, and had taped dozens of pens together to try to fill as many books as possible so they could get out of the police force and get on with more fun things, like crime.

Plug looked at the building his master was about to attack. The pub was full. Better than full – heaving.

Oh yes, the Dog & Fist was crammed with bodies! So many people jammed together! Half-stomped escapees from Justice Week ordered drinks to soothe their flattened, battered heads! Candleboys drank with no hands, to keep their wicks dry! Businesspeople told loud, boring stories about their quiet, boring days! The place was packed! The place was rammed!

The place was as ready for a battle as an ex-assassin and a boneless thief could possibly make it.

Rialto Grande stomped up, his gruesome troops lurching behind his big banana jaw. Sergeant Plug saluted, which earned him a withering glance.

'Thet's a looooovely hat, Sergeant Plug,' Rialto jeered as he casually adjusted his cape, 'and this eeees a lovely night for *violence*.'

He patted Barney the dog on his little armoured head. Truly, Rialto had a mission for everyone tonight.

Inside, Boneless Charlie flipped into the air and caught a tray of drinks.

Outside, Rialto picked up Barney. He kissed his armoured dog on the visor.

Inside, Calo poured drinks for laughing men and women.

Outside, Rialto tossed the armoured Barney towards the Dog & Fist's lovely front window.

Inside, a man turned to his friend and asked, 'Have you noticed there's an armoured dog flying towards the window?'

'No, I haven't noticed anyth—'

The glass shattered. Barney clanged against the man who never noticed anything. He didn't notice.

Calo walked over to the window. 'Oh, about time!' she said.

21
THE RUMBLE

Rialto Grande strode into the Dog & Fist. To the terrified people inside, he was a creaking monolith of crooked teeth and cracking knuckles. To Barney the dog, he was all that, with added licking.

People automatically pushed and shoved to get as far from Rialto as possible, which was impossible; the place was so full there was nowhere for them to go. They slipped into each other's laps; they tried to shove their heads into each other's armpits; fingers went into noses and feet got trodden on by backsides. For here was the Chief Wrecker himself – and all any sensible Marrowvillian wanted to do was avoid meeting him.

He raised a gloved hand in the air. 'My naaaame is Rialto Grande! And I am herrrre on Wrecker business!'

The bar fell silent. Of course it did – it was made of wood. Everybody in the pub was pretty quiet, too.

'You people do not seem . . . sufficiently alarmed.'

With one flaming kick from his enormous fight-boot, Rialto shattered the nearest table. The wood flew apart in burning splinters. Glasses smashed. Barney sneezed. Rialto picked up the shivering dog, flipped up his visor and licked his snotty little face. Anyone disgusted by his dog-licking was too terrified to say anything.

'Theeeere eeees a squadron of Wreckers outsede, and they weeelll wreck anywern who leaves this rooooom.'

Rialto's faithful team of Wreckers put their heads through the windows. This wasn't much fun for them, since most of the windows were closed. The Morton Brothers did their headbutt at the same time, so headbutted each other, then fell over, and started fighting.

'Theeeere eeees also . . .'

'Mum loves me more!' Left Morton screamed at Right Morton from the pavement outside the pub.

'No, she loves me!' said Right Morton, still burning with shame from the ordeal of the pants chocolate.

Rialto coughed, and tried to talk over their idiot argument. The other Wreckers tried their best to look very scary, which was easy, since they were.

'There eees also a –' Rialto continued.

'You were adopted!' said Left Morton.

'There eeeees also a –' Rialto started again.

'We're joined together! That means you were adopted, too!'

'No, they added you later! They added you later! I was happy and then they stapled you on!'

The Morton Brothers had got up and were now wrestling each other. Their argument had also risen in volume. Both these things conspired to raise Rialto Grande's blood pressure. The pulsing veins on his forehead made it look like his head was suffering an earthquake.

Rialto snapped. One massive hand grabbed a stool. The next thing the Morton Brothers knew, a seat was being hurled straight at their faces.

'As I was saying, therrrre is a team of Wreckers outssiiiide who weelll wreck anywern who goes outsssiiiiide . . . but therrrrre is also a team coming in here. NOW!'

His twenty extra men dug their way into the room. How do you dig into a crowded room? By grabbing people and shovelling them out through the nearest exits. In this case, those exits were the broken windows.

Businessmen went flying into the street, businesswomen made the short journey from inside to outside and the Fishflinger cried out with delight. He'd never had so many customers. He threw fish at them. It was a big night for these fine citizens of Marrowville; they'd only wanted a drink – then they'd been tossed through windows, now they were being pelted with haddock by a laughing man who was jumping from foot to foot and screaming 'POPULAR FISH!'

Twenty young thugs stood at Rialto's back. They were a shadow of force behind a man whose soul was poisonous and whose heart was shaped like a bulging fist.

'The cheldreen who killed Howard Howard are here.' He pointed at Calo and Charlie. 'They are being held by this clanking half-human and this feeeelthy thief.'

Boneless Charlie was hanging from the ceiling. He waved. His moustache twisted upward in its own hairy smile.

'I want the cheldreeeen. I want them now. Anywern who can give them to me will be able to walk out of here alive. Anywern who can't give them to me will be broken for their failure.'

The room was still. A man raised his hand.

'What eees eeet?'

'Do you mean that somewhere, hidden in this pub, there's a Secret Giraffe?'

The crowd murmured. Life had just got more interesting. Sure, the Wreckers could mutilate them, but now there was a chance that, before that happened, they might see a boy who could turn into a giraffe. They wanted answers.

'Tell us about the Secret Giraffe!'

'Is he really a giraffe?'

'Yeah, tell us! Tell us about the Secret Giraffe!'

'NOBODY IS REALLY A SECRET GIRAFFE! IT WAS JUST A BIT OF GRAFFITI!' Rialto had had no idea he could feel so angry. He was only in the pub for vengeance. This was getting strange.

'You know, I've always felt that, on the inside, I was secretly a giraffe,' said one of the men who'd been enjoying his drink before Rialto exploded his table.

'My wife was secretly a giraffe the whole time we were married. Not that I noticed,' said the man who never noticed anything.

Behind the bar, the Secret Giraffe and the Girl Who Isn't Here stifled giggles.

'Gentlemen, ladies, what Mr Grande has said is totally true.' Boneless Charlie seemed to have had a change of heart.

The children froze. Calo looked shocked.

Charlie spread his arms wide to the people. 'For the last few weeks, my blessed wife and I have been keeping a secret from all of you . . .' Boneless Charlie looked so sad, his guilt unbearable, his confession monstrous.

'Go oooon,' said Rialto.

Charlie walked over to the bar.

Rialto laughed. 'Look at him – he's betraying the cheldreen to save himself! What a goooood bad guy you are, Charlie.' The Chief Wrecker cooed his approval. He adored what he saw. Soon there would be no more talk of secret giraffes, and a whole lot more stuffing two children into instruments of extreme torture.

Charlie took a piece of paper from his pocket. He scribbled on it.

'I want you all to watch me as I write this.' He read each word aloud as he scribbled. '*I, Boneless Charlie, humble purveyor of fine liquor, owner of the best facial hair in Marrowville, killed Howard Howard. It was terrific, and I would do it again, especially if he came back as a zombie.* Oh God, Calo! I've finally told them the truth! Oh boo-hoo! Oh booey-hooey-hoo!'

Dramatically, he slapped the confession on to the bar. It slipped off and he fell over. He'd spent too much time polishing the wood. Charlie tumbled to the ground as the precious bit of paper slowly wafted behind the bar and, unseen by all, landed at the children's feet.

'*You* did it?' A Candleboy on the floor was intrigued. He wasn't alone in his curiosity. Another great murmuring filled the room.

'I knew a child couldn't kill a Wrecker!' said a woman who'd been hiding under a table since the Wreckers arrived.

'I'm so glad he's gone! I know there's a young fella using my head as a football right now, but no Howard

Howard! How wonderful!' said a man whose head was being kicked by a Wrecker, but whose heart was being gladdened by circumstance.

'Good on ya, Charlie!' shouted a chap in the process of disappearing backwards through a window. Boss Smasher's skull-spanning palm was crushing his forehead, but not his spirit.★

'Old Charlie killed Howard Howard!' cried a voice.

'Oh, thank God!' said another.

'We hated that guy!' said yet another. The crowd burst into applause. Yes, they were getting beaten up, but Howard Howard had been such a jerk for the length of time they'd known him, and everybody loved Charlie even before they thought he was the slayer of one of the town's stupidest demons. Some people were so happy they started singing. They weren't all singing the same song, since no songs existed for an event they'd never even dared imagine would arrive. Instead, about forty different songs happened, each including made-up phrases like '*twelve-fingered filth-sucker*' and '*I'm glad you're dead, so glad you're dead, deadetty-deadetty-dead-dead-dead*'.

'Stop that clapping! Stop that singing!' shouted Rialto Grande. 'Stop eet!'

'*DEADETTY-DEADETTY-DEADETTY!*

★ Then, of course, he got outside, where the rest of Boss Smasher crushed his spirit along with his kneecaps.

'*DEADETTY-DEADETTY-DEADETTY-DEAD!*'

That last song was getting quite popular.

Charlie's moustache curled up with pride. Making sure the Wreckers came when the pub was full was clever, but the fake confession had been a masterstroke. He folded his arms and rocked on his heels.

It was such a good plan. A plan he'd quickly cooked up in his cunning old brain – it had bubbled up so fast that his entire mind was like a frying pan for plots and schemes.

He had confessed to a crime, in front of everybody. He'd committed plenty of crimes, but he'd never confessed to one before. Especially not one he hadn't actually done.

It was a great distraction. The Wreckers were confused – and they had such little tolerance for being made fun of. It would drive them mad, which, since they already nearly were, would surely cause what was left of their sanity to drool out of their ears. 'Maybe Barney could lick it up,' Charlie pondered. 'I wonder what sanity tastes like? I suppose it tastes sensible.'

'*DEADETTY! DEADETTY! DEADETTY! DEADETTY!*' Now everyone was singing.

He sang along, too, and why not? Oh, the Wreckers would torture him and probably kill him, but it didn't matter. Blasting Aubrey through the roof had shown the Wreckers he had the children, and the fight-boots.

He was also about to show them they couldn't have the children, or the fight-boots.

And, on top of that, he'd taken this opportunity to remind them that everybody in Marrowville hated them.

He was at once a criminal, a hero and a sacrifice. And he knew the truth. The Grinders were coming. He didn't know what they wanted, but he suspected they had big plans for Aubrey and Aubrey's sister.

And, as long as the children were alive, whatever mind-bending terrors the Grinders had planned for the town would far eclipse the mundane menace of Rialto Grande.

Charlie chuckled. It really had been a terrific spur-of-the-moment ploy.

A terrific spur-of-the-moment ploy ruined only when a small high-pitched voice suddenly joined in on a stray '*Deadetty*'.

Huddled behind the bar, held tight by his sister, the happiness in Aubrey's tiny body had bubbled to the surface. And he laughed. '*DEADETTY-DEADETTY-DEAD!*' he giggled.

Everyone went quiet and turned towards the bar.

The noise was unmistakable. A child's laugh doesn't sound like an adult's. It is a high-pitched thing that pierces the air and seeks out the ears of adults who are busy (or hungover).

Rialto pointed at the bar. It was as though there was an invisible line leading from his huge finger through the wood, through the metal, straight through Aubrey's back and into the little boy's heart.

And then pain surged through Rialto's finger. There really was an invisible line, but it led from Calo's arm, across the bar, and straight through Rialto's hand. Her string-sword had pierced his enormous fingernail. She tugged, and suddenly the pompadoured warlord found himself pointing directly at her. And she was smiling.

'Rialto,' said Calo.

'Calo Steeeeel-Shins.' He giggled and grinned a sick grin, saliva leaking from between his yellow teeth. 'When I am dern with youuuuu, I theeenk I'll keep those metal legs. Use themmm to wreck your husband.'

'Try that, and your terrible hair will be the last thing I cut off you.'

Rialto rolled his green eyes. 'Yourrrr woman is much braver than you, Charlie.'

'Oh, she doesn't belong to me, old fellow. We're just married.' Charlie was now sitting cross-legged on top of the bar. His good humour suggested he was blissfully unaware of the twenty-one-man death squad that was taking up most of his favourite place.

Charlie was, of course, exceptionally aware of the twenty-one-man death squad. He was also aware that

Calo had just started a fight. And he was aware that the children would be very easy to find, and that he almost *definitely* didn't quite *totally* have a plan any more.

And then he noticed that Rialto had used his other arm to point at the bar, and had ordered his men to wreck everyone in the joint.

Poor Charlie. He really should've been paying more attention.

Flames erupted from every fight-boot. The Wreckers ran screaming into the terrified crowd, swinging fists and chains and fire. They howled with joy. They felt power. They felt invincible. They felt the glory a cruel man feels as they drag someone weaker than them through a window.

Calo twisted the length of cord round her arm and pulled Rialto a step closer towards her.

Aubrey's sister dropped her string-sword and put her hands over her brother's ears. She heard bodies being thrown against the bar. She heard screaming. She heard crunching. She heard Rialto's braying laugh.

Five Wreckers dashed forward to grab Boneless Charlie, and all five grabbed each other as Charlie slipped between them.

One Wrecker swung a punch. Charlie spun. The same man found his wrist grabbed by the strands of Charlie's moustache and flung across the room.

Charlie crouched on the floor. With one hand, he pulled his moustache off his face. Wreckers flew at him from all sides. He stretched his arm and cracked his moustache like a whip. It snapped round a young Wrecker's wrist and stayed there – a coil of steel wire wrapped round weak flesh.

Charlie stood up, the other end of his long, thin facial hair held delicately between his fingers and thumb, the way an orchestral conductor would hold his baton, if that baton was a moustache, and partially wrapped round another man's arm.

With a flourish, he raised his arm. The Wrecker's trapped arm rose, too.

Charlie nodded at the confused young man, and then laughingly yanked the Wrecker's fist into another Wrecker's face. Then into another one. Then another. He flipped the Wrecker into the air and stopped his fall with a table and another Wrecker's spine. He pinched his weaponized moustache and it sprang straight again. It was time to snare another wrist.

A chair was thrown at him. He flipped into the air and sat on it cross-legged. It sailed into the wall and shattered, dropping him on an unsuspecting Wrecker. He whooped with glee as another thug became his puppet, thrashing and bashing his way across the floor.

He did it till he got sick of it – and he never got sick

of it. He moved like a dancer, kicking in teeth. He was an acrobat, twisting against weapons. He was a puppeteer who didn't like his puppet very much. He was Boneless Charlie, and he was cleverer and nobler than his opponents, even if he was a bit absent-minded and occasionally stole things.

Across the room, Calo dragged Rialto towards her. Despite the pain in his hand, the madman was enjoying himself immensely. He loved a bit of carnage. He carelessly plunged his free arm into the wall and dragged his fingers through the plaster. He laughed. In the mass of screams, it just looked like he was baring his teeth.

The new Wreckers weren't thinking like people any more. Bloodlust and gunpowder had transformed them into burning machines that existed just to break bones. These machines ran entirely on other people's fear. And fear was everywhere.

They smashed people. Some tried to fight back and were smashed harder. Flames burst out all around the room.

Behind the bar, the children worked on a plan. It was easy – Charlie had given them a clue.

Aubrey's sister had picked up the confession. It wasn't a confession of any kind. Charlie had drawn a picture of himself talking. There was a speech bubble that said:

Hello, children! Could I possibly trouble you, if it's not too inconvenient, for the sudden and unexpected appearance of a Secret Giraffe? PS We are in extreme danger! Isn't it wonderful?

Aubrey turned to his sister. 'Do giraffes wear fight-boots?'

'Of course,' she said.

A young Wrecker was thrown over the bar. He landed next to them with a thud. He really was very young. Like the others, he'd smeared his body with fruit to make himself look tough. But, unlike the others, he hadn't had any strawberries, just bananas. His brown shirt was covered with big splotches of yellow.

'Do you think he's part of the plan?' asked Aubrey.

'Yes,' said Boneless Charlie, popping his head over the bar while simultaneously kicking two men.

'What happened to your moustache?' asked Aubrey's sister.

Charlie waved it in the air. 'War!'

He looked around and took in the fight. His beloved Dog & Fist was in pandemonium. Everything that wasn't broken was being broken. A dog in armour was sneezing on the bar. Charlie patted him.

The Morton Brothers slammed their hammer down next to Charlie. The bar cracked. Charlie tumbled to the floor. They slammed the floor. He tumbled away from them. They slammed it again. He tumbled between their legs. They sat on him. He stopped tumbling.

When Rialto Grande was ten steps away from Calo, he plucked the string-sword's point out of his finger. The ease with which he did this sent a message, and that message was: 'I could've taken it out at any time.'

Calo stopped smiling. She retracted the blade. She planted her feet shoulder-width apart and held her weapon against her chest, the tip pointing over her right shoulder. It was a traditional battle pose. An elegant way of showing respect to your opponent before showing them what the inside of their guts looked like.

Behind the bar, Aubrey's sister forced her brother into the unconscious Wrecker's shirt. This was hard, since the Wrecker was still inside the shirt. And harder still because Aubrey was going into the shirt upside down. But he didn't worry about that; he worried about why his sister was drawing eyes on the Wrecker's boots.

Rialto loomed over Calo. The yellow teeth parted and his voice oozed out. 'You doooo realize, don't you, Calo, that if you're theeeeenking of having a duel I am totally unarmed?'

'That's a lie, Rialto.'

'Yes, but eeeeet was such good fun to say.'

Gorgo and Boss Smasher stood behind Rialto. They watched their boss clench and unclench his fists. There was a sizzling sound.

Gorgo flinched. Instinctively, he covered his chest.

Calo saw the rock-man shudder, and knew something terrible was coming.

Rialto's smile was too wide for it to just be something conventional, like a hidden blade, or the news he'd managed to infect her with a deadly poison. He was a man who enjoyed a joke, especially when it really hurt.

And even more alarming, aside from Gorgo, Rialto's other henchmen seemed amused. Normally, they'd have lumbered over to protect their boss, but the Mortons were sitting down. Rodney was hissing and dancing. Boss Smasher had a sly grin on his face.

Boss Smasher spoke. 'Did you know, assassin, that we don't just use fight-*boots*?'

The gloves on Rialto's hands burst into columns of flame. He launched himself at Calo. Every punch was an inferno. He could melt a person. He could melt steel. He would do both.

Calo darted forward beneath the jets of fire. The huge man misjudged an upper-cut. She stepped round the blow and jammed the tip of her sword into Rialto's chin. She pressed forward.

At that moment, Calo, former assassin, now bartender, now adoptive parent, saw seven things.

She saw a laughing man made of fire grab her sword.

She saw her sword melt.

She saw the laughing man grab her arms.

She saw her husband leap into the air.

She saw her husband stride across the shoulders of fifteen men and kick Rialto Grande in his enormous stupid face.

She saw Boss Smasher's fist knock Charlie out of the air.

She saw defeat.

Boneless Charlie's body met Boss Smasher's fists and cracked apart. Rodney Paste jumped on his head, hissing and spitting. Boneless Charlie had bones to smash, after all.

Rialto Grande laughed. Every finger on his hand had become a white-hot column of flame. And every one of those fingers had just been jammed through Calo's shoulders. He laughed as he dropped her.

Calo and Charlie lay helpless on the ground.

'Come out, cheldreen!' called Rialto Grande. 'Or your friends will surely die!'

The children stepped out from behind the bar. Or one did and the other didn't.

One was a girl. She held a string-sword in one hand, and pointed it directly at Rialto.

'Rialto Grande! I haven't seen you since you and

your men had lunch with my father!' she said. 'Are you sure you can see me? Because I am not here.'

Rialto clenched his fist, squashing the fire-lizard inside his glove. He threw a punch, and a column of flame burned a course for Aubrey's sister. She flung herself to the side and hurled her sword at Rialto's face. The big Wrecker snatched the blade from the air with one snap of his horrible teeth.

From behind the bar, a small voice said, 'Please don't burn my sister.'

'Thank you!' called Aubrey's sister.

(It doesn't matter if you and your friends might be about to die, there's always time to be nice.)

The little voice continued. 'My name is Aubrey Howard, and I am . . .'

There was a pause, and a sizzling sound. 'And I am . . .'

The sizzling got louder. Rialto, Boss Smasher, the Mortons and everybody in the room turned to look at the bar.

'. . . A SECRET GIRAFFE!'

There was a *boom*. Aubrey's sister threw herself to the floor. Aubrey had stomped his fight-boots – and what launched itself over the bar and hit Rialto Grande in the chest was so fast that nobody was quite sure what they'd seen.

To them, it was a yellow-and-brown blur wrapped

up in a fireball. To us, it was a little rocket-propelled boy stuffed upside down in the front of a big, dirty Wrecker's shirt, with the big, dirty Wrecker's legs flailing madly above him.

To Rialto Grande, it was pain.

Aubrey and the unconscious Wrecker had become a missile. They crashed into the giant, who crashed through the wall and out into the street.

Unfortunately for Rialto, the street wasn't empty. Sergeant Plug, huge, humdrum and going home, had just got on top of Terry the Terrible Horse. The giant flew rump-first into the horse's head-spikes. Terry, not accustomed to sudden butts to the face, panicked. He galloped down the road, his sharp barbs digging into Rialto's posterior with each hoofbeat.

'I'm sorry, Mr Grande!' said Sergeant Plug.

Rialto Grande said nothing. He'd never been embarrassed before tonight. He didn't like it.

'Yayyyyyy!' Aubrey was zooming around the Dog & Fist, the unconscious Wrecker's legs whacking Gorgo, the Mortons, Boss Smasher and a whole bunch of other Wreckers, who were pretty dangerous, but not important enough to have names.

'The Secret Giraffe!' cried a man on the ground. 'It has two heads and can fly!'

'It has the head of a small boy and two heads that

look like shoes with eyes painted on them!' A woman was amazed.

'What Secret Giraffe?' asked the man who never noticed anything.

The people in the pub who could stand up did so. Then ducked again as Aubrey zoomed over them.

Calo and Charlie and Aubrey had thumped most of the Wreckers, and those they hadn't whacked were suddenly surrounded by people who weren't particularly scared of them. Why should they be scared? They'd just seen a two-headed giraffe that could fly.

Calo and Charlie got up. Calo took the melted stub of her sword and placed it at Boss Smasher's throat.

'Get out.'

Charlie smiled helpfully as he reaffixed his moustache. 'I think my wife would like you gentlemen to leave.'

Barney sneezed.

'And would somebody *please* take that dog to a vet!'

22
Breakfast with Family

Calo and Charlie sat up in bed, the morning's brown sun streaming through the curtains. Aubrey was pouring tea the colour of the sky. Aubrey's sister was buttering toast the colour of burnt. It was breakfast time at the Dog & Fist, and one weary adult had bruises and two bandaged arms. The other weary adult had bruises and two bandages on his moustache.

'However did you manage to get the toast so wonderfully . . . crisp?' asked Boneless Charlie.

Aubrey's sister nodded over at Howard Howard's fight-boots, tossed carelessly on a chair in the corner of the room. (Not too carelessly, obviously, or this chapter would just read, 'The children dropped the shoes, every-one was incinerated, nobody had breakfast. The End.')

Charlie beamed as he took two plates from Aubrey's sister. 'Thank you, my tiny darling.'

Everybody ate their breakfast. The toast was buttery

and delicious. The tea was warm and soothing. The children had done a good job. The happiness in the room seemed to spill out into the street, where folks chatted pleasantly amid the occasional squeaking and creaking of bicycles and food carts.

'Big night last night,' said Calo. She hadn't spoken all morning.

It had been a huge night. The downstairs bar was a mess. No windows were unbroken, no drinks were unspilled, and almost every visitor had left with a free handful of their own teeth.

'It was horrible – and amazing!' Aubrey's sister was more animated than anyone had ever seen her. She jumped around the room.

'Calo, you would've destroyed Rialto, but who knew he had exploding hands? I hope he scratches his bum!' said Aubrey's sister. 'And you, Charlie, we thought you were going to throw us to the Wreckers, but no . . . it was –' she stood up – 'FAKE CONFESSION TIME! BOOEY-HOOEY-HOO!' The young girl was bubbling with glee, her pent-up emotions spilling out in a hyperactive frenzy. This was very unlike Aubrey's sister. Her guard was totally down.

Aubrey jumped up, too. He excitedly pretended to be everyone in the fight. 'Boom! Bang! Urgh! Mummy loves ME more!'

Aubrey's sister grabbed her string-sword. She pretended to hurl it at an imaginary Rialto Grande. She shuffled; she danced; she felt the same way she had when Howard Howard had gone into that mincer.

She cocked her head back and laughed. Relief was blasting through her whole body. She beamed at her friends.

'You two were tremendous!' Her eyes were shining. 'Thank you for looking after my brother and me.' She beckoned her brother to her. 'Come here, Aubrey.'

Aubrey was busy pretending to be both of the Mortons *and* Rialto *and* Charlie *and* a broken table, but, being a good brother, he came over to where 'here' was.

'Say thank you, my . . . darling.' She giggled to use one of the words Charlie and Calo always did. It felt like they were a little family. A happy little family who spent their lives fighting off menaces who wore leather and kicked down doors and husbands and wives and children.

'Thank you, Charlie and Calo.' Aubrey was shifting from foot to foot. He was happy, but embarrassed. He'd never needed to thank anyone before. Who had ever done anything for him and his sister? Not his father, not horrible Mrs Dalrymple. Just these two strange people, the clever one with the big moustache and no bones, and the clever, no-nonsense one who had made his sister feel so special.

Charlie's blackened eyes glimmered. He raised a weary hand to wave away the praise. 'Oh, my loves – last night wasn't anything much. My darling wife fights too honourably, and I'm just a sneaky old ratbag.'

'The important thing is that neither of you are hurt.' Calo was being serious. For a street-smart warrior, she sounded very tired.

Aubrey's sister decided she wasn't having that. She had woken up absolutely exhilarated. She and her brother had been defended! They felt wanted. They felt like they were at home. She would make her friends feel better.

She leaned over the foot of Calo and Charlie's bed. 'The really important thing is that both of you will be all right soon. Until then, Aubrey and I will look after the pub. Won't we, Aubrey?'

'I don't think . . .' Calo began.

'It'll be superb! The Wreckers know we're here, but we thrashed them! And we'll do it again! And *everyone* hates them! I'm sure, if they ever come back, we'll all just devise another genius plan – and rip them apart!' Aubrey's sister was usually guided by caution with a side order of fear and anger, but victory and excitement had turned danger into a game. She wanted to show her friends how brave she was, and how happy she was to be with them.

'What do you think, Aubrey?'

Aubrey didn't do much thinking, but he was great at imagining. He was now pretending to be a car that delivered toast. 'Vroooom!' he shouted, driving a plate up to Calo's side of the bed. 'Toast!'

Calo smiled, but the happiness didn't reach her eyes.

'Oh, I'll have a spot of dead bread,' Charlie said. He took the food, but left it on his plate.

Aubrey's sister glanced at the plate. Happy as she was, she could still sense that something was wrong. She paused.

Charlie noticed. 'Oh, don't worry about us, my love. We're old. We get injured just by sneezing,' he said.

As though to emphasize this point, he sneezed. He sneezed so hard his head sank between his shoulders and deep into his chest, like a turtle suddenly going home. He popped his head back up and waggled his eyebrows. 'I'm sorry, everybody. It seems I just wiped my nose on my heart.'

'Old Snot-Heart,' said Aubrey's sister, realizing fun was back on the menu.

Aubrey laughed. 'Snot-Heart! Walrus-Head Snot-Heart! Whom! Whom! Whom!'

Calo glanced at her playful husband. He was hurt, but it was wonderful to see him trying to make the children laugh. It was also wonderful to see two healthy children finally having fun. She was the only person in the room who didn't look joyful. And she knew she was the only one who was right.

The night before, the two ex-assassins hadn't had the energy to feel proud. Half an hour after the battle ended, they turned off all the inside lights and sat on the only remaining chairs in their wrecked pub. They'd talked softly and tended each other's wounds, the floor strewn with broken glass that reflected the moonlight. They were, for a long time, a small island in an ocean of pale, glimmering shards.

'I took down an army once,' Calo had whispered.

Charlie had kissed her forehead. 'You certainly did.'

To the children, sitting on the stairs, the scene had looked beautiful. But they couldn't see Calo shivering in pain, or Charlie's lower lip quivering as he held his injured wife.

Later, the kids had offered to help Calo up the stairs, but she insisted she could do it herself. The swordfighter had limped to bed, her determination alone dragging her exhausted, broken body up each step.

She'd been in too much pain to sleep for long, and, when she did, her dreams had been hellish. She'd seen Rialto's crooked yellow teeth as he laughed through the flames, and giant shadowy figures that marched through the razor-mist and crushed cities beneath their feet. Then the Grinders had smiled at her and waved, like they knew where she was.

And now, on a morning when her room was filled with toast and butter and giggles, Calo knew something the children couldn't know. Last night hadn't been a victory. It had been a deadly loss. And what was to come would be worse.

Calo tried to adjust the pillow behind her back. She was in agony, but, as always, there were more important things to do than suffer. She tried to smile and failed.

Aubrey's sister saw Calo struggle. She could sense

something was about to happen. And she wished it wouldn't. She looked at her brother. He was happily trying to deliver toast to an unresponsive cushion. She looked back at the bed; neither Calo nor Charlie were smiling any more. They had placed their hands next to each other, their fingers lightly touching. Aubrey's sister realized they were in too much pain to actually hold hands.

Calo coughed. Words weren't coming out easily. She croaked, 'Come here, you two.'

The children walked over to the adults. With one arm, Calo gave Aubrey's sister as much of a cuddle as she could manage. Charlie gave Aubrey a weak squeeze, angling his head so he didn't injure his moustache further. The little boy hugged him back. The injured Charlie winced in pain. For a moment, they all looked like the family Aubrey's sister wanted them to be.

It didn't last long.

Charlie spoke. His voice was quiet, and weak. 'My loves, we have had to make a difficult decision.'

The tone of Charlie's voice chased away any trace of a smile from Aubrey's sister's face.

'We've all had the most wonderful time together, but we can't keep you two here any more.'

Aubrey's sister, who could cope with almost anything, felt tears well up in her eyes. She dug her fingers into her hands to stop herself crying. Weeping in front of other people wasn't a luxury she ever allowed herself.

'Oh, my darling! It'll be all right.' Charlie was perceptive – he could see that Aubrey's sister was trying to be very strong.

Aubrey's sister was perceptive, too; she knew that nothing was going to be 'all right'.

'We're sorry,' said Calo.

'I'm sorry!' said Aubrey's sister. The news felt like a knife, and seeing two people she loved in pain was dreadful. 'I'm sorry we put you in danger!' She didn't want to yell at her friends, but she couldn't stop herself. As happy as she had just felt, that happiness was gone now.

'I'm sorry, too!' Aubrey was no longer being a car. Aubrey knew how to apologize. His first word had been 'Sorry'. (It was part of a longer sentence: 'Sorry I'm alive.')

Calo shook her head. 'Sweethearts, Charlie and I aren't in any danger. We're old enough and ugly enough to look after ourselves. It's just we can't . . .' She hesitated. 'We can't look after you.'

Calo had never felt truly bad about anything she'd done, but saying that to the children had made her soul feel cold.

'We thought we could, my loves. But we've failed.' Charlie's moustache drooped unevenly, as though its left side was a broken leg. 'Last night was just the Wreckers' first attack, and they outsmarted and out-gunned us.'

'That's not true!' said Aubrey.

'Little man, the next time they come we won't be able to do a blasted thing. They will sweep through this building and cart you and your sister off to a hole somewhere.'

Calo spoke up. 'We spent our lives building up a level of mystery and rumour. "He's a great thief!" "She's a great warrior!" But now they know our limits. If you stay here, you will both die. Probably tonight.'

Charlie cut in ruefully. 'It'll be tonight. They're still hideous cowards. They won't come during the day.'

Aubrey's sister shut her eyes as firmly as she could. She tried to keep her voice flat and unwavering. 'I'm sorry we did this to you.'

Calo sighed. It wasn't the response the girl had really needed.

Aubrey's sister ran to the other end of the bedroom and turned her back so nobody would see her cry. Aubrey didn't turn his back. He bawled. He'd never known that anyone other than his sister could be kind. He'd never slept in a bed. He'd never laughed so much. And it was all gone with a few words.

Aubrey's sister heard the creaking of bedsprings as

the two injured adults got up. They were moving as quickly as they could.

'You haven't done anything to us, lovely. You misunderstand.' Calo spoke as she walked.

'We've just, well . . .' Charlie was stumbling for the right words.

'Just say it, Walrus-Head.' Calo's voice was sad – even her favourite nickname had lost its sting.

'We have to send you somewhere.' Charlie crouched. It hurt his body, but it was worth it to be eye level with Aubrey's sister. 'We have a plan, you see.'

The girl turned round, confused and angry. She began to shout. 'What's the plan, Charlie? More bees that aren't bees? And where will we go? The mist? To join our mother in the flying razors?'

She really hadn't wanted to yell at her friends.

Calo put one hand on Aubrey's sister's shoulder. 'Sweetheart, you are one of my four favourite people in the world, and I owe you an apology.'

The girl looked straight ahead. She wouldn't make eye contact with anybody.

Charlie spoke. 'We need both of you to be very, very brave.'

Calo continued. She didn't want any of this. 'We have to ask you both to do something we would never do.'

'We have to throw you at something more dangerous

than anything else we've ever known,' said Charlie. 'Oddly enough, it's the only way we can protect you.'

Calo was looking out of the window. Aubrey's sister followed her friend's gaze. Calo was staring at something nobody else could see. That didn't mean it wasn't there, however.

If Aubrey's sister could have seen through the Victory Finger, and through all the streets and alleys and churches and bridges and houses and spires of Marrowville, she would've known that Calo was staring directly at the One Tree.

'Regretfully, my loves, we're going to need to send you,' said Charlie, 'to the Grinders.'

23

THE TERRIBLE CONDITION
OF SERGEANT PLUG'S SKIN

Deep in the basement of the Marrowville Police Station-and-Jail, one of the sinks in Chief Superintendent Sergeant Lorenzo Plug's private washroom was filling up with warm, soapy water. Yes, Sergeant Plug's office was a cell, but he had a lovely bathroom. It had lots and lots of taps, and several dozen showers. All he had to do was wait for the prisoners to stop using it, before he got a go.

He sighed. The night before had been devastating for his career, and he knew it. After all, his horse had skewered his boss. He'd done what he could to help, but he'd fallen off Terry ages before Rialto had. The last time he saw the Chief Wrecker, he was screeching through yellow teeth as Terry galloped down an alley and out of sight.

'Better make use of this luxury while you've still got

a job,' he said to his reflection in the mirror. He felt terrible. If he was fired, he'd miss every part of being a police officer. Even the hats.

He looked in the mirror. There were bags under his eyes. His skin looked tired. He peered closer.

Tired and . . . *lumpy*?

I can't have . . . he thought. *I'm too old for . . .*

He sighed. 'Pimples.'

The word echoed around the bathroom:

PIMPLES
PIMPLES
PIMPLES
PIMPLES.

'Just another indignity,' he muttered sadly. He inspected the lumps in the mirror again. They didn't look normal. For a start, they burned.

He splashed his face with water. It didn't help. He looked again. The pimples didn't just burn – they were much, much larger than the pimples he'd had as a boy. Those had been little reddish spots – these were like massive bubbles. They made his face look like it was covered with batches of crimson hard-boiled eggs.

In fact, they seemed to be getting bigger as he looked at them.

'Oh well,' he said, his voice echoing off the tiles in the huge room. His echo came back, *Oh well, oh well, oh well, oh well*. But he knew he wasn't well.

He looked over at the Sacred Police Officer's Charter. He'd propped it up next to the mirror for company. He wasn't sure exactly why, but he wasn't exactly sure about anything any more. At least the Book wasn't open, and he didn't have to see the word STOMACH scrawled in such big troubling letters again.

He looked at his arms. Did they have pimples on them, too? They certainly did.

'Going mad,' he said to himself.

He washed his hands and prepared to do something he'd had to do every night as a teenager.

'Time to bring back my squeezing fingers,' he murmured to himself.

At that point, the echo asked him a question. *How are you?*

Sergeant Plug looked round.

Keep going, Sergeant Plug. The echo's voice had such authority that he fixed his eyes back on the mirror.

'Who are you?' asked Sergeant Plug.

Let's just say that you love me.

Sergeant Plug realized he wasn't hearing an echo. The voice was coming from the Book.

It spoke again. *Go ahead, Sergeant Plug. Squeeze a pimple.*

Sergeant Plug felt adoration course through his body. Of course he loved the voice! It was all he'd ever wanted. He pressed his two index fingers to his forehead and found the sides of a particularly sizeable egg. It was time to make his face smooth and presentable – to make himself the shining beacon of law and order the town so desperately didn't need.

Sergeant Plug, you have a miserable life, don't you?

He nodded into the mirror.

We'll change that. I will give you a new purpose, Sergeant Plug.

'Oh, thank you!' Sergeant Plug was filled with relief. Tears of gratitude welled in his eyes. The voice controlled every part of him.

Now squeeze, Sergeant Plug.

Chief Superintendent Sergeant Lorenzo Plug, whose father had named his children for the best jobs he thought they could get, jammed his fingers into the pustule. He thought of his brother, whose full name was Untended Private Toilet, his sister, Loud Unpopular Potato, and, of course, his father, whose name had been Lord God Emperor Bigballs.

Are you ready for your new purpose, Sergeant Plug?

Sergeant Plug squeaked out a mewling 'Yes!' The pimple was big and it hurt.

Pop it, Sergeant Plug.

He pulled his fingers to either side of his forehead, and breathed deep. This would be the final blow to his swollen foe. Sergeant Plug rammed his nails right into the bloated zit. It burst, splattering the mirror with a warm shower of yellow pus.

The big man's eyes widened in horror. He gaped at his reflection. It wasn't just that the mirror was now filthy – it was more that there was now something much more alarming than a pimple on his face.

Staring out from where the pimple had been was a human eye.

Sergeant Plug gulped. He could see out of all three eyes, and his three eyes made him notice just how very many large pimples were covering his face. And arms. And legs. And hands. And everything.

The Sacred Police Officer's Charter laughed at Sergeant Plug. The hateful, living eyes on its cover had returned – once again, the Book could wink, glance, stare and glare.

Do you know me, slave? asked the Book.

Sergeant Plug touched his tongue. There were pimples on it – and on his fingers. He had boils in his ears. He had cysts on his wrists. There were lumps all over him.

He shook his bumpy head. His whole body burned.

The Book laughed at him. *You worshipped me as the*

Sacred Police Officer's Charter, with your face – and then when you took off your lovely gloves. Don't you remember?

The big policeman nodded. Tears were running down his face, which had the added side effect of making his pimples sting.

That has been my name before, and one day it may be again, but now you will worship me under my real name. Are you proud?

Sergeant Plug nodded his head. He didn't feel proud. He didn't feel anything. He also hadn't told his head to nod, but it had done it.

You will call me by my preferred title, the Book of Eyes. Do you understand?

Sergeant Plug nodded again. It wasn't against his will, since it seemed he had no will left at all. He just couldn't control his body.

Then, slave, I have one command.

He stared helplessly at the Book.

Pop ALL your pimples!

Sergeant Plug reached for his face. He screamed.

Three-and-a-half disgusting hours later, Sergeant Plug was a new man. Which is to say he was entirely eyes. He had blue eyes on his fingertips, purple eyes on his earlobes, black eyes beneath his chin and a brown eye where you'd expect.*

* If you're wondering what this means – here's a clue: the eye wasn't always brown.

He cradled the Book of Eyes with fingers that blinked. If he could still think for himself, he might have realized he was weeping. Not out of any of the new eyes, just the two he'd had all his life.

Once, those two eyes had shown him his entire world – but now they were just another thing he couldn't control.

Take me out, slave.

Chief Superintendent Sergeant Lorenzo Plug walked out of his bathroom and through his empty office. He could see everything in the room, but he didn't know that the Wreckers had called all his officers away to a secret meeting. The fact he didn't know that was what made it a secret.

He didn't know anything any more. He only knew that he had to serve the Book of Eyes – and the Book of Eyes wanted to go on a journey.

He stepped outside. The sun was too bright. His entire body shut itself in discomfort. Blinded, he stumbled back into the shade of his office.

He wondered, 'What can I use to protect myself?' The answer he came up with was, 'Two hundred pairs of sunglasses.'

Or night-time, you fool, said the Book of Eyes. It could read his thoughts. It could also, if it wanted, make sure he never had a thought of his own ever again.

The Book had known everything about Sergeant Plug from the moment his face had hit its pages in the town square. And now it wanted him to go and find someone else who had touched it.

It wanted him to go and find the boy.

It wanted to see one of its sons.

24
RIALTO'S ARMY

Inside the cave, 400 pairs of police boots were standing to attention. The blue-suited buffoons were standing stiffer and straighter than they ever had before. They did this because they were petrified. For today the officers were seeing a leader whom they truly feared.

Every man and woman on Marrowville's police force had abandoned their post, picked up their sack of notebooks and tromped towards an uncertain fate. Even Officer Jenkins, the constable whose eye had been taken by Terry the Terrible Horse's endless quest for sugar lumps, was there. In fact, he'd turned up early.

The cave went deep into the rocky face of Wrecker Bay, like a blackhead that would take an absolute eternity to pop. It had been the Wreckers' property ever since the shipwreck that had brought the notebooks that had brought law (but not order) to Marrowville.

The Wreckers called it the Hall of Righteousness.

They didn't use it often, preferring instead to spend their days enjoying random evil.★

Rodney Paste staggered inside, the daylight behind him turning his bent body into a crooked shadow. He was trying to blow a trumpet. A strained note sounded. It was a hideously strangulated fart of a noise.

The police officers turned to him in mild confusion. Was the trumpet blocked? It seemed to be causing Rodney extreme physical pain.

The little man bent backwards. His face was crimson. He grabbed the trumpet with both hands and pointed it straight at the sky. His shabby body shook with effort. He blew.

A fire-lizard blasted out. It splatted against the cave's stone ceiling and exploded. The trumpet sounded one true note as bits of flammable reptile fell to the floor in a rain of medium-rare meat.

Rodney collapsed. He lay on the ground, gasping for air. A sizeable boot stood on his throat. The gasping stopped.

'Thank you for that leeeeeetle show, Rodneeeeeeey.'

★ Random evil is much easier than having total power. The Wreckers lived in Marrowville and there was nowhere else to go. However, if they totally controlled the place, there'd be boring questions to deal with. Questions like, 'Where does our water come from?' and 'Where does all our poop go?' No, they left those questions to the mayor, who was a wise one. All the way up there in that office. If only anyone knew who the mayor was.

Rialto Grande had arrived. The terror of the town was flanked by a halo of daylight and the sizzling debris of a recently charred reptile. He stepped over his hissing underling and strode through the assembled police.

His heavy frame ascended the cave's iron stairs. You or I might 'walk up' some stairs, but Rialto *ascended*. As well he might have – he was walking to a throne. His shower-curtain cape billowed behind him, majestic in its waftiness, ridiculous in its shower-curtain-ness.

At the top of the stairs was a magnificent chair made from broken barrels and the skeletons of penguins. When Rialto reached it, he turned and locked his eyes on the assembled force below. He didn't sit down. Getting impaled on Terry the Terrible Horse will do that to you.

Barney sneezed. The dog's nose-rain echoed wetly. It was so loud that everyone felt like they'd been splashed.

'My name is Rialto Grande, and I have a teeeerrible problem that only you splendeeeed people can help me weeth.' He stretched out his massive arms.

The police officers saluted him.

His usual Wreckers tromped inside. They stood as close to attention as they could. The Mortons picked each other's noses. Boss Smasher flexed his arms.

Gorgo grunted and squeaked at the flaming remains of the fire-lizard. Rodney scrambled to stand up. Rialto addressed his troops.

'My brotherrrrs and I have spent a *colossal* amount of teme trying to deeeeal with the tiny *parasites* that keeeeelled Howard Howard. And every teme some-theeng has gone catastrophically wrong. Now the town laughs at the Wreckerrrrs! They think they can taunt us with their "Secret Giraffe" and say they hated poooooor Brother Howarrrd. They think they can say such things to our faces! Thieves think they can take what is ourrrrrrs! Marrowville must, wernce again, learn to fear the Wreckerrrrs because with fear comes respect! Say that with meeee.'

'WITH FEAR COMES RESPECT!'

'You weeeell have dreaaaaamed of becoming Wreckerrrrs from the first day you were allowed to become poleeeece. Immunity from Justice Weeeeek! Freedom to do *anytheng* you want, any time you want! To be the enemy people treat better than a frieeeeend. But there was always something stopping you!'

He gestured at the sacks.

'So many noteboooooks! The one rule between Marrowville and *utter* anarchy! Filling out these booooooks was the one thing that kept our numbers down! But today that changes!'

He stomped a booted foot. It wasn't loaded, so it just made a point, not a boom.

'Bring eeeet out, brotherrrrs.'

Deep inside the cave, fifty neckless Wreckers attached ropes to the leather harnesses bolted across their chests. These were squat, strong, filthy men covered with sweat and soot. Their hair was a broken mass of half-burnt clumps, and their hard muscles jutted out from under scorched skin.

They stepped forward as one, sweating and swearing and cursing the weight they pulled. It was a shadow as large as a volcano, and from within it came a horrible, shrill scratching noise.

Again, Rialto spread his arms out to the assembled police officers.

'Today, I will make each of youuuu a Wreckerrrr.'

The colossal black shape was being dragged on wheels. It was dreadful in the darkness and, when it hit the light, nightmarish. But, like all good nightmares, it wasn't revealed at once. It was too massive for that.

The recruits watched it come closer and closer. Whatever it was, it was large enough to eat buildings.

It was breaching the light now. Black shadow turned into brown rust and pale white bone.

Gorgo squeaked and shook.

The thing was made entirely of cages. Cages of steel,

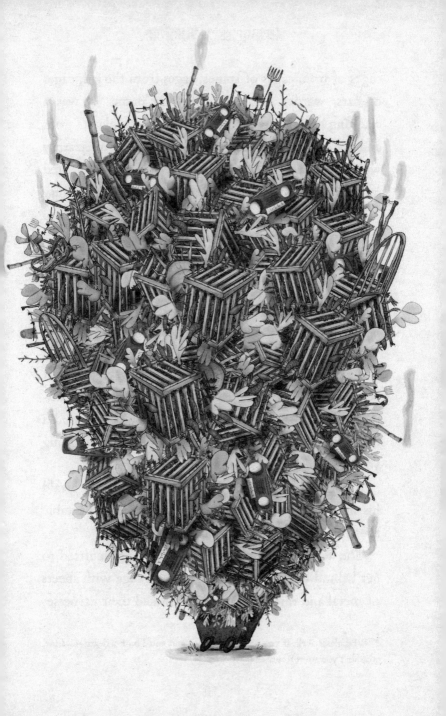

cages of iron, cages of spines, cages from the jail, cages of cars, warped cages of cribs and prams. It was a clanking cacophony of criss-crossing bars, planks, rods and locks, ribcages and rusted scrap, all haphazardly welded and bolted and nailed and latched and twisted into a hollow dome the height of a ten-storey building.

And each of its hundreds of cages was crammed to capacity with panicked, shrieking fire-lizards.

'This, my dangerous friends, is the Sky of Fire!' Rialto shouted. Behind him, hundreds of thousands of reptiles writhed in distress, their misery expressed in yowls of noise and random jets of flame.

The assembled police officers went pale. To see the Sky of Fire up close was to realize that anything caught beneath it would immediately know a future of screaming and ash. Its sheer scale meant it could surround a building, or a neighbourhood. It could engulf anything you'd ever loved, with no exits or escape.

It was the perfect toy for someone who was afraid his men might vanish in a thunderstorm – a portable firestorm that could make anything disappear.

The Wreckers tending the infernal cages scurried to get behind them. They'd backed each cage with sheets of metal and thick glass.* They hooked their harnesses

* Why glass? Well, if you were a Wrecker, and you'd built a death machine, wouldn't you want to watch it work?

to wrought-metal beams and clambered up the beast.

'Onnnne frightened fire-lizard can burn down a buildeng. But drive everyyyy fire-lizard in town into a frenzyyy – and we will make Marrowville an inferno! Everyone will burn to the sound of the Wreckerrrrs' drums!'

The men who'd climbed the back of the Sky of Fire spread out to its furthest edges. They removed thick wooden rods from their harnesses.

As one, they struck the iron and glass. In the cages around the furthest rim of the dome, fire-lizards freaked out and slammed themselves against the bars. Jets of flame erupted.

Rialto Grande had spread his arms wide again; the monstrous thug was now a triumphant silhouette backed by the incinerating breath of his very own monster.

The ground thrummed. Rialto's words now had a thudding undercurrent of shrieks and drums and the rush of flames.

'We will leave no memoryyyyy of the place! Tonight we go to the Dog & Fist! We lowerrrr the Sky of Fire over that ratty little dump, and we leave notheng but a scorch mark where Calo Steel-Shins, Boneless Charlie and those tiny parasites used to be. Join with us!'

The new recruits looked at one another. They were frightened. Was this *good*? Was it right to burn down the entire town? Was this what they'd wanted? Constable Jenkins closed his one eye in rueful contemplation. *Was this right?*

'Remember, my friends! Anywern who doesn't fearrrr the Wreckers can spend a few minutes inside the Sky of Fire, and see how they feel afterrrr.'

The new recruits suddenly agreed that everything Rialto had said was totally fine.

'Throw down your notebooks!'

They did. Sacks filled up with decades of observations and knowledge were tossed into a large pile in the middle of the cave.

'The Sky of Fire will take care of those for you now.'

He slammed his hands together and then wrenched them apart. At his signal, twenty of the Wreckers harnessed to the Sky of Fire dropped to its base and yanked at the metal poles that secured the infernal machine to its wheeled platform. The other thirty Wreckers clambered madly up the back of the cages to its very top.

Rialto stabbed the air with his fist, then curled his fingers into a claw. He dropped his arm forward.

The thirty Wreckers at the top of the Sky of Fire leaped off the front of the machine, the ropes around their bodies snapping taut as they used their weight to tip the Sky of Fire over.

With a horrendous groan of metal, and thirty horrendous groans when the jumping men finally landed, the Sky of Fire crashed into the dirt.

The piled-up sacks of notebooks were now surrounded by an enormous patchwork dome of jagged metal and glass, its inside a junkyard nightmare of twisted cages, shrieking lizards and jets of flame.

There was muffled yelling. One of the thirty Wreckers had accidentally landed inside the dome. If you looked through the glass, you could see him trying to detach his harness. Everyone could hear him begging to be let out.

Rialto picked up a stray bone. He walked all the way round the dome, absent-mindedly running it against the backs of the fire-lizards' cages. He nodded. Every harnessed Wrecker who could still stand began to strike the outside of the Sky of Fire.

Just as they had before, the fire-lizards inside freaked out. Their gasoline glands went into overdrive. They began to vomit flames in terror.

In exactly zero seconds, the Sky of Fire had turned the notebooks into a blazing bureaucratic bonfire.

Rialto cackled, the flames reflecting in his bloodshot eyes. He called to his new army, who stood in awe as their old lives burned. Against the roaring fire, they saw the silhouette of a man throwing his powerful arms into the air in triumph.

'We are all Wreckerrrrs! We snap bones, we eat *veins* and we are *respected*, because respect has a friend, doesn't heeeee? What is the name of respect's friend?'

'FEAR!' his troops chanted in the light of the flames. 'FEAR! FEAR! FEAR!'

'Drag the Sky of Fire to the Dog & Fist!'

The new Wreckers set to, grabbing ropes and pulleys. The old Wreckers polished their fight-boots.

There were no more notebooks left.

And nobody heard any more begging, either.

And nobody noticed Gorgo getting up to leave.

25
PreParaTions

Night had fallen on the little family that lived inside the Dog & Fist, and soon, once again, the Wreckers would come knocking. Then smashing. Then tearing. Death was on its way, even if the little family couldn't possibly know the terrible form it would take, or how many cages it was made of.

And yet, upstairs, Aubrey and Aubrey's sister were relaxed. They were bundled up in their warm, long coats and were quietly going to sleep. Calo and Charlie had said they could have the big bed tonight, so they slept in the adults' room. They just wished they weren't about to leave their heroes.

'I don't want to go, sis,' said Aubrey.

'Neither of us wants to go, Aubrey,' his sister replied.

Before the rest of his body went anywhere, Aubrey's brain had arrived at the place where sad little boys' brains go. It's a fragile place, where the littlest thing is the hinge that opens up the tears. His tiny voice threatened to get soggy.

'Do you think . . . (sob) that there'll be . . . (sob) *food*?'

'Yes, there will, my tiny stomach-on-legs.' Boneless Charlie tottered into the room carrying a basket. He sat down and placed it beside him on the bed. The kids rummaged around inside. Injured though he was, Charlie had gone out thieving for them. There were bits of cooked chicken, there was fudge, there were apples and there were drinks.

'There's something special in there, too,' said Calo from the doorway.

Aubrey's sister pulled out a leather tube attached to a short buckled strap. Both objects were covered with an intricate design. Silver lines danced and wove along the surface of the leather, as though each stroke traced the strikes of a master swordsman's finest battle.

'It's a scabbard for your string-sword.' Calo nodded at the girl. 'Take care of it.'

Aubrey's sister immediately slid her weapon into its new home. She buckled the strap round her waist. Calo had given her another thing she would keep forever.

'Thank you.'

Calo chuckled, getting up. 'We don't know what the Grinders will do when you arrive, but at least we know you'll be fed, warm and well armed.'

The adults had done so much to cheer up the children. The scabbard may have been a wonderful gift for Aubrey's sister, but there was one thing really keeping the fear away: for the first time, the adults had told the children exactly what their plan was.

Charlie had even been honest about how well he thought this plan would work, and the kids took solace in the fact that, if the plan failed, at least Rialto Grande would suffer. Or get very messy. It all depended on where exactly the children landed.

From the hallway, the adults craned their heads towards each other, and watched the children.

'Goodnight, Aubrey,' said Calo.

'Goodnight, young lady,' said Charlie.

'Goodnight, Calo,' said Aubrey's sister.

'Goodnight, Walrus-Head Snot-Heart,' said both kids.

Calo smirked. Charlie snorted. His moustache flared up. The children's good humour had made him forget his injuries. And then he remembered he would probably never see the source of that good humour ever again. Calo turned off the light.

The adults couldn't see the kids smile as they settled down to sleep, and neither child had to see the fear in their protectors' eyes.

It was the last time they would all be together.

26
THE GREAT WRECKER BARBECUE

Calo and Charlie went downstairs.

'You put them all in where you wanted them?' asked Calo.

'My lady love, you saw me install the blasted things. I put them where *you* wanted them.'

'You were right to do so.'

They stood behind the cracked bar, the beautiful wooden bar they had carved and polished themselves. Charlie rubbed a spot on its surface. He really liked rubbing that one particular bit of timber. In fact, he'd done it so often it had become discoloured.

Calo gently squeezed her husband's shoulder. He turned and gave her a hug.

The downstairs bar was still ruined, but, for a moment, Calo and Boneless Charlie were at peace. It was like when they'd first opened the place. They'd built it, they'd shaped it, they'd moulded it and they'd lived a quiet life. It had been just the two of them, and no more war or fighting.

Now they stood, hand in hand, and waited for whatever was going to come through the front door.

In the street, something rumbled. Something huge.

'Heave!' came Boss Smasher's voice.

The ground started to shake. The murky street lights outside were snuffed out.

Calo called out, 'Fishflinger! Are you there?'

'Fish!' said the Fishflinger. He stood up on the towel that he'd made a little nest in.

'What's out there?'

The Fishflinger looked down the road. What he saw made him run for his cursed life. He was so frightened he didn't even mention fish. Not even once.

Two hundred Wreckers were wheeling the Sky of Fire up the cobblestones. They were pulling the great-wheeled war machine through the main square. Even next to the Victory Finger, it was colossal. It was a menacing multi-faced prison, thundering up the road. Its fire-breathing inmates shrieked panic and spat flame. The Sky of Fire was an inescapable death for anything that became trapped inside its dome.

But Calo and Charlie didn't look outside. They waited. They heard the trudge and grunts of an army, and the inhuman yowling of terrified fire-lizards. They heard clanging metal. They heard heavy wheels digging into the pavement. They heard the crumbling of plaster walls as nearby buildings met the edges of something huge. They heard their neighbours dashing into the street, and the laughter of cruel men.

They heard Rialto Grande shout, 'Drop!'

There was a rushing sound. The whole of the Dog & Fist shook. Every light in every room went out. The Sky of Fire had been lowered over the building.

The air was a cacophony of shrieking reptiles.

In bed, Aubrey pulled back the curtains. Outside, a wall of fire-lizards smashed themselves against the inside of their cages. He screamed with pure fear.

'Don't get out of bed, children!' called Calo. 'Whatever you do, don't get out of bed!'

'It's a nightmare!' called Charlie. 'It just looks and feels exactly like real life!'

Through the window, Calo could see Wrecker men crowded behind the fire-lizards' cages. They carried steel rods.

'He's brought an army,' said Calo.

'I've brought my moustache,' said Charlie. He unwrapped his bandanna, as he always did when it was time to fight. His eye tattoos stared sightlessly from his head, which was very frightening for a human opponent, but sadly meant absolutely nothing to a devilish menagerie of panic-stricken lizards.

Rialto's voice came through the walls. Rodney Paste and Boss Smasher were holding a great metal cone to his lips.

'Hello, cheldreen! Hello, thief! Hello, half-steel, half-meat! This is the voice of Rialto Grande, and this whole building is now surrounded by my veeeeery good freeeend, the Sky of Fire. In a few seconds, three thousand torrents of flame will turn everything you are, and everything you've ever had, to ash. Your skeeeen will boil, and your braiiiiins will *pop*. The ground will become so hot that what you once called home will be a scorched hole in the road. But don't worry – once you're dead, we'll fill the hole with water and call it a swimming pool! Give it a name. Something like the Howard Howard Memorial Pool for Good Boys and Girls.'

At the mention of her father's name, Aubrey's sister unsheathed her string-sword.

'Stay in bed, children! And put the sword away!' called Calo.

'How did she hear that?' wondered Aubrey's sister.

The Wreckers began to drum on the outside of the cages. There was no rhythm to it, just hundreds of thudding strikes from homicidal men. Jets of flame began to lash the Dog & Fist.

The pub sign fell off in the heat. Inside, Calo roared.

'DESTROY!' screamed Rialto Grande.

Every Wrecker piled on to the outside of the Sky of Fire and started shaking and thumping the backs of the cages. Two hundred human bodies clambered up and down the demonic structure, shouting and punching at the creatures inside. Fire belched and blasted from every angle, every cage, from every lizard's mouth. Inside the Sky of Fire, the night became a furnace.

'I love you, my darling angel-dumpling,' said Boneless Charlie.

'I love you, Walrus-Head,' said Calo.

Charlie punched straight through the discoloured patch of wood on the bar. He flipped the switch hidden underneath it. It was attached to wires that led to a little something underneath their bed.

He looked up. The last thing Boneless Charlie and Calo saw was a wall of orange fire rushing towards them. The former assassin grabbed her husband. He kissed her forehead.

And the little world that Calo and Charlie had made together burned.

Aubrey and Aubrey's sister heard an explosion from the downstairs bar.

They waited for Calo or Charlie to say something, but no sound came.

Aubrey's sister wailed. Aubrey jumped up on the bed, but was forced back into the pillows. Four explosions went off directly underneath the children, and the bed was launched into the air. Aubrey, Aubrey's sister and the bed were blasted through the ceiling. Then through the roof. Then straight into the firestorm.

In an instant, the bed was ablaze. It wasn't a bed any more: it was a fireball hurtling straight to the top of the Sky of Fire's burning dome. Fire danced on the children's coats. Cages and cages of fire-lizards blocked out the night's shadows, their gasoline screams turning the darkness to immolating* light.

Deranged with anger and pain, Aubrey's sister lashed out with her string-sword. The cage of bones above them shattered. Makeshift bars and upset lizards clattered and splatted to the ground. The bed rocketed upward so quickly that she stabbed through the brass barrier and the Wrecker behind it without even noticing.

She'd made enough of a gap for the bed to shoot

* If you don't know it yet, 'immolate' is a cool word for burning something. It's one of those words you can use to describe something violent, while also looking a bit clever. Other ones include 'defenestrate', which means to throw someone out of a window, and 'eviscerate', which means to cut out someone's guts. 'Once, I immolated my mum's birthday dinner, so I defenestrated her before I was eviscerated!' There you go.

through. The Girl Who Isn't Here was exactly where she needed to be – and had sliced a hole in the face of Rialto Grande's new toy.

The flaming bed flew through the gap and streaked out into the night with two crying children on it. The sheer force of the wind snuffed out the flames and pressed them both into the mattress.

Below the children, on each bed leg, there was a loaded fight-boot, blasting like a rocket.

And high above them dark clouds began to swirl in preparation for a thunderstorm.

Calo and Charlie really did have a plan. And it had worked, after all.

It wasn't bad for a final gift.

27
SERGEANT PLUG GOES OUT WALKING

Sergeant Plug had no police uniform left, which was fine, since Marrowville no longer had a police force. All he had was a body covered with eyeballs, and a book that was much the same. The Book of Eyes had let him open its pages and look inside. Every chapter had been, as you'd expect, a catalogue of eyes. The eyes had names written under them. He'd even found his grandfather's name. His new master was fascinating.

He'd wanted to ask about the inscription, STOMACH, but his brain had become fogged when he tried. Yes, he knew his every thought was being controlled, but he didn't mind. And he didn't mind that the reason he didn't mind was that his mind was being controlled and being told not to mind. At least with this job he didn't have to wear a stupid hat.

He was marching now. He had waited until nightfall, as his master wanted. He waddled along, an eager servant to a strange commander.

He turned left out of the police station. The road was deserted, but he could hear a crowd a few streets over. And he could see a huge black shape moving down the street. Of course he could see it, he was made of eyes – and it was taller than any of the tumbledown buildings in this part of Marrowville.

A man ran down the other side of the street. It was his old second-in-command, Officer Jenkins, the fellow who'd once had such a horrible time with Terry the Terrible Horse. Officer Jenkins was dressed as a Wrecker.

Sergeant Plug had wanted to call out, 'Bit of under-cover work, eh, Jenkins?' but a signal in his brain told him not to. He kept walking forward and arrived at a T-junction. The eyes on his right side saw the black shape lit up and unfettered by darkness. He saw the cages reaching up to the sky. He saw the appalling mass of frightened beasts. Last of all, he recognized the people dragging it. They were his officers, all dressed as Wreckers.

In that moment, Sergeant Plug realized that the entire police force had been promoted above him. He was, as of now, the only police officer left in Marrowville, a town filled with criminals, all of whom had been trained as police officers. Maybe, when he came back from whatever the Book of Eyes wanted, he would once again ask Rialto to burn his notebooks, and he could join in, too.

NO BURNING BOOKS! I'M MADE OF PAPER. YOU THINK I LIKE FIRE? said the Book of Eyes, deep inside his head.

Oh, of course! Sorry, thought Sergeant Plug.

He kept walking. There were alleys to wander, and you knew when you'd arrived in the middle of town because the buildings were suddenly hugely tall. Each was a tattered, cloud-tickling tower, a hodge-podge made over centuries. You couldn't really appreciate looking at something like that until you had over two hundred eyes.

He could see everything around him, and yet he still ran into something hefty. His whole life had been like this. He bruised the lids of his kneecap-eyes. What had he bumped into?

In the shadows, Terry the Terrible Horse gave him a terrible horsey grunt.

'Terry!' said Sergeant Plug, the words squeezing out around the little eyes that had colonized his tongue. 'I'm so happy to see you!'

Sergeant Plug had never had much luck, but at least on this occasion he'd managed to bump into the one part of Terry that wasn't covered with spikes.

For his part, Terry the Terrible Horse heard his name

being said by a familiar voice. He looked at the strange thing in front of him. Unfortunately for Sergeant Plug, Terry's big long head did not contain a big long brain. In fact, Terry the Terrible Horse only knew a few things. These were:

1. I am Terry.
2. Running is good.
3. Do you have any sugar lumps?

Terry looked at what was in front of him, and tried to make it fit into one of these categories. He knew it wasn't Terry because he was Terry. Running really was good, and maybe he would do that in a moment. He knew sugar lumps were white bumps, and what he saw looked a lot like white bumps. In fact, it looked like a lot of white bumps . . .

Could this thing be . . . could it possibly be . . . ?

Yes!!!! SUGAR LUMPS!

Terry tentatively reached forward to lick the delicious sweets. Sergeant Plug tried to shoo the horse away.

What is going on? asked the Book of Eyes.

'Bad Terry!' said Sergeant Plug, taking a step away from the Terrible Horse.

Terry heard this and was confused. Sugar lumps didn't normally talk, or move away! He would eat them!

Stop moving, sugar lumps!

Sergeant Plug held the Book of Eyes in front of Terry. When it had been the Sacred Police Officer's Charter, it had been the source of all authority in his life. Now that it was the mind-controlling Book of Eyes, it was essentially his god. He shoved his god into his old horse's face.

This was very confusing to the horse. The moving sugar lumps seemed to be holding up a big sugar lump. Terry leaned forward and began to chew on the Book's cover.

Urgh! said the Book of Eyes as a horsey tongue splattered its cover. The front of the Book blinked away spit. *It's eating us, slave!*

Sergeant Plug froze. In an uncontrolled moment, he realized that if his horse ate the Book he would probably be free. He wondered whether his new skin condition would clear up. He wondered whether he was going to be in trouble with Rialto.

DO SOMETHING ABOUT THE HORSE, thought Sergeant Plug, though the thought wasn't his, since he'd never had enough confidence to think in capital letters. He'd received an urgent command from his master, and he would do its bidding with the cleverest plan he could think of.

'Very bad Terry!' said Sergeant Plug. That didn't

work. No human being had ever listened to him, so why should a horse? Terry kept chewing away.

GET ME OUT OF THIS BEAST'S MOUTH, SLAVE!

Sergeant Plug sighed. The Book had come up with its own plan. He felt his right arm rise up, out of his control. He extended two fingers and poked Terry in his gigantic horsey nostrils. It wasn't something he'd ever imagined he would do, and the snotty grotto his finger-eyes witnessed is not something you need to know about.

Terry whinnied with outrage. He let the sugar lump flop on to the ground. It didn't even taste like sugar. It was just lumpy.

RUN! commanded the Book of Eyes.

Sergeant Plug heard the command and began to run.

Terry the Terrible Horse saw the strange thing running. He knew how to do that. *Running is good!* he thought. He began to run, too. He chased the big strange thing that might still have been sugar lumps.

PICK ME UP, YOU FOOL! commanded the Book of Eyes.

Sergeant Plug ran back and picked up the Book.

This was the trouble with controlling someone's brain. The Book's slaves always did exactly what they were told. The Book would have to teach this new one how to think for itself, within the appropriate limits, of course.

Terry came trotting round in a big circle, enjoying the new game. He ran straight at the Book, his hooves clip-clopping joyfully, the barbs and spikes on his body glinting menacingly. The Book commanded its new slave to: *GET US OUT OF HERE!*

The road led downhill. Sergeant Plug saw a rubbish bin and tried to leap over it. Like a trained athlete who'd practised for this moment all his life, he fell head-first into the filth.

Terry wanted the thing inside the bin to not be inside the bin any more. He nudged it with his nose-spikes. Then he turned round and kicked the bin with his hooves.

CLANG!

CLANG!

CLANG!

The bin came loose! It hit the pavement. It began to roll downhill. Sergeant Plug whirled around inside. He was rolling in rubbish, as his father always said he would. The Book of Eyes was cursing him.

WHY MUST MY SLAVE BE A COMPLETE FAILURE? it asked.

Man and book and bin went clattering and bouncing down the hill. The noise inside was so loud that Sergeant

Plug didn't hear the series of deafening explosions from up at the Dog & Fist.

The noise inside his head was loud, too. The Book of Eyes wasn't controlling his brain any more. It was too discombobulated by spinning and rubbish and horse spit. Sergeant Plug was miserable again.

He had always suffered. Nothing had ever worked out. Nobody had ever liked him. Why, being stuck inside this bin was like being at school! When others had been made captains of sports and other activities, he'd been told he was the school Fart Monitor. His job was to locate the source of all classroom wind.

He had performed his duties with honour and enthusiasm. He had never lied and said one fart belonged to another child. He had never farted and said it wasn't his. He sniffed out these crimes against clean air and told the relevant teachers. But had they been grateful? No. The head teacher claimed nobody had asked him to do any of that and that he was just sniffing farts for fun. It all meant the other children wouldn't play with him. He'd just been trying to do his job.

The roaring Wreckers and their monstrous machine were far behind him now. He was rolling his way out of town.

CLANG!

Terry had caught up. He kicked the bin into the air. And then eyes began to appear all over the horse's body.

The Book of Eyes was laughing again. It seemed that it could implant itself in almost any creature, as long as they touched it for long enough. It had still been gross being trapped inside a horse's mouth, though.

Terry? thought Terry.

Run? thought Terry.

Sugar lumps? thought Terry.

TAKE THE BOOK AND THE BIG MAN WHERE THEY NEED TO GO, thought Terry.

Which is how Sergeant Plug found himself back on his horse, cantering happily along the South Town Bridge towards the One Tree. His new master had tamed his old horse!

He brushed a bit of rubbish off himself. Things were looking better already! And, with his body, he could see everything that was going on. He'd already dealt with his father during Justice Week, maybe he could find that old head teacher, too . . .

And then three remarkable things happened. First, as the Book of Eyes approached the One Tree, the Book began to glow and the tree began to hiss.

Second, a bolt of lightning hit the One Tree and Sergeant Plug heard the most beautiful music he had ever come across.

And third – Terry, the Book and Sergeant Plug were all so distracted that not one of them paid any attention to the full-size bed that was falling out of the sky. Not until it landed on them.

Especially not when it landed on them.

The Book was flung into the grass.

The One Tree hissed.

Sergeant Plug suffered.

Sugar lumps? thought Terry.

28
THE LANDING

Aubrey's sister sprang out of bed. It was a luxury she'd got used to at the Dog & Fist. When her father was still alive, she'd quite often had to spring out of piles of rubble, or hollowed-out engines, or rusty old cars.*

Today, however, the bed was outside, and things were stranger than they had ever been. Aubrey lay dazed, his head pressed into a pillow that had miraculously survived the fire. Seeing Aubrey sleep on an extraordinarily lucky pillow was the only normal thing about this situation. Aubrey's sister loved her brother, but he had two settings – unconscious and clownish. However, it was good to see him safe. For a half-second, she forgot that the people who had taken care of her and her brother were probably gone forever.

---

* Mostly, though, the Girl Who Isn't Here had sprung out of the cellar, though that didn't necessarily happen in the morning. It had always depended on when Howard Howard wanted to unlock the door to the place he claimed she wasn't inside.

And then the half-second was over.

She had flown through flames; she had seen the Sky of Fire incinerate the Dog & Fist. Her thoughts were filled with the terrible image of a field of ash, with no sign of her heroes, not even a few strands of Charlie's finely groomed moustache.

Aubrey's sister was grieving, which is the kind of rage and despair you may experience when someone you love passes away. Sometimes it arrives long after your loved one is gone. For Aubrey's sister, it had arrived the moment she heard the first explosion beneath her.

She was angry and she had a weapon. She glanced around. This was not where she thought she'd be. She and her brother were back at the One Tree, the place Charlie had taken them that one beautiful sunny day.

'Where are you?' shouted Aubrey's sister, her sword up, her breath ragged. 'The tall man and the old woman! Where are you?'

The One Tree hissed. If it was an answer, it wasn't the answer she wanted. She swung her blade into the artificial tree's thick metal trunk. It clanged. It was as though she was trying to summon the whole town and had struck a bell to get their attention.

The ocean roared below the rocky cliff face beside her. The wind was picking up. A few rays of brown sunlight stabbed through the blanket of grey mist that hung low in the sky, the sodden, silent home of the whirling blades that tumbled through the air.

It started to rain. Far above the mist, dark clouds twisted. There was a distant roar of thunder.

'Oh good. Rain,' said Aubrey's sister. 'Of course it's raining. Dead friends and rain. What a perfect day.'

Aubrey's sister was so preoccupied with her rage that she hadn't noticed the groaning man under her bed. Sergeant Lorenzo Plug was woozy. All his eyes were out of focus. He hadn't thought his day could get any odder, but then a bed had hit him on the head. He was pinned underneath it.

He looked for the Book of Eyes. Looking was, in his condition, a full-body activity. He didn't see the Book; he saw the springs of a bed. Then he saw a little face looking at him. The face was upside down.

Aubrey was looking under the bed. When it landed, he had been lucky not to bounce off and straight over the cliff. Fortunately, the bed's fall had been cushioned by something large. And horsey. And policeman-y. And eye . . . y.

'Sis!' shouted Aubrey, which is a sensible thing to do if you find a monster under your bed. If you love your sister, she may protect you. If you don't, maybe you can feed her to the monster.

Aubrey's sister spun round. As numb and angry as she

was, she always knew the sound of her brother in trouble. She dashed towards the bed, sword at the ready. That was when she saw the horse.

Terry the Terrible Horse was a formidable enough sight back when he wasn't covered from head to hoof with human eyes. His big muzzle was calmly chomping some grass. It really was a sight to see: the eyes in his big nose were misty with mucus, and the eyes on his teeth were getting irritated by the grass. The eyes that weren't eating or misting up gave Aubrey's sister a look of half-interest. It was like being judged by a crowd of people.

She paused. Of all the things she had seen in her life, this was very nearly the strangest. It nearly made her forget her brother. It nearly made her forget everything.

'Sis!' shouted Aubrey again.

Aubrey's sister looked blankly at the horse-shape in front of her. It seemed strangely familiar. She cast her gaze over it. Did she recognize some of the eyes? She had only really ever met a few people: Calo, Charlie, the Wreckers, Howard Howard, Mrs Dalrymple, and she didn't quite remember what her mother had looked like. Was this what the Grinders were when they weren't an old man and an old woman? Was this a Wrecker? Was this a bunch of Wreckers jammed together? And why were they encased in such tangled armour? Was this a new kind of portable jail? Was this . . .

The *armour*!

Her natural practicality kicked in. She recognized the spiked horse. She remembered the big policeman who had chased her brother at the Justice Week celebration.

'Aubrey!' she called. 'Get off the bed!'

Aubrey bounced up and ran towards his sister, just as Sergeant Plug's arm snaked out from under the bed and made a grab for where the little boy had been. The dazed officer slid out from under the mattress. His multiple eyes took in everything at once. He could see two familiar-looking children, his Terrible Horse, the One Tree, the clouds, the grass, a bug in the grass, the bed, the town, the ocean, but not, unfortunately, the Book.

He called out to the children. 'You two!'

In a hummingbird's heartbeat, Aubrey was at his sister's side. He saw a man-shaped bundle of eyes slowly lurching towards them. Then he saw a horse-shaped bundle of eyes not lurching at anyone. Then his hand started hurting. He fell to his knees.

His sister stood still; her brother was grimacing in pain. Normally, she would have reached out to hold him, but right now she didn't know what she could do. They were in serious trouble, and all she could do was feel cold inside. The loss of Calo and Charlie had stripped away almost all her feelings, leaving behind only 'numb' and 'angry'. She couldn't even be amazed by the strange policeman and his horse, or wonder how it was they had come to end up like that. She just looked at the One Tree and remembered a happy day, full of bees.

Sergeant Plug moved towards Aubrey. 'You are the one I was looking for! Howard Howard's little murderer!'

Aubrey glanced up, wincing in pain. The man-thing was still blundering towards them.

'The citizens of Marrowville only respect me once a year! And you *ruined* it! You tried to steal my Book! You TOUCHED my Book! My wonderful, wonderful Book! The Book that contains all the wisdom anyone ever needs to know!'

It's a horrible thing to watch 200 eyes crying at once, especially if they're all on the same body. Sergeant Plug was a sad little boy who had grown up into a sad giant man.

'And Mr Rialto made me wear an awful hat! And everyone *laughed* at me! And then he took all my police officers! And *you touched my Book*! My wonderful, special Book! Where is my beautiful Book?'

He was sobbing now. The tears from all his eyes ran on to the grass, making it incredibly wet. He slipped on his own tears. He kept crying. Every part of him was crying. He tried to pull himself up with his hands, but his hands were weeping. He kept slipping further and further away from the children, towards the edge of the cliff.

'Where is *my Book*? Where are you, master? I can't hear your wonderful voice!'

Down below, the water of Wrecker Bay looked like the whole world would if Sergeant Plug cried for long enough. He was thrashing around in a salty tantrum.

Would this be how Sergeant Plug finished his days? Washed off a cliff by a tide of his own sadness?

STOP CRYING, YOU BLOATED FOOL, said the voice of the Book.

Sergeant Plug's tears dried up. He was no longer slipping off the edge of the cliff. He just lay there, exhausted and inert. His whole body complied with its master's command.

When the children and their rocket-propelled bed collided with Sergeant Plug, the devoted slave had lost his grip on his beloved master. The Book went on a small journey through the air and landed at the foot of the One Tree. It had been stunned by the impact, and why shouldn't it? It may have been malevolent, mysterious and magical, but it was still a book, and it really hurts a book if you bend its spine.

The Book wanted to speak to the children, but it could only speak to people it could control. Sergeant Plug had touched its pages and cover so often it had infected him. Terry the Terrible Horse had got a mouthful of pages. Aubrey had only touched its cover once. It wasn't enough.

BRING THE CHILDREN TO ME, THERE'S A GOOD HORSE.

Terry the Terrible Horse snorted. Every eye on him opened wide. He trotted towards the children, trying to nudge them with his barbed nose.

'Get away!' said Aubrey's sister.

'Yeah! Shoo!' said Aubrey.

'Shoo?' asked Aubrey's sister.

'Yeah, it's what you say to animals to make them go away.'

'Do they know that?'

Terry didn't know that. He knew 'Terry', 'running', 'sugar lumps' and a new one: *HURT THE CHILDREN!*

The nightmarish horse swung his massive head at the children. Clusters of eyes rocked back and forth under spikes that would take out any other eye that got too close. Terry was thrashing at them, herding them back towards the tree with blades and snorts. (The kids counted their blessings – at least they weren't being forced over the cliff.)

Clang.

The children felt the hard metal of the One Tree through the back of their clothes. The Secret Giraffe and the Girl Who Isn't Here had nowhere to go. Before them lay the flesh-tearing menace of what had once been just an armoured horse, but was now a blood-curdling mass of spikes and snorts and eyes. The horse leaned in and held himself centimetres from their faces. They were trapped.

PICK ME UP, came the voice of the Book in Sergeant Plug's brain. He waddled over to the One Tree, and felt around its huge roots. Yes, the One Tree, despite being mostly metal, had roots. They were steel drums that had been mangled and painted, but they looked very convincing.

'I found you!' he said, his voice full of joy. He picked up the Book of Eyes and hugged it. If the Book could've squirmed, it would have.

The rain started to bucket down. A deluge had begun.

Mouth open and heart aflame, Sergeant Plug carried the Book over to the children. He proudly shoved it in their faces.

I WILL SPEAK THROUGH YOU, SERGEANT PLUG, said the Book, its voice heard only in the big policeman's tiny policeman's brain.

'Please, master,' drooled Sergeant Plug.

'Who is he talking to?' asked Aubrey's sister.

'Why is he holding up a picture of our mother?' asked Aubrey.

It was just like the last time Aubrey had seen the Book of Eyes. The Book didn't appear monstrous to him. It seemed to have a picture of his mother on the front, even though he had no idea what his mother had looked like.

'That's not a picture of her!' said Aubrey's sister. 'It's a picture of Calo and Charlie! Look!'

And look is what they did, and look back at them is what the Book did. The pictures they'd each seen melted away, like a mask slipping off to reveal the Book's true face.

The children stared. The dozens of eyes on the cover of the Book stared back. The big man holding the Book spoke, but the voice wasn't his. This was a commanding voice, a voice that was used to being listened to.

'I AM NOT COVERED WITH A PICTURE OF YOUR MOTHER OR YOUR FRIENDS. I CAN AND WILL APPEAR AS WHATEVER WILL BRING MY PREY CLOSEST TO ME.'

'Who are you?' asked Aubrey's sister.

'THE MAN WHO IS TALKING IS CHIEF SUPERINTENDENT SERGEANT LORENZO PLUG OF THE MARROWVILLE POLICE FORCE. HE BELONGS TO ME NOW.'

'You look different,' said Aubrey to the thing that used to look like Sergeant Plug.

'THE VOICE YOU ARE HEARING IS *THE BOOK OF EYES*.

'FOR A LONG TIME, THE PEOPLE CALLED ME THE SACRED POLICE OFFICER'S CHARTER. I AM THE HEART THAT PUMPED THE HORRIBLE BLOOD OF MARROWVILLE.

'I AM ORDER. I AM LAW.

'AND I WOULD HAVE BEEN THAT FOREVER IF I HADN'T BEEN TOUCHED BY YOU, YOUNG MAN.'

Aubrey trembled.

'A LONG TIME AGO, THE PEOPLE OF MARROWVILLE WARNED EACH OTHER NOT TO TOUCH ME.

'IF I LIE UNTOUCHED BY HUMAN FLESH, THEN I AM JUST A BOOK.

'AND I CAN BE *ANY* BOOK.

'SO I BECAME THE CHARTER – THE PRIZE THAT CAME WITH JUSTICE.

'AND I BECAME SO IMPORTANT THAT IT WAS ILLEGAL TO TOUCH ME.

'THEY WOULD ONLY TOUCH ME WITH THEIR GLOVES.

'BUT YOU TWO CAME ALONG, AND I WAS FINALLY TOUCHED.

'AND I COULD RETURN TO MY TASK.'

The children remembered Sergeant Plug falling off his horse in the town square. They remembered the Book opening in mid-air and enveloping his face with its pages. Had . . . had the Book moved itself? Had the Book done that to him deliberately?

'WHEN I AM TOUCHED BY A PERSON, I CAN TAKE WHAT HAS BEEN LAID INSIDE ME – AND I PLACE IT INSIDE THEM.'

Aubrey's hand began to burn again. He gasped.

'YES, AUBREY HOWARD. YOU TOUCHED ME WITH THE FLESH OF THAT HAND. SOON

YOU WILL SUFFER WHAT MY CREATORS HAVE DONE TO YOU, AND DONE TO HUNDREDS MORE BEFORE YOU.'

Aubrey's sister had slid in front of her brother. She pointed her string-sword at the Book. She shouted, 'We don't know you! Don't you touch him! Don't even talk to him!'

The Book was laughing. Coming out of Sergeant Plug's huge lungs, the laugh rumbled like thunder.

'YOU DON'T KNOW ME? I DIDN'T HEAR THAT, AUBREY! I DEFINITELY DIDN'T HEAR THAT! AND THE THING I DEFINITELY DIDN'T HEAR DEFINITELY DIDN'T TRY TO TELL ME *A DAMNED THING*.'

Aubrey's sister was shocked. The blood drained from her face. She shook her head. The Book hadn't spoken to her – it had spoken to her brother. It was like she didn't exist. It was like . . .

Sergeant Plug opened the Book. Inside were the names of every citizen of Marrowville, but over some there were pairs of living human eyes. All alive, all moving – and all labelled. Almost all were Wreckers.

He squinted at a particularly nasty-looking pair. They were hateful little things that glared contemptuously. They were balls of rage that looked like they would hurt children and wreck lives, just for fun.

And they had a name printed under them. Or one name, twice.

HOWARD HOWARD.

29
DADDY

Howard Howard's old weapons were alive again. Two six-fingered hands slid out from between the pages of the Book of Eyes. Soon they dangled from two arms of knotted, brawny muscle. He curled his fingers into the tattooed fists that had made such an unforgettable impact on other people's faces. His bloodshot eyes glared furiously from their prison on the page.

With the Book clasped in his meaty palms, Sergeant Plug screamed five words that weren't his, in a voice that the children recognized from too many angry nights.

'YOU LET THEM TAKE ME!'

Aubrey whimpered. His father had been frightening enough when he was alive, but this was him in death, apparently clawing his way back into the world. Aubrey's sister mentally cursed the cruel reality she lived in.

Sergeant Plug roared. His throat was a hole that spat the rage of a mad Wrecker.

The arms lashed out. Aubrey and Aubrey's sister were each aware of the name HOWARD rushing towards them, at speed, and written across gnarled knuckles.

There's a children's song in Marrowville that sounds a lot like one you might already know. It goes like this:

IT'S RAINING,
IT'S POURING,
YOUR OLD MAN LIVES INSIDE A BOOK.
RUN, YOU FOOL.*

The children were cowering. Well, Aubrey was cowering. Aubrey's sister would later insist that she was crouching tactically, but I can tell you she was far too numb for that. She'd reached the point where she didn't feel much of anything any more. She just hunched over and took whatever was coming.

A fist flew over Aubrey's head and slammed into the One Tree. Once again, the steel trunk clanged like a gong. The arms of Howard Howard thrashed in a frenzy. His blows thudded into the tree until it rang and

---

* It's not the best song, but it does have extra verses, including: *'If any part of the Book your father lives in touches you for long enough, you'll soon be able to see the inside of your own ear'* and *'I've never seen anything survive a trip down a grinder, except a cow this one time, but we don't talk about that, oh no, seriously, I was sick for weeks.'*

rang like a cathedral bell yanked by an insane monk. His rage was a storm of pain, and his blur of fists wouldn't miss Aubrey forever. In fact, they'd stopped missing him a while ago. I just wanted you to feel better.

Deafened by the clanging, Aubrey saw the world in front of him. There was a policeman, sadly changed. There was a horse, sadly changed. There was mist, about normal. There was violence, as always. Far away, there were the shadowy buildings of the little town of Marrowville. Up close, fists rushed forward, then retracted, then rushed at him again. His sister wasn't moving. He screamed for her, but she did nothing.

He saw the Sky of Fire being wheeled down the far side of the valley. If he had heard anything above the clanging of the One Tree, it would surely have been the grunts and shrieks of desperate Wreckers and enslaved fire-lizards. But it wasn't.

Instead, he heard, in the midst of the racket, a hiss. And then a slow, creaking, wheezing tune that seemed to come from the air, and also from far, far below the ground. It sliced through the world and snaked up into his ears.

Aubrey's sister heard the music, too. She knew the tune. She knew who was coming. Calo and Charlie's plan had worked. She stood up and pushed Aubrey to the side, away from the Terrible Horse, the obese policeman, the Book and their father's fury.

Blood rushed through her body. She felt alive again. She was a girl with problems to solve and, luckily, she was a born solution.

She picked up her weapon. Her father's fists sailed at her face. She flicked the string-sword straight up between his oncoming hands. With two quick strikes, she whipped each wrist with the blunt of the blade. Howard Howard's arms were knocked so wide that the Book threatened to fall out of Sergeant Plug's hands. He fumbled with it, shouting angrily at himself in a voice that wasn't his.

Aubrey's sister smiled. She raised the tip of her string-sword at the Book, and directly between her father's bloodshot eyes. She was elegant, she was smart and she hadn't been broken, after all.

And, best of all, she had a sword.

'Howard,' said Aubrey's sister, 'you never gave me a name, so I won't swear by that.'

'Why would I give it a name, Aubrey? I never wanted it!' Howard's voice boomed out of Sergeant Plug's throat. 'And, when I've stopped it talking, you've got an appointment with my fists, son!'

Aubrey's sister had defended her brother her entire life. 'You won't hurt him, Howard!' She had already swung the string-sword before she realized she'd even moved.

Howard Howard's fist knocked the blade away. Sergeant Plug's mouth echoed Howard's voice: 'Shut up, nameless.'

The girl tumbled and grabbed her weapon. There were tears in her eyes.

'Howard, I swear, if you are alive in that book, then I'm going to fix that. And if you aren't alive, then I am going to shred this so-called Book of Eyes, just for making me have to see you. And *anyone* who has a problem with that, man or beast or Wrecker or Grinder or big eye-covered things . . . oh, whatever you guys are –' she glanced at Sergeant Plug and Terry – 'then I want you to understand that I was trained in the fine art of the string-sword by its greatest champion: Calo the Dentist –'

She didn't finish her speech. An enormous bolt of fire hit the top of the One Tree. The bark burned. The leaves turned to ash that blew away in the wind. The wind that blew them carried a braying laugh, and a sniffling dog.

30
THE PARTY BY THE SEA

'TRAINEDDDD BY CALO? I *keeled* her dead! An' eeeef she trained you, I hope you had teme for a couple of classes in the art of failure from that old dustbucket, Hopeless Charleeeee . . .'

Rialto Grande was laughing from the window of his rust-covered truck. He and his goons had piled into the Cockroach and followed the flying bed from the second it had crashed through the Sky of Fire and streaked through the night's shadows. The truck smashed into the bed now, sending the fight-booted piece of furniture tumbling to the edge of the cliff. A pillow flew over the side and down towards the water.

Aubrey's sister had pressed the string-sword against the cover of the Book. Like all eyes in the presence of sharp things, it winced.

She squinted over Sergeant Plug's shoulder at the new ghoulish arrivals. Of course, Sergeant Plug and Terry, both being made of eyes, saw them without turning round.

Rialto kicked his door open. Behind him, his army was slowly dragging the Sky of Fire out of the valley. It stood on its cart, its cages criss-crossing the sky like a hideous net. It spat out another fireball. It hit branches. Sister, policeman, horse, book and father were blasted into the dirt.

The One Tree became an inferno.

The tree was no longer a false piece of greenery. Its bark and leaves had been stripped away. Against the storm clouds above, it looked just like a metallic hand engulfed by flame.

Aubrey's sister considered this from her new position, which was flat on the ground, once again, slightly singed.

Aubrey huddled in the grass. He watched hooks on ropes bite into the edges of the cliff. It wasn't just Rialto and his army of thugs that had shown up. More Wreckers were clambering up the steep cliff of Wrecker Bay. He could hear them cursing and scrabbling in the mist.

'Oh good,' said Aubrey, who hadn't learned anything about string-swords, but had been trained in the fine art of sarcasm by his sister.

'Now what areeee you *doing*, parasite?'

Rialto Grande didn't just step out of his vehicle; he strutted with his chest thrust forward like his whole body was a ship built to shatter icebergs. His grinning mouth was a red-and-yellow sunrise of decaying teeth and bleeding gums. There had been a fire, a massacre and now the certainty of more of the same. Rialto Grande was having the most wonderful day.

'What ees that?' he asked, pointing at the eye-covered Terry the Terrible Horse, who whinnied as he struggled to get up. 'And what ees that?' He pointed at the similarly afflicted Sergeant Lorenzo Plug, who whined as he struggled to get up. 'And what ees *that*?' He pointed at the Book of Eyes.

Aubrey's sister cursed herself. The fireball hitting the tree had disorientated her, which meant she'd lost track of her quarry. The Book of Eyes was using Howard Howard's arms to drag itself away from her. She reached for it. A small rock hit her in the face.

'Parasite!' barked Rialto. He'd picked up some pebbles and was jovially lobbing them at her, a murderous thug turned back into playground bully. She covered her eyes with her sword arm. Stones cut through her skin and pride as her tormentor stepped closer.

'Are you having a *lovely* time, parasite? Is it all you hoped for?'

She planned the man's death. She would not be humiliated. Oh, she was exhausted and burned and torn apart by grief, but she *had things to do*, and revenge would be first on the list. Yes! Rialto would die! For Calo and Charlie, Rialto would die!

It was a shame Rialto had made her so upset. She'd completely missed the Book of Eyes scuttling towards the long grass where Aubrey had been hiding.

Rialto Grande wasn't afraid of the child on the ground, or of the monsters he saw before him. Or of the storm clouds overhead. He had no reason to be. He was an all-conquering chaos king commanding so many Wreckers that there was no way they could be beaten, or, he whispered quietly to himself, just vanish in the rain.

A platoon of his new men were hoisting themselves over the lip of the cliff. His forces surrounded every non-Wrecker in a perfect ring. And, if this measure failed, all he had to do was lift his arm. Once the signal was received, and his troops had sufficiently agitated the Sky of Fire's fire-lizards, his pet inferno would obliterate everyone on the cliff, regardless of how many eyes they had.

He walked over to Aubrey's sister and drove his foot into her stomach, knocking all the air out of her.

'A string-sword! Oh my!' He yanked it away from the staggering girl. Rialto couldn't stop laughing. With the fire above him, he was a shock of yellow hair dancing on a massive shadow. He slicked his hair back, and again lost his accent. 'When I'm done with you and your brother, I think I'll use this tiny stabber to pick my teeth.'

He laughed again. 'In fect, why wait?' The accent was back. He began to jab the sword between his cracked, decaying molars.

His goons joined him on the grass. Boss Smasher was laughing. Rodney Paste was laughing – as well as he could.

'Ha ha ha!' laughed Left Morton, who was trying to understand if a joke had been told.

Right Morton wasn't laughing. He remembered the last time he was at the One Tree. He was looking around for bees.

Gorgo wasn't there. They didn't notice. He usually said so little that nobody noticed when he was there, either. Except the times he'd cried and squeaked about fire. Oh, and that great time with the flower. They'd liked that a lot.

Hidden from view, Aubrey was watching Rialto Grande with great concern. The Secret Giraffe desperately wanted to save his sister. He rummaged in the pockets of his coat for something useful. He found fudge instead.

'Fudge!' said Aubrey.

Then he didn't say anything else. The Book had reached him. Two six-fingered hands closed around his neck, and began to roughly pull him towards the pages that would brand him forever. Aubrey curled his body away and kicked at his father's elbows. He beat the man's huge forearms with his little fists. He writhed as every eye inside the Book sparked with excitement.

'Look at this!' shouted Boss Smasher, standing over the tussle between boy and book. Rialto casually strolled over to his underling, still picking his teeth with the string-sword.

'The boy's getting smacked by a book!' Boss Smasher was excited.

'Weeelll, we can't have thet,' said Rialto, kicking the Book away. 'This ees the boy-boy who murdered Brother Howard! I weel be the one who deals weeth him, in honour of my great friend!' He kicked the Book again.

That had always been the nice thing about Rialto Grande: 75 per cent of him was a professional murderer, but 25 per cent was a complete idiot. The Book fell near the burning tree. If only Rialto had thought to read the name on its knuckles.

Snuffling and wet, Barney the dog came over and sniffed the Book. Then licked its cover. Nobody paid any attention as Howard Howard's hands shot out of its pages and grabbed Barney.

Rialto stood over Aubrey. He picked his teeth again. A voice called out. Sergeant Lorenzo Plug was standing up.

'YOU TURD-SUCKING MORON, RIALTO!' he shouted in Howard Howard's voice. The words were Howard's, but, unfortunately, the man most afraid of Rialto Grande was the one actually speaking them.

Sergeant Lorenzo Plug was trembling. There were two strong minds fighting for control inside the Book: sometimes it was Howard Howard who spoke, sometimes it was the Book. However, he only had one weak mind and it followed both of them.

And now his old boss had noticed him.

Sergeant Plug knew he had just made an appalling mistake. He had yelled an insult at probably the most dangerous monster on two legs he would ever know. He dreaded to think what type of hat he'd be made to wear. Every eye on his body started to get moist.

'Hmmm?' mused a curious Rialto Grande. 'Who eeees theees rotund freak that speaks to meeee?' He walked towards Sergeant Plug, his eyes amused and vicious. 'Who would speak to Rialto Grande like thet?'

Sergeant Plug thought, *Not me, not me, not me, not me, not me*.

Unfortunately, Sergeant Plug's mouth said, 'STOP LICKING ME, DOG.' It said it in the voice of the Book. Howard's voice was gone.

'HEEEEEEMMMMM?!' Rialto's eyebrows nearly shot up and off his face. His shower-curtain cape rustled.

'I am not a doggg! I do not berk! And I only leeeek my adorable . . . Barneyyyyyyy!' The dog had padded over to him. The giant man picked up his beloved wet pet. 'You brought meeeee a *present*!'

It seemed that Barney had, indeed, brought Rialto a present. In the dog's mouth was a large book covered with pictures of other cute dogs. Yes, the Book of Eyes could always tell what its prey wanted, even if it was drenched in the kind of spit and snot only an unwell animal can create.

Rialto cooed with delight at the pretty doggies and licked his canine friend. He clenched the string-sword between his teeth and took the Book in his free hand. He was in love with it.

Barney opened his mouth. There was an eyeball on his tongue. He made to bark, and instead spoke with the voice of the Book:

'LICKING DOGS IS WEIRD.'

Amazed, Rialto twisted his head to look at his suddenly talkative pet.

He didn't see Aubrey's sister stand up. And he didn't see that she was smiling.

'Rialto Grande! Boss Smasher! Left Morton! Right Morton! Rodney Paste!' She called to every Wrecker she could see.

Rialto looked up. They all did.

They'd never let Aubrey's sister speak much, but, right now, she was pretty sure it was her turn to talk.

'Boys, I have known you all for years, and never once have we been properly introduced. My father never gave me a name. My mother wasn't allowed to give me one. You all pretended I didn't exist, unless you felt like a bit of target practice.'

She adjusted her belt.

'You knew my brother existed. You hurt him. And you never stopped Howard Howard from hurting him, either. You are sacks of scum, destroyers of lives and murderers of good people. Which is why today is the last day any of us will ever see each other.'

Her voice rose in volume.

'Calo and Boneless Charlie were the best people I have ever known. And you took them away from me.'

Rialto debated signalling for the Sky of Fire. On the downside, the firestorm would probably get him, too. On the upside, he wouldn't have to hear the parasite talk.

'But that's OK because, as I was saying before, I was trained in the art of the string-sword by a woman named Calo.'

She laughed. 'Calo the . . . Dentist.'

She twisted her hand. The nice thing about a string-sword is that the string is pretty much invisible. And the nice thing about being underestimated your whole life is that all your hits will be good ones, since nobody's expecting them.

And the nice thing about cruel men is that you should never be a cruel man because eventually someone crueller will come along and deal with you. And maybe they won't even be cruel, just smart – and right. And, as I said before, not a man.

Realization hit Rialto Grande. He had taken the string-sword away from the girl. She had let him do it. She had wanted him to do it. She had held the string in her hand the entire time. She had just twitched her finger.

The blade jerked in Rialto's mouth. Its point lodged deep inside a rotten tooth and down into an inflamed gum. Rialto grabbed his face, which meant he smacked himself in the head with a book and a dog. The girl clutched the string with both hands and pulled.

Rialto, the Book and Barney lurched into Sergeant Plug. Rialto was hooked like a fish. Sergeant Plug's whole body was crying again. He slipped over, taking the giant Wrecker with him.

Now the giant Wrecker was on a teary, soppy-eyed sled. And Aubrey's sister had one destination for them – the rocket-propelled bed.

Rialto's troops swarmed to stop Aubrey's sister as she dashed towards the bedframe. Unfortunately for them, she had a very useful little brother.

'FUDGE!' shouted Aubrey. 'FUDGE!' He stood up and tossed the block of fudge he'd found. It landed brownly on the sheets.

'Fudge', of course, was only one word. Aubrey would

say a lot of sentences in his life. Some would be long, and some would be short, but very few would be as important as the words he'd just shouted.

Terry the Terrible Horse, now made entirely of eyes and spikes, used every terrible eye he had to follow the path of the sweet treat the boy had thrown. The Book of Eyes wasn't ordering him to do anything, which meant he had gone back to his normal thoughts. Of course, he only ever had one of three thoughts, and the best one had just arrived.

SUGAR LUMPS!!!

He barrelled towards the bed. Every Wrecker in the way was slashed or pricked or kicked off the cliff. Thugs and muggers and murderers and bandits were cannon-balled into the air and fell down, down, down into the ocean far below. Officer Jenkins, one eye missing, one arm missing, one leg missing, realized too late that what was left of him was once again standing in the wrong place at the wrong time.

'I hate you, Terrry!' shouted Officer Jenkins as he took a one-armed, one-way trip head-first into Wrecker Bay.

On the hill, Rialto's new Wreckers cradled their clubs and wondered if they should agitate the fire-lizards and shoot again. Then a man made of rocks and moss began smashing open the cages.

'Stop that!' shouted a new Wrecker. A stone fist

whomped him so hard he flew halfway back to town. The other new Wreckers started to wish they'd kept their notebooks.

'FLOWER!!!!!' shouted Gorgo.

The freed fire-lizards threw themselves out of their cages. There were so many falling down the huge structure that they became an unbroken green waterfall of tumbling reptiles. They hit the ground and scurried straight over to the hordes of Wreckers, each fire-lizard a tiny green warrior burping fire and mewling for revenge.

Gorgo watched singed Wreckers fleeing in every direction.

It would take a team of eighteen strong men with pickaxes about three weeks to get inside Gorgo's head, but, if we could read his thoughts, we'd learn one thing: he didn't do any of that to help the children – he was still a murderer. Just a murderer who hates fire and likes flowers.

A fire-lizard burped near him. Gorgo squeaked and ran home as fast as his rocky legs would carry him.*

Rialto slid off Sergeant Plug's tear-sodden body. He was simply too slippery.

Aubrey's sister slid over grass and under the bed. The motion jerked Rialto's neck up. He stumbled forward,

---

* It wasn't very fast. In fact, after this book's over, he'll still only be about halfway there.

flames spurting from the front of his fight-boots. He tried to throw away the Book so he could snap the string, but the Book was panicking. It opened back to Howard Howard's page. The dead thug's arms came out and grabbed his boss's head.

Rialto's eyes widened at the words he read and the eyes he saw. 'Brother Howard?' he asked.

It didn't matter. Rialto and the Book were the final obstacle between Terry and the fudge. Rialto felt the familiar sensation of being pricked by barbs. He was again flung into the air by what could only be that idiot Sergeant Plug's horse. He landed on the bed. It was much comfier than the spikes – and he had a good book to read. Why, it was basically an outdoor hotel.

Terry nibbled his fudge. If a horse could dance, this Terrible Horse was dancing. He whinnied and kicked and clopped and stomped.

Aubrey ran up to his sister's side. It was, and would always be, the safest place he knew. The children stood next to the bed.

Rialto Grande smiled at them. It was the smile of someone who doesn't care about anything that's just happened because they are about to win.

He clenched his gloved fist. It burst into flames.

Unfortunately for Rialto, there was one thing left on the cliff that didn't like fire.

Hands shot out of the Book of Eyes and frantically began to strike the Wrecker. Howard Howard's six-fingered hands made a mess of their old boss's hideous visage. Over and over again they stamped Rialto's face with HOWARD HOWARD HOWARD HOWARD HOWARD.

And, unfortunately for everyone else, there was still one person left on the cliff who didn't like people hurting the Book.

'DON'T BURN THE BOOK!' The weeping Sergeant Plug had slid under the bed. He was trying to climb on, but his moist, puffy eye-hands couldn't quite get a grip. It was the story of his entire life. He kept flopping on to the scorched mattress and sliding off. It was ridiculous.

Rialto punched back at the hands that thumped his face and squeezed his neck. He kicked at Sergeant Plug as the moist policeman wetly grabbed at his leg. The blade of the string-sword was still lodged in his mouth, and its string was still in Aubrey's sister's hand. He was a murderer and an idiot and a braggart and a brute. And he had no idea what was coming.

Aubrey knew when his sister was in control of a situation. And she was in control of this one.

'Howard Howard and Rialto Grande, there are two things I want you to know.'

Aubrey's sister was talking to her father and chief bully, but, as usual, they didn't listen. It was a shame: they really should have.

'The first is, as I've tried to tell you, I'm here . . .' She didn't shout it at the warring brutes. Softly, to her brother, she added, 'I'll always be here, Aubrey.'

Aubrey wrapped his arms round her waist. He smiled up at her. It was all very nice. It was almost like she wasn't going to kill these appalling men. She was, though.

He let her go. She put her hands on her hips. It was time to get back to business.

'The second thing is: I don't need a name. I just need the people I love . . .'

Rialto wasn't listening. He had pulled back his fiery fist and swung it at the Book.

'. . . and a few less people I don't.'

Aubrey's sister jerked her wrist down, the same way Calo used to catch fire-lizards in the pub.

Rialto's head snapped into the mattress. His body twisted to one side. The string-sword whirled through the air and back into its scabbard.

The fiery punch went wild. It curved under the bed. Rialto's burning hand smashed straight into one of the fight-boots Charlie had stolen from him.

'Give me my beautiful Book!' Sergeant Plug had

clambered on to the bed, despite his whole body being slick with tears. He'd finally accomplished something. He was just in time for the fight-boot to explode.

The bed flipped into the air and over the cliff. Sergeant Plug and Rialto Grande plummeted towards oblivion. Both men screamed. Plug wanted his Book. Rialto wanted Plug to shut up.

They smashed through the waves like a baseball through a glass window. The bed splintered on impact; the men didn't. They just sank in Wrecker Bay.

And down, down, down, down they went into the deep blue ocean, both men senseless and forever still. They sank until they hit a shipwreck. It was the ship that had brought the notebooks to town, back on a day nobody could remember, but everyone believed in.

The children turned away from the sea. The fire that had engulfed the One Tree was now being slowly dampened by rain.

Aubrey had a question for his sister. 'You don't want a name?'

She shook her head.

'No. Just you.' She hugged him tight.

It was a good answer.

They noticed the Book of Eyes was floating in the air.

They didn't have an answer for *that*.

31
DINNER

The Book was panicking. Frantically, it changed its cover. What would the children like to see? It flashed gold. It showed their mother. It showed Calo and Boneless Charlie. The pictures warped. Calo's head became fat. Charlie became a skeleton.

The Book showed the Grinders.

Its entire cover was a black-and-white etching of the round woman and the skeleton man. The Book's eyes opened again. Each one now had two misshapen pupils – one wide blob, one thin line.

The sky was thick with black clouds now. The rain was getting heavier. The mist was getting lower.

And under the sound of the rain – music. Music only for the ears it was meant for.

'They're back, Aubrey!' shouted Aubrey's sister. She called into the wind, 'Where were you when we needed you?'

The fire that had made the One Tree glow had finally died. Without its bark, the tree was a metal hand whose jagged fingers splayed out into the sky, as though a giant was trying to tear out the heart of the sun. The shadow it cast flowed down over the hill like rivulets of black oil.

Over by the Cockroach, Rialto Grande's usual gang of Wreckers was struggling to understand what had just happened. Their army had scattered. The Sky of Fire was a wreck. Their boss had gone over a cliff, and there was a horse covered with eyes doing a happy little dance. Each of its eyes had two misshapen pupils.

'What we do now?' asked Left Morton.

Rodney hissed and pointed over at the children and the Book.

Boss Smasher saw them, too. 'Murder,' he said.

Right Morton shook his head. 'We should leave them alone.'

In that moment, he really *was* smarter than his brother. He was smarter than any of them. It was the single smartest thing any Wrecker had ever said, or would ever say again. And, being Wreckers, they all ignored it.

Aubrey tugged on his sister's arm. 'Wreckers.'

Aubrey's sister stepped in front of her brother.

Rodney bolted towards the children. His feet splashed in the shadow cast by the One Tree. The splashing told him it wasn't a shadow but a liquid as dark as a shadow. Too late he realized it had pooled beneath all the Wreckers' feet.

They glanced at it. No reflections glanced back. Not of them, and not of the raining sky. Unless, of course, the sky was full of teeth. But that was silly – there were only razors in the sky.

There were teeth in the liquid. Curved white teeth. And machine parts. And razors. And hands. And eyes. A bolt of lightning hit the One Tree.

Right Morton was the first to recover his vision. He blinked and rubbed his knuckles against his eyelids.

The river of shadow wasn't flowing from the One Tree but from an object that had appeared in front of it. It flowed from the gaping mouth of a black pram. Music did, too. Beautiful, haunting music.

A skeleton undertaker in a top hat and black suit was turning a crank on the pram's side. A round woman pottered next to him.

The music made Right Morton want to waddle over there. The eyeless sockets of the couple's faces made him wish for death. And, in a moment, his wish would be granted. The smart part of his brain tried to walk away, but his feet were stuck in the black shadow.

'Boys!' he called – a wise decision, since this was a threat he couldn't entirely understand.

Boss Smasher was no help. The massive fists that he walked on were submerged in the murk. His tiny legs kicked helplessly in the air.

The skeleton man cranked the pram's handle. The Wreckers

were being slowly pulled towards the pram. They had become a production line: first Rodney Paste, then Boss Smasher, then the Morton Brothers. Of course, they didn't know what exactly they'd produce (or what produce they'd become).

'The mallet! Give me the mallet!' Right Morton called to his brother.

But Left Morton was enjoying the music. Right Morton grabbed the weapon himself. He tried to smash the shadow. It didn't work. He tried to smash his legs to get free. He successfully broke his own ankle. The shadow didn't let go.

He was closer to the couple now. He saw Rodney Paste's skinny legs disappear into the pram. The pram belched up a fine red paste.

Boss Smasher was next. His arms were so big they wouldn't fit. The round woman had to jump on top of him until he disappeared into the gurgling maw. The pram shook violently. Thick strings of crimson shot out.

The Morton Brothers were at the lip of the pram now. Left Morton bopped his head to the music.

'I think we'll be OK,' he said, a final idiot thought gracing his dim-witted skull as the Morton Brothers' world became a black void of curved teeth and whirling blades.

Right Morton screamed.

He was always smarter than his brother.

32
A Family Reunion

Halfway to town, half-fried Wreckers were limping home. Fire-lizards frolicked happily in the grass. They'd do that until one belched, and then there'd be no more grass to frolic in. Then they'd head into town, to the delight and worry of everyone everywhere.

Back at the One Tree, Aubrey's sister had covered her brother's eyes. It was a little late. They'd both been temporarily blinded by the lightning, but his vision had come back just in time to see what had happened to Rialto's band of Wreckers.

Now Aubrey was puking. It was good to puke: it took everything horrible the world had poured into his eyes and poured it out again, this time on to his shirt. And at least it took his mind off the fact that his hand had started burning again.

Aubrey's sister patted his back. She looked up. The Lady Grinder was leaning next to the One Tree; there

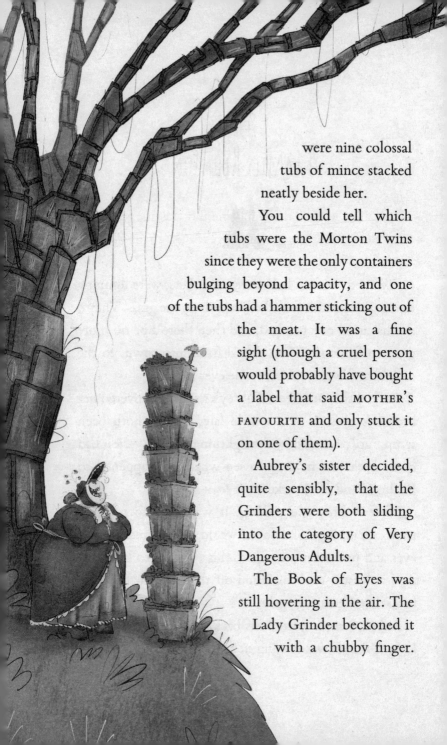

were nine colossal tubs of mince stacked neatly beside her.

You could tell which tubs were the Morton Twins since they were the only containers bulging beyond capacity, and one of the tubs had a hammer sticking out of the meat. It was a fine sight (though a cruel person would probably have bought a label that said MOTHER'S FAVOURITE and only stuck it on one of them).

Aubrey's sister decided, quite sensibly, that the Grinders were both sliding into the category of Very Dangerous Adults.

The Book of Eyes was still hovering in the air. The Lady Grinder beckoned it with a chubby finger.

It floated lazily towards her, as if drawn by her magic.

A thought arrived in Aubrey's sister's brain: *She's controlling the book!*

'Not yet,' said Aubrey's sister. She shot her string-sword into the air and speared the Book's cover. She coiled up the string in her finger and drew the thing closer. The ease with which she did this suggested she was doing nothing more strenuous than flying a particularly ugly kite.

The Gentleman Grinder creaked up next to his wife and held her hand. They looked peaceful and content, just as they had back on the children's doorstep.

'I have questions to ask you,' said Aubrey's sister.

'So do I,' said Aubrey, wiping his chin.

They both stepped round Terry the Terrible Horse, who was still on a sugar rush and happily prancing about. The Book didn't stop him with a terse command. It didn't seem to want to talk any more.

The Gentleman Grinder hissed a greeting. The Lady Grinder chortled and clapped.

'Hello, lovelies,' she cooed. 'It's nice to see you again.'

For once, Aubrey's sister didn't care if it was nice to be seen. She had, as she'd said, questions.

'What is this?' she asked. She nodded at the Book; its airborne state was keeping it a safe distance from her.

'Oooh, still *so very* direct, I see. The name it likes to

use is the Book of Eyes. Didn't it tell you? It's meant to tell you,' she simpered, 'eventually.'

'It has our father in it,' said Aubrey. 'He tried to strangle me.'

The Gentleman Grinder was hissing again. It was definitely the same hiss the One Tree had produced day after day.

'What have you done?' asked Aubrey's sister.

'We saved you from your lives, my love,' replied the Lady Grinder. 'We gave you hope, and adventure, and a family. Why, we even gave you a child to rescue.'

'But the Wreckers destroyed everything! They –' Aubrey's sister thought of Calo and Charlie – 'destroyed everyone.'

'Well, that is what Wreckers do,' replied the Lady Grinder.

'You gave us a *child*?' asked Aubrey, who didn't remember having to change any nappies.

The Lady Grinder was amused. Her little face dimpled. 'Yes, my dear, and your sister has it now.' She turned to Aubrey's sister. 'That book you're holding hostage (which you're doing very well, if I may say so) is our child.'

The Gentleman Grinder mimed rocking a baby in his arms.

Aubrey's sister narrowed her eyes at the Lady Grinder.

'Holding hostage' was a little too dramatic. And the word 'child' was flat-out wrong. And whatever the Gentleman Grinder was doing was just alarming. The book wasn't a 'child'. A child just grows up – this thing destroyed people.

'Are all your children objects?' Aubrey's sister went for sarcasm. It would give her time to think of something better. 'When we met you, you said the pram was your baby! I'm just asking in case the One Tree turns out to be your nephew or something! HA HA HA HA HA HA.'

Aubrey's sister fake-laughed. It was noisy and abrupt and literally just her loudly saying, 'HA HA HA HA HA HA.'

The Gentleman Grinder shook his head. He hissed out words.

'Not our nephew . . .'

Above him, the steel and iron of the One Tree began to flake away in the wind, as though dissolving at the Gentleman Grinder's command. Aubrey's eyes widened. With all its metal stripped away, the One Tree was nothing but bone.

The Gentleman Grinder nodded. '. . . our ancient *enemy.*'

The cliff overlooking Wrecker Bay had once been a

beautiful place where the children had spent a perfect sunny day climbing up a giant dead tree. Now it was a wrecked, scorched crater surrounded by tubs of mince, a hostile Book, two mysterious pensioners, a dancing horse and what appeared to be the remains of a giant hand. The fingers of an enormous skeleton were jutting out of the ground. It was like a human hand, but extra finger bones sprouted from the side of every finger and then extra fingers jutted out of those. Imagine a nest of wriggling centipedes, but all made of pale, dusty bone.*

'What is *that*?' asked Aubrey.

'Do either of you know what's out in the mist?' The Lady Grinder answered with a question of her own.

'Razors,' the kids said in unison.

'Maybe our mother,' said Aubrey's sister.

'Definitely some ducks,' said Aubrey.

The old lady was walking towards them. 'No,' she said. 'The word you're looking for is *beasts*.'

She stood right in front of the children. She smelled of vanilla and sherry, but now her tone was acid.

'There are beasts outside Marrowville,' said the Lady Grinder. She gestured at the giant hand. 'Why, this one is so massive beneath the earth that its skull wears your little town like a crown. But we deal with it.'

To emphasize her point, the Lady Grinder tilted her head to the sky. A bolt of lightning struck the hand. The massive fingers turned to shadow in the flash. And Aubrey's sister stopped dead. It was the shadow from her time in the mist. She shook her head. The memory had come back, and it was tearing through her brain.

---

* Now try to sleep tonight.

Her mother had run into the razor-mist. Her father had thrown her in after. The endless shadows were there. They had shielded her from the blades. They had picked her up. She'd been lifted out of the mist by a giant hand. But they'd only rescued her, not her mother.

Aubrey's sister clenched the wire of her string-sword until her knuckles went white.

'Is the One Tree dead?' asked Aubrey.

The Lady Grinder scoffed. 'Oh, young man – everything my husband and I want to be dead ends up dead, and precisely when we want it to.'

The Gentleman Grinder gave them a thumbs-up. It was scarier than when he'd pretended to rock the baby.

'You'll give me back my child now, girl,' said the old lady. 'Because I, that Book, that pram and that handsome man over there are the only reasons you and your brother even have a town to be miserable in.'

The Gentleman Grinder doffed his hat. Centuries together and she still called him 'handsome man'! Oh, it was enough to make his bleached bones blush.

The Lady Grinder continued. 'As far as you're concerned, everything outside Marrowville is dead. Every city, every monster and every monstrous person is safely, wonderfully dead. As long as they stay out there in the mist . . . which they will if you give me that Book. Otherwise . . .'

The giant skeleton hand twitched. Again, lightning struck the hand.

The Lady Grinder darted forward and snatched at the Book. Quickly, Aubrey's sister jumped back. Now she really had taken it hostage.

The old lady smiled. 'Don't do that, lovely.' She stretched out. She was so wide that it took ages. 'Do you see what the One Tree really is?'

Aubrey looked up at the tower of jutting bones. It had been so pretty before the burning. And the lightning. And whatever was happening right now.

'We defeated him. Buried him here.'

The Lady Grinder laughed. 'He's been buried underground so long that the idiots of Marrowville forgot what he was and dressed his fingers up like a tree!'

She tilted her head to the sky. 'Of course, nobody remembers any of that – we don't let them.'

Miles away, a bolt of lightning hit an alley in the middle of town. 'Fish!' screamed the Fishflinger. Another bolt hit the hand.

Again it twitched. Thunder roared as another bolt of electricity sizzled out of the sky.

Sensibly, the children turned and ran.

'I wouldn't bother running, lovelies. Go into Marrowville and we'll destroy you. Run outside Marrowville and the mist will do it for us. And if you manage to get through the mist, well, there's hundreds more of these beasts.'

Aubrey's sister was hurtling down the valley as fast as she could, the Book trailing behind her in the air. Her brother sprinted behind.

The Gentleman Grinder twisted the pram's crank, and a simple burst of music meant she and Aubrey were suddenly back on top of the cliff.

'I know you're enjoying playing with my child, lovely, but is there a chance you could put it back in my frail old hands? I have missed it so.'

Again, the Lady Grinder beckoned to the Book. And again it began to float towards her.

'No,' said Aubrey's sister, 'that isn't a beast – and this isn't a child.' She flicked her wrist and the string-sword jerked the Book to the ground. She placed one foot on its cover and yanked out the sword. She pointed the blade at the Lady Grinder.

'Either let us go, or tell me what this *thing* is. It burrows into people's heads and takes them over. It *hurts* people – and Howard Howard is inside it.'

The Lady Grinder took a step forward. A child's blade meant nothing to her.

Aubrey's sister aimed her blade straight at the Book. She wasn't sure she knew how to threaten a book, but pointing sharp things at people tended to work, so it would just have to do.

The old lady giggled. 'If you'd like to know what it is . . . why don't you read it?'

Aubrey's sister shook her head.

'Open it up with your sword, lovely. It won't hurt you if you don't touch it.'

Reluctantly, Aubrey's sister released the Book from under her foot. Carefully, she prised open the cover with the string-sword's tip. She saw the ugly, burned-in STOMACH that defaced the inside cover.

The Lady Grinder saw it, too, and it was news to her. 'Who did that to you?' she asked the Book. Her little hands grasped feebly towards it. 'Did those awful police do that to you?' She looked up at Aubrey's sister, genuinely horrified. 'They've scarred my baby.'

Aubrey's sister blocked the old lady out of her mind. She flipped some of the pages. Every citizen of Marrowville had their name in there, and their address. But some of those names belonged to dead people, and some of those names had a set of living, moving eyes above them. She turned to the back of the book and saw fresh eyes appear: Boss Smasher, Rodney Paste, Left Morton and Right Morton all glared back at her, each dead thug now just as alive and fuelled by hate as he'd ever been. She saw Sergeant Plug's name, but without the eyes. There were so very many names. So very many eyes. So very many Wreckers. And, of course, one man with two names, or the same name twice. And next to him, with no eyes above his name: Aubrey Howard. And next to that . . . a space with nothing but a question mark.

'Do *you* have a name yet, lovely?' The old lady was frowning at Aubrey's sister.

The children hadn't seen the Lady Grinder frown before. If she and her husband could mince up Howard Howard and all Rialto's crew when they were happy, what would they do if they were upset?

'Please,' said Aubrey, 'you saved us from our dad, and the Wreckers. Please tell my sister what the Book is.'

Aubrey's sister's voice was cold. 'They didn't save us, Aubrey. They put Howard Howard inside this Book, and then he tried to kill you. Wait –' She remembered falling down the tunnel that had led to the Dog & Fist.

She wheeled on the old woman. Her voice was white-hot again. 'You sent us to Calo and Charlie! Did you want us safe, or were they just some more people you wanted dead?'

The Lady Grinder shrugged. 'Not everyone matters, my love.'

Those five words sliced into the children's hearts. Aubrey started to cry.

A better person might have regretted saying such a harsh thing to two exhausted, grieving children, but the Lady Grinder wasn't technically a person. And she'd hurt the children deliberately.

She tilted her head to one side. Her voice became soothing. 'Oh, don't cry, Aubrey. Why, it's just what's happening. And you, my girl, wouldn't you like a name? There are lots of lovely ones in that Book. Pick one.' The dimples were back. 'Come, come – think of one quickly. It'll make everything hurt so much less.'

'This book told us it was the heart of Marrowville,' said Aubrey's sister. She was keeping her focus. She wanted so desperately to point Calo's favourite weapon at the old lady, but what could a string-sword do to a creature as powerful as a Grinder? Her arm was trembling; she would just have to keep threatening the Book.

'The *heart*?' Despite herself, the old lady chuckled. She smiled kindly at the Book. 'My, my, you did get some ideas while you were away.' She glanced back at Aubrey's sister. 'Lovely – this isn't the heart. As you can see, it's the stomach.'

'The stomach?' asked Aubrey.

'Oh my, yes. When something gets eaten, wherever else would it go?'

Eaten. The word hit Aubrey's sister hard. 'Where's the mouth?'

With great care, and a flicker of warmth in his hollow eye sockets, the Gentleman Grinder fondly patted the top of the black pram.

'The mouth . . .' he hissed.

'Our child,' said the Lady Grinder.

The black pram and the Book of Eyes were parts of the same creature.

33

MARROWVILLE

The Grinders were half right about the dangers outside Marrowville. Sinister shapes loomed in the swirling razor-mist. Brutal bands of outlaws struggled for life in a world of darkness and flying blades. Every city and village was isolated, locked off from its neighbours, and memories of its neighbours even existing. Birds flew as far as they could before landing in pieces on someone's plate.

And then there were the beasts. Beasts that could kill even a Grinder. But that wasn't necessarily a bad thing. It was a cornucopia of horrors, all lost and locked forever in the swirling, fatal mist.

But the Lady Grinder had left out an important detail. 'Our little family controls the mist.'

She clapped her hands. 'Be grateful, children – we three keep away the monsters outside Marrowville.'

The Lady Grinder simpered. 'Just my husband and me and our beautiful baby.'

Aubrey's sister narrowed her eyes. 'What about the ones inside Marrowville?'

The Gentleman Grinder looked offended. He stroked the top of the pram as though its feelings had been hurt.

The old lady shook her head. 'My dears, our child separates the good from the wicked. Good people stay on the outside; bad people go through the mouth and into the stomach.'

'No they don't,' said Aubrey's sister. 'I've seen the Book hurt good people. Or at least people who tried to be good.' She remembered Sergeant Plug's pathetic addiction to the thing before and after his sudden outbreak of eyes. 'It lures people in.'

'Oh no, lovely – our lovely little tum-tum just makes people happy so that they'll take care of it. There's nothing at all wrong with that. It works very well for kittens.'

'EYES! Why is it full of people's eyes?' Aubrey's sister would not be distracted by jokes or kittens.

Both the Grinders chuckled.

'Well, how else would we see what everyone in Marrowville is doing? If you touch the Book with your skin, we put an eye in you, and we see everything. If nobody touches it, well –' the old lady dabbed her empty eye sockets – 'we can't see the Book any more. So it gives people what they want until they touch it . . . no matter how long that takes.'

The Book changed its cover back to the Sacred Police Officer's Charter, then to an image of Aubrey's mother, then it took a guess and showed some fish.

'You see? All it does is show you what it thinks you want to see. It's been giving Marrowville its laws. Feeding the strong, and wrecking the rest.'

She addressed the Book. 'We're sorry it took us so long to find you! They made you so important it was a crime to touch you!'

She was weeping now. 'We lost centuries of work.'

There was a hissing. Was the Gentleman Grinder sobbing, too? Can skeletons sob? What do they cry? Dust?

The Lady Grinder spoke again, her voice racked with sobs. 'My dears, we couldn't find our baby for so long. Please give it back.'

Somehow, Aubrey's sister found a smile. 'Oh, absolutely not.'

The Lady Grinder stopped weeping. She turned to her husband, and coldly and calmly sighed a threat. 'Don't try to hurt us, children – we play the music that stops the pain forever.'

The Gentleman Grinder slowly started to turn the crank on the black pram. He was wheeling it towards them, the wheels squeaking as the organ churned.

The Lady Grinder folded her arms. 'It's always such a shame when you people think for yourselves.'

'But you saved us.' Aubrey was still blubbing. He was broken. He was bruised, bereaved, covered with vomit and, when he wiped the snot from his face, his tears and phlegm were the only things that cooled the burning in his hand. 'You sent us to our friends! You killed Howard Howard! You killed the Wreckers!'

'No, we don't *kill* the people who matter, just the ones who don't.' The old lady shook her head. 'The strong ones we harvest. We grind their earthly bodies into mince, and we turn what's left behind into something better. Something that lasts forever.'

The music was getting loud now. It swirled on the wind.

'An army.'

The skeleton hand was twitching and twisting against the sky.

'Do you matter, children? Would you like to fight forever?' To Aubrey's sister the Lady Grinder said, 'What's your name, lovely?'

'Get behind me, Aubrey,' said Aubrey's sister.

She leaned all her weight on the string-sword's blade. It pierced the Book's cover.

The old lady tutted. 'Your little foot is standing on an eternal collection of the strongest, strangest bashers, brawlers and thugs we could find. We built them a township where brutality flourished, and now there they are, indexed, filed, catalogued and ready to be released for a perfectly delightful war.'

'Who are you going to war against?'

The old lady nodded at the giant hand. 'Them.'

Aubrey had not got behind his sister. He marched up to the old lady.

'Is that what Marrowville is?' he demanded. Aubrey had grown up with one little dream, which was to see the town. 'Is Marrowville just where you grow your monsters?'

The Lady Grinder laughed cruelly. 'Yes, Aubrey, and the spineless cowards they feed on.'

Aubrey's sister shouted over the wind and the rain, 'You control everything, don't you?'

'Oh yes, dear. In fact, the only thing we don't seem to be able to control is that dancing horse.'

Everyone looked over at Terry, who had been whinnying it up the entire time.

'That horse should be doing nothing, but it seems

as though something more powerful is making him dance.' The Lady Grinder was confused; what could be more powerful than the Grinders and the Book of Eyes?

SUGAR LUMPS! SUGAR LUMPS! SUGAR LUMPS! thought Terry.

The wind howled and the Lady Grinder howled with it.

'Give me the Book, children! One day, the mist will fade – and every creature left in this appalling world will pour into Marrowville. And we will need to win that fight, or everyone here will be slaughtered.'

'I don't believe you!' The wind was deafening. Aubrey's sister could barely be heard, but the Gentleman Grinder heard her. He nodded and sighed.

The Lady Grinder's wrinkled finger stabbed out at Aubrey's sister. 'What's your name?' She opened her hand to Aubrey. 'Young man, what do *you* call your sister? Do you have a name for her?'

If Aubrey had still been concussed, he might have unthinkingly said, 'Sis.' If he had felt playful, he might have said anything. But this was Aubrey at his most serious. This was the Aubrey who'd defended his sister when Rialto had grabbed her in their house. This was the Aubrey who'd always tried to make her feel better after she'd dealt with Howard Howard. This was a boy who'd seen two of his favourite people burn.

The only difference between him then and now was that this Aubrey was able to *talk*. And he defended his sister by saying his own name.

'I'm Aubrey Howard.'

The Lady Grinder scowled. 'We don't want you, idiot. We want the warrior.'

But the 'warrior' she wanted was laughing. Her shoulders were shaking. Guffaws blasted out of her, the great, gasping bursts of mirth you get when you've finally lost all control.

'You're trying to harvest *me*!'

The Grinders froze.

'You killed my friends . . . you're attacking my

brother, and all so you can have *me*!'

The Lady Grinder grimaced. 'We made you strong, girl! You could be a general in our army.'

Aubrey's sister cracked a half-smile. 'Then why don't you mince me up?'

The Grinders looked at each other.

'You can't do it, can you?'

The Gentleman Grinder tried to push the pram towards her. It wouldn't budge.

She laughed. 'It's because I'm not here, isn't it?'

The Gentleman Grinder put his long fingers to his temples, like he was nursing a headache.

'That's why you keep asking my name!' cried Aubrey's sister. 'I'M NOT HERE BECAUSE I DON'T HAVE A NAME!'

The Grinders were both trying to push the pram forward. Its wheels might as well have rusted over completely. There was no way of getting it towards Aubrey's sister. It refused to move.

Marrowville was based on rules, and the Grinders were the people who'd made those rules – and Aubrey's sister had broken the main one just by having a father who didn't like her.

Aubrey was shouting now. 'You need your little Book to know everybody's name, don't you, Grinders? You knew who our father was, and you knew my name . . . but you don't know my sister's name!

'You made the rules for Marrowville! The Wreckers run the police who can only be Wreckers if they fill out notebooks and become the best at crime! Nobody can leave Marrowville, so they stay and either get stronger or weaker. And then you harvest the strongest – but everyone in Marrowville has a name, and they have to have a name, or they don't exist, which means you can't write them in your Book . . .'

He took a breath.

'. . . and the Book finds out what people want and tells them what to do without them even noticing that's what it does! And you only want the strongest for your army, but you need their names to go in there! And she doesn't have a name!'

Aubrey's sister was clapping. 'A hundred and forty-nine words, Aubrey!'

Aubrey was running around like a mad thing. 'I pretend to be stupid, but really I'm listening!'

He ran up to the Lady Grinder. 'It's called strategy!'

He farted. 'That wasn't a strategy – that was a fart and I'm not sorry!'

Aubrey's sister was cackling. She was fairly certain her brother was irritating a god. After all, he had just passed wind before a creature that literally controlled the air. But that wasn't important.

I don't have a name!

Aubrey's sister thought of Howard Howard. Every memory she had of him was of a vicious, violent, vindictive drunkard, but was there the slightest glimmer of a chance he'd known this would happen? Then she remembered everything he'd ever done. Probably not, she decided.

Neither child noticed when the Gentleman Grinder slowly turned the pram towards Aubrey. He tested the wheels. When they weren't pointing at Aubrey's sister, they worked just fine.

The elongated undertaker rushed at the boy, the black shape inside his pram slobbering with hunger.

Aubrey's sister hadn't liked any of what the Lady Grinder had said. Nothing she'd proposed was worth the deaths of people as decent as Calo and Boneless Charlie. Even the beasts had helped her more than the Grinders ever had.

And that was before the big Grinder had started running towards her brother.

An army? As far as she was concerned, the hell that was Marrowville deserved to meet the hell outside it, and she wanted to see what was out there.

Aubrey's sister turned away from the Grinders. With a flick of the string-sword, she tossed the Book at the thrashing, dancing, whinnying, snorting and spitting form of Terry the Terrible Horse. He was so full of sugary excitement that his armour shredded it from cover to cover.

The black pram howled and collapsed. Of course it did – she'd just cut out its stomach.

34
Dessert

The Grinders' pram was dying. It sank into the dirt, the spokes melting into a black tar. The music went with it, as though the notes themselves were drowning.

The old lady showed no signs of being upset. She smiled, as always.

'That's all right, lovely,' said the Lady Grinder. 'We'll just have to make another.'

She turned round and held her husband's hand. Their rings interlocked.

'We're going to leave now.'

'I'll never be your soldier,' said Aubrey's sister.

The Gentlemen Grinder hissed.

'He says he doesn't care. We'll just kill you. Another time.'

'Really?' said Aubrey's sister. 'Why not now? Everyone else has tried.'

'Oh, we don't kill horrible children. Just adults who don't matter.'

The Grinders began to melt into the shadow of what had once been the One Tree.

'But don't worry – you won't be a child forever.'

><)))*>

The children began walking back to Marrowville. The future was uncertain, but everything always was.

A car drove towards them. A familiar face was at the wheel; he looked past them to the One Tree, right where the Grinders had been standing. Then he popped his head out of the window.

'Fish!' called the Fishflinger.

'Fishflinger!' said Aubrey's sister. 'You can . . . you can drive?'

'Of course I can drive! I can say things that don't involve fish, too.' He winked. 'Do we know each other?'

Aubrey laughed. 'We've never actually met, but we caught fish from you one night.'

'Oh!' The Fishflinger clapped his hands. 'That was you? I'm so sorry – literally all I've had on my brain lately has been fish. Climb in – I'll drive you back into town.'

They motored their way back towards familiar buildings, though obviously the one that really mattered would be gone forever. They saw that the town's population of fire-lizards was once again free to roam, but it saddened them to see the little green critters burp flame at teenage boys once more. The night of the Sky of Fire would stay with the children forever.

'Do you want to see what happened to the Dog & Fist?' asked the Fishflinger.

'No, thank you,' said Aubrey sadly. 'Not today.'

The Fishflinger nodded. He parked his car next to Skyline's Ruin, the great spire that was allegedly the office of the mayor. He opened the front door with a key, and bent down to take a newspaper from its over-stuffed metal box.

Aubrey's sister nudged her brother in amazement. 'Fishflinger, are you the mayor?' she asked.

'Oh yes. Have been for ages. I just lost my keys.'

'And your mind?' asked Aubrey.

'That too.'

On the outside, Skyline's Ruin was the most magnificent structure the children had ever seen. Inside, it was still the most magnificent structure they had ever seen, but with couches. Nothing was crumbling. Everything was marble. The mayor asked them to join him in the lift.

One hundred storeys (and a boring story that was still a bit about fish) later, the children stepped out into the mayor's office, a palace of plush chairs and an enormous wooden desk framed by the uppermost window in all Marrowville.

The children ran to it. Their whole world was spread out beneath them. Every crumbling speck, every dusty, misty nook and cranny. Aubrey had been blasted out of the Dog & Fist, but neither he nor his sister had ever been this far up in the air.

'Let me see if we've any food in the house.' The mayor dashed off. The children suspected the imminent arrival of fresh, popular fish.

When the mayor returned, he had no fish, just toast.

The children gratefully took it. It reminded them of a happier time, and anything was better than looking out of the window at the burnt-out crater where the Dog & Fist used to be.

Along with the toast, the mayor had brought a roll of parchment, and a question.

'There's been a bit of rain lately . . .' he began, 'and I couldn't help but notice that the One Tree appears to actually be the hand of an extremely large skeleton . . .'

He unrolled the parchment on the desk.

'You two haven't, by any chance, seen this Book?'

An etching of the Book of Eyes glared sightlessly up from the table.

'Yes, yes, we definitely have,' said Aubrey.

'Is it destroyed?'

'Yes, Mayor Fishflinger, yes, it is,' said Aubrey's sister.

'Tremendous!' The mayor rolled the parchment back up. He was so pleased he didn't even mind being called 'Mayor Fishflinger'.

'I take it, then, that you have met its owners?'

The children went pale.

'Repeatedly,' said Aubrey's sister.

The mayor clicked his fingers. 'Outstanding!'

Aubrey found himself checking the mayor for a top hat and a pram.

'Oh, what superb news!' The mayor was very pleased. He did a little dance and clicked his fingers again. 'I'd just figured out where this one was! I was on my way to collect it, but then, well, I was struck by lightning. Then I couldn't talk about anything but fish for a while.'

'How do you know the Grinders?' asked Aubrey's sister.

'Well, they've been in Marrowville a long time – and so have I.'

The mayor got up. He pulled out his keys. They were beautiful and brass and . . .

. . . one of them was decorated with a design that looked familiar – an eye with an 'x' for a pupil, resting on a bed of normal eyes.

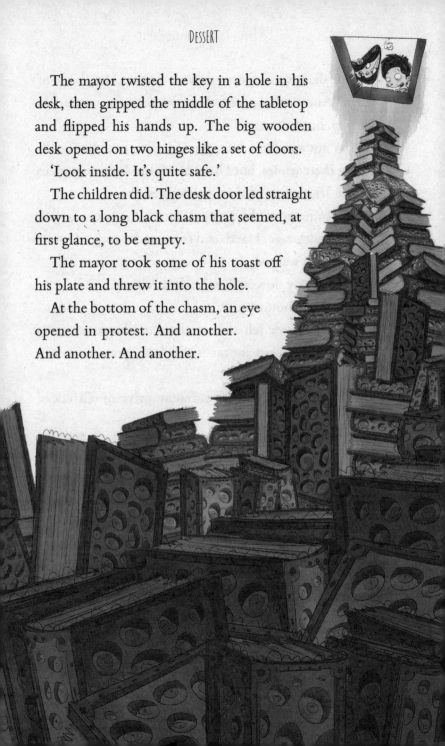

The mayor twisted the key in a hole in his desk, then gripped the middle of the tabletop and flipped his hands up. The big wooden desk opened on two hinges like a set of doors.

'Look inside. It's quite safe.'

The children did. The desk door led straight down to a long black chasm that seemed, at first glance, to be empty.

The mayor took some of his toast off his plate and threw it into the hole.

At the bottom of the chasm, an eye opened in protest. And another. And another. And another.

The shaft was crammed with books. Hundreds of them. And each one of those books was covered in glaring, hateful eyes.

'I'm not sure how long the Grinders have been collecting their armies, but I have been alive long enough to steal at least a few of their precious books.'

The inmates of the prison beneath the mayor's desk howled with rage. Hands slid from under pages. Covers twisted and warped.

'How many do you have?' asked Aubrey.

'At least a thousand.'

Aubrey's sister felt sick. A thousand books meant a thousand stomachs meant a thousand prams meant a thousand mouths meant . . .

'There's thousands of different pairs of Grinders, aren't there?'

'Oh yes,' said the mayor. 'Oh, absolutely yes.'

The children stared into the pit of books.

It was a shame. If they'd looked out of the window at that moment, they'd have noticed something.

The mist was gone.

In the town below, a number of things happened.

At the crater that had been the Dog & Fist, a small shivering dog was startled as two figures opened a trapdoor and jumped out of the blackened ground. One was a lady wearing a mask. Her legs clanked. The other was a man wearing a mask, with a moustache that was wearing two masks.

'What are our names this time?' asked the man.

'I'll be . . . Caro; you can be . . . Spineless Charles,' said the woman.

'Excellent, my incognito sweetheart – nobody will ever figure that out.'

On the outskirts of town, the roads that had once ended in mist finally stretched out into the world. And Marrowville had its first visitor in quite some time. It wasn't, as the Grinders would've hoped, a fearsome, roaring beast. It was tiny. And it quacked. A single, solitary duck had landed safely on the ground.

History had been made. There was, however, a problem. The ground was a rock. And the rock was a man.

Gorgo ate the duck in one bite.

It had only been a few minutes, but Marrowville hadn't changed that much.

And up in Skyline's Ruin, in front of the biggest window in the tallest building in Marrowville, Aubrey's sister – the Wrecker-Killer, hero, strategist and string-sword enthusiast – looked out at the future. It was uncertain, and disturbing, but she'd handle it.

It didn't matter that she could see that the giant hand that used to be the One Tree was clearly moving, and starting to claw at the ground.

Her brother, Aubrey Howard – the Wrecker-Killer, hero, explosives amateur, master of the Fatal Coconut and part-time Secret Giraffe – looked at the palm of his right hand. There was a big red pimple on it. He touched it.

An eye opened.

And the sun rose over the little town of Marrowville.

And music played.

Acknowledgements

I'd like to thank my wonderful wife, Jo, and our good friend Jess. Some of the best ideas in this book came from all of us sitting up at night together, and without Jess's sketches when I was writing, my imagination wouldn't have fired half as much. Thank you both – and, JoJo, thanks for fifteen years of tolerating the phrase, 'Listen to this bit!'

Anthony and Wendy, for all the support, the trips to second-hand bookshops and all the movies with subtitles.

Jude, whose absence of nonsense makes her a delight.

I'd also like to thank my agent, Cathryn Summerhayes; Mark Watson, who has been more generous to me than is totally necessary; superb editor Sharan Matharu, Wendy Shakespeare, Tom Rawlinson and Gary Panton, without whose leap of faith none of this could have happened.

Also, my sister-in-law Megan, who won't be even remotely impressed that I've stolen the name of her cat.